Mother and Child

Works by Rochelle Ratner

Fiction

Bobby's Girl
The Lion's Share

Poetry

A Birthday of Waters
False Trees
The Tightrope Walker
Quarry
Combing the Waves
Pirate's Song
The Tarnished Chain
Graven Images
The Mysteries
Sea Air in a Grave . . .
Practicing to Be a Woman
Someday Songs
Zodiac Arrest
House and Home
Beggars at the Wall
Balancing Acts
Toast Soldiers
Leads
Ben Casey Days

Mother and Child

A Novel

by

Rochelle Ratner

H\S

HAMILTON STONE EDITIONS

Library of Congress Cataloging-in-Publication Data

Ratner, Rochelle.
Mother and child / Rochelle Ratner.
p. cm.
ISBN-13: 978-0-9801786-1-6 (alk. paper)
1. Interpersonal relations--Fiction. 2. Parent and child--Fiction. 3. New York (N.Y.)--Fiction. I. Title.
PS3568.A76M68 2008
813'.54--dc22
2008002944

Cover by Claudia Carlson

H\s

HAMILTON STONE EDITIONS
P.O. Box 43, Maplewood, New Jersey 07040

For Ken

Mother and Child

CHAPTER ONE

BREAKING FREE OF THEIR MOTHER'S HANDS THE MOMENT they're in the playground, two identically dressed sisters race to the slide. The smaller one goes up the ladder while the older one starts crawling up from the slippery bottom. They crash two thirds of the way down, laughing.

Ellyn never ceases to be amazed by happy children.

The past year or two, she's made it a point to get to the park every weekend it doesn't rain, if only for a half hour. A little down time, a chance to sit back and enjoy the sun or snow, sucking in enough stillness to carry her through the week ahead. Days when she's had enough of making small talk with some asinine guy whose dog or ferret attracted her, she'll often excuse herself and head for the nearest playground (of which Central Park seems to have hundreds). No homeless guys stretched out on benches there. No one upending the trash cans. Only parents and babysitters seem to hang out by the sandbox.

Kids are fun, so long as they keep their distance.

"Heads up!" Phil shouts.

His daughter's long, scraped legs swing toward her.

Ellyn smiles. Draws back in mock alarm. Leans forward again, elbow resting on knee, chin propped on her hand. She watches the shadow Phil's thinning blonde hair makes along the side of his face. His whole body gets into the act of pushing his daughter on the swings.

Here Tiffany comes again: innocence personified. Full cheeks, growing fuller with each swing until it looks as if her freckles are going to burst. She leans her head all the way back and closes her eyes as the swing sails out and up. She'll probably be gawky in a few years, but right now she looks slightly younger than eleven, with enough baby fat left to compensate for her height.

It's herself, The Child, Ellyn's seeing there.

No. No one ever pushes TC.

Fragments of red nail polish that clashes with Tiffany's hair can be detected on her cuticles, the rest of it picked or bitten off. Now she's swinging without holding on. Tiffany stands on the swing, using the weight of her body to propel herself.

The next swing opens up and Tiffany grabs it. "Quick, Dad, get on!"

Phil defers to Ellyn.

There are only three swings, and a lot of kids, here. She really shouldn't.

Tiffany says don't worry about the little kids, they don't belong here anyway. They're supposed to use the baby swings over near the gate. Or they can go swing on the tires and get as rough as they want to.

Sure, sure, don't bother with the little kids. Ellyn knows that script only too well. When she was younger than Tiffany her sister would take her to the park, then get involved with a group of girls her own age. She could have gotten hit over the head with a metal bucket and Joan probably wouldn't have noticed.

"Come on," Tiffany calls. She's going to lose her balance if she has to hold this rope any longer.

Ellyn sits down, walks back and forth a few times. All of the sudden Phil gives her a push. She loses her footing.

"Hold on," he screams, pushing again, and again.

She gets carried away.

Phil can't get the two swings to work in unison, so his strong, confident hands push one sweaty back, then the other. Tiffany and Ellyn reach out their arms to touch as they pass. They call to each other, the calls getting sillier and sillier: Peek-a-boo! Boo! Knock knock! Scaredy cat! Nice kitty! High Ho Silver! Whamo! Presto! Abracadabra! Cock a doodle do! Fiddlesticks! Tick tock!

OUT OF BREATH, PHIL STEPS ASIDE for a moment. Beads of sweat make his eyes tear, still he can't bring himself to look away: the two women of his life together on the swings. Five years, three months, twelve days, then all of the sudden it picks up where it left off.

He always knew it would be this way.

ELLYN HASN'T BEEN ON A SWING in over twenty years. Suddenly she's invigorated, the way she feels after a few drinks and good sex, only freer. Happier.

She runs her fingers up through her hair, and then lets it drop from way up there. "I used to lean my head back even further than you do. My chin pointed straight up to the sky," she tells Tiffany. Phil's gone to get them all sodas.

"Wasn't that weird for the person pushing you?"

"Well, usually no one was pushing me."

"That's how it is on the swings at school."

"The closest playground was in this lot where the swings had sand beneath them," Ellyn says. "If I leaned my head back, I came home with sand in my hair. My stepmother had a fit." Then again, RuthAnn always had fits.

"Didn't you have to wash your hair all the time?"

"Yep. But that's okay, I love washing my hair."

"I hate washing my hair."

Ellyn runs her fingers through the little girl's hair. "It's a bit thicker than mine, Tiffany. I'll bet it's hard to get the soap out."

"It's torture!" She reaches up, runs her fingers through Ellyn's hair. It feels like the fur of this collie her friend used to have. "You can call me Tips," she says. "That's what my father calls me."

Ellyn smiles. Promises to show Tips a few tricks that might make hair-washing easier.

Tips pulls a few strands of Ellyn's hair loose and holds them next to her ponytail. "If we had a scissors, we could, like, cut a few hairs and mix them all together. I'll bet we wouldn't be able to tell which was which."

"And the next beautician who cut my hair would be my enemy for life," Ellyn laughs. She takes a sip of the Diet Sprite Phil hands her. Catches her distorted reflection in the top of the can. She's glad now she gave in and agreed to meet Phil's daughter. Usually, she makes it a habit to be busy those weekends guys have their kids, especially at the start.

Then again, Phil was different from the start. So into the bar scene no consenting adult would ever suspect he had a kid. She'll never forget that night she found out.

It was a Thursday, four Thursdays after they'd met. Phil was cooking dinner to celebrate their one-month anniversary. It couldn't have been a more perfect night. It was warm, and they set up a Hibachi on his terrace. She didn't even know apartments on Riverside Drive had terraces, let alone imagine herself eating on one. She took a deep breath: the only fumes were from the inviting charcoal. Trucks aren't allowed on the highway, and the occasional Number 5 bus on the Drive didn't seem to matter. They looked across the river and watched the lights come on in New Jersey.

"That's where I'm from, out there," he said, placing an arm around her. They clinked glasses again – to New York, here and now.

Two hundred feet below them, the last of the homeless were probably retrieving their belongings from the alleys where they'd hidden them a few hours earlier and wandering into Riverside Park to bed down for the night.

Phil checked the coals, went in to get the London Broil, returned carrying it one-handed high above his head: the perfect waiter. Pouring herself another glass of Brouilly, she watched as he turned the beef, then turned it again, and again, and again, and again, giving each side equal care.

Rare meat, rare wine, will you be my valentine? Ellyn muttered under her breath. How silly could she get? There was something about Phil. All month he'd been bringing out these delightful, corny thoughts in her.

He set the meat aside to let it stand, went in for candles. He put them on the table, she lit a match. It went out before she was anywhere near the wick. Laughing, he tried; didn't come any closer. Determined, they stood together against the railing, trying to block the wind. They each struck a match, came at it from both sides at once. Still no luck. She threw up her hands; he embraced her.

"At least my match lit," Ellyn laughed. She told him about pledging for Delta Phi in college, and one of the things they had to do was light the members' cigarettes. "I practiced for two solid weeks before I was able to light a match with one strike. I always managed to bend them or wear the sulfur off rubbing it so frantically."

"So that's the real reason you don't smoke."

"Don't worry. My sister Joan smokes enough for both of us."

He took the candles inside, lit them, brought them back out. By the time he had the salad on the table the wind was in control. He gave the candles one more shot, lighting them inside again. This time she watched closely, made a wish the moment the flame went out. Not a wish, a hope: may this balcony never fall into the river, may there always be nights like this.

He placed the candles on a table right inside the door, lit them one more time, put on a CD of Haydn string quartets, turned off the living room lights, whipped up one of the best bearnaise sauces this side of Café Des Artistes.

"You've got skills I never would have expected," she teased.

"Hey, I wasn't always a thrillionaire. Besides, when Tiffany was an infant, cooking was our only option."

"Tiffany?" Ellyn gulped her wine. Christ. She picked another married one.

"My daughter. You'll meet her one of these weekends. She lives with my parents in Cherry Hill."

The Balsamic vinaigrette made her mouth feel raw. She knew the Daddy Dearest type. He was always the one who either went back to his wife because he missed the kids so much, or spent weekends moping around the house because he couldn't get to see the little martyrs-in-training.

No, Phil was different. As they slowly worked their way through course after course (including cheese and fruit, along with a light dessert wine), he told her about his wife's death, his daughter's life with his parents in Cherry Hill. They looked toward New Jersey again. It wasn't even 9:30, yet some of the lights were starting to go out. It was a different world over there.

The wind blew her hair across his face and he made a futile stab at catching it. Behind them, the candles were burning down. It was getting chilly. They carried the dishes inside, sat down in the living room.

She told him about her mother.

"MY MOTHER'S DEAD TOO, you know," she tells Tips as they start walking home.

"How old were you when she died?"

"A little over three."

"I was five."

"I know, your father told me."

"You never told me you were so young," Phil comments.

She explains it's not usually something she finds herself discussing on the first few dates.

Tips asks if she thinks about her mother much.

"Sometimes. I used to more than I do now. Sometimes it hurts too much."

"Same here," Tips says, taking Ellyn's warm hand. She chatters on about how, two years ago, when she was in third grade, her grandmother saw her moping around the house, and started her on piano lessons. Grandma promised that sitting around on rainy afternoons being able to play her favorite songs would make her happy. It doesn't, all it does is take time away from things she'd rather be doing, hanging out in the schoolyard and stuff. But she doesn't want to tell her grandparents, or they'd be sad too.

She follows Ellyn's arm up to her shoulder. "It's not nice to stare at people," Grandma always tells her. And Grandma tugs to make sure she keeps moving, even when it's only the homeless woman who sleeps curled up in the doorway to the drugstore. Still she sneaks stares at Ellyn every chance she gets.

"I REALLY LOVE THE BARBIE you gave me," Tips says. It's one of those Barbies whose arms and legs twist and bend and you're supposed to be able to put them in all sorts of dance or athletic positions. She didn't think it was so great at first, but she smiled and said thank you, just like Grandma, Grandpa, her father and the whole world seems to have taught her.

That Barbie cost $10, tops. She's learned to judge her father's girlfriends by how much they spend on a present. Some of them spend a whole lot, and then expect her to be so excited she'll go off and play by herself and not bother them for hours. Those are the worst.

No, the worst are the ones who don't bring her anything. Or the ones who show up with a stuffed animal, as if she's a four-year-old.

She sure didn't expect Ellyn to be so great. When they were driving here Friday night, her father told her Ellyn was tall and thin. He described her long strawberry-blonde hair that's heavy on the strawberry side, and how she'll sometimes twirl a few strands around her finger when she's lost in thought. The large blue eyes that seem to gaze at things forever. The freckles she tries to cover with makeup but can't completely hide, and how they deepen when she smiles.

Staring straight ahead, she'd responded even then that it sounded like Mommy.

"She does look as if she could be a gym teacher, or maybe a dance teacher," her father laughed. "Only she's not. Ellyn works for one of the largest advertising agencies in the city."

Her mother was a real gym teacher. Before she got pregnant, that is. It took two years for her body to get in shape enough to teach again, and then it turned out the only job she could get was in Great Neck, all the way out on Long Island. She was driving home late one night, it was raining, and the car skidded off the road. That was that.

She reached into her backpack and pulled out her science book. They have to answer the questions at the back of Chapter Sixteen and bring them to school on Tuesday. Plus write an essay on transportation for civics class and a book report for English. Monday's Memorial Day, they've got three days off, that's why her father decided to bring her into the city this weekend. It's a holiday weekend, but they still have homework.

That's Ellyn, with a "Y," her father told her.

At least these weekends with her father she doesn't have to practice piano. Most of the time he lets her do whatever she wants. She can log onto AOL and spend all the time she wants in the chat rooms without anyone complaining that it's tying up the phone. She can send ten e-mails to Melissa even though they only saw each other yesterday. And her father takes her goofy places, like to a pizza place when they've just had lunch or when it's almost dinnertime. Except sometimes one of the women he's with decides they have to plan things, and she ends up being dragged to dopey places like puppet shows or street fairs.

She grabs hold of Ellyn's wrist. "I'm glad we went to the Wild West playground. It's my favorite."

"Worth going all the way to 94th Street for! Though sometimes we end up taking a cab home, because this heavy swinger here is overtired." Phil ruffles his daughter's hair.

"I was sort of, like, scared at first," Tips confesses. "I thought we might head for the jungle gym, and maybe you'd, like, try to get me to stand up straight on the very top."

"Do I look like the a person who'd do that?" Ellyn laughs.

Tips lets go. Stands so still you'd think they were playing statues. Their eyes meet.

"My mother said she'd teach me how to stand on top when I was older," Tips says at last, taking Ellyn's hand again. It feels really smooth and soft. "But Grandma gets nervous when I climb too high, so I haven't had a lot of practice. This one girl at my school, she's not my friend I just see her around all the time, she can, like, walk along the top bar and keep her balance."

"I'm scared of heights, too," Ellyn commiserates. "I have this vivid memory of standing up on a chair and my mother screaming at my father or sister to grab me, terrified I'd fall off."

"A chair's not very high," Phil laughs.

"It depends upon your perspective," Ellyn and Tips say together.

"Race you to the building," Tips shouts, taking off without waiting for an answer. Rounding the corner, they literally run into a mother and her two kids Phil and Tips know from the neighborhood. "This is our friend Ellyn," Phil says, making introductions.

Our friend. Ellyn's ears curve upward at the phrase.

And here comes a woman carrying a rabbit! Phil sees it first, and points it out to the kids, who run over to the woman holding him.

Tips asks if they can pet him.

The woman nods. Tips immediately cradles the rabbit's head in her palms. The other two kids hang back a bit. Finally the girl takes a step forward, reaches a tentative finger to the rabbit's ear. Jumps back as if expecting it to bite. Tips is stroking the rabbit between his ears, whispering in the tip of an ear, telling him how soft and beautiful he is.

"She's so gentle," Ellyn whispers. "How can she be that rough on the swings, run down the block without looking where she's going, then all of the sudden be so calm and soothing?"

"She's been gentle with animals ever since she was a toddler," Phil says.

Ellyn stands there beaming, delighted to know such a child.

"She has her mother's touch," Phil continues.

"ORDER ANYTHING YOU WANT, except chow mein," Phil tells his daughter as they weave in and out of the crowd along Mott St. No matter what time you come down here, there's a mob.

"How about if Ellyn orders chow mein? I can have some of hers, can't I?"

"If Ellyn orders chow mein it's the end of our friendship."

"Don't order chow mein," Tips tells her. "Please."

Ellyn promises she won't.

They stop to look at these plastic water guns a guy's selling on the corner, get squirted once, then continue walking. Every time they get down to Chinatown Phil silently vows to bring his daughter there more often. It's the kind of neighborhood you don't find in Cherry Hill.

"And no putting sweet and sour sauce on everything, the way Grandma does," he continues as they head into Kuan Sing. "As a matter of fact, no sweet and sour."

"Suppose I want sweet and sour fried rice?"

"Nope."

"Sweet and sour chow mein?"

They're laughing nonstop till the food comes.

Trying to pick up a dumpling with chopsticks pushes Tips over the edge. Ellyn shows her how to brace it on her middle finger and steady her wrist, but she still can't manage.

"Mommy was so good she could pick up a single grain of rice," Phil announces.

Ellyn pays no attention to his challenge.

After dinner they start walking uptown, but Ellyn steers them off onto Bayard St.: The Chinatown Ice Cream Factory. As they're waiting in line they stare at the list of flavors: Green Tea, Lychee, Ginger, Red Bean . . . "If you ask, they might even have sweet and sour," she whispers to Tips.

"Where'd you find this place?" Phil asks.

"Believe it or not, I've known about it since high school. Some of us used to come into the city on weekends. They make all their own."

"I'll bet they do." He orders a green tea cone, gets a ginger cone for Ellyn and a chocolate chip double-dip cone for Tips. He also buys his daughter one of those bright yellow T-shirts with a green dragon eating ice cream on it that says Chinatown Ice Cream Factory. Ellyn asks for a few extra napkins.

Cones in hand, they walk up as far as Canal Street. Phil tries to steer them west. "The fish market might still be open," he says. "I thought the two of you might enjoy seeing all the fish with their heads still on."

Ellyn backs away. Tells him about one meal down here where she ordered fish and one of the people she was with made its mouth move. "The sight of whole fish has made me sick to my stomach ever since."

"Too bad."

Tips insists that the sight of whole fish makes her sick, too. Even in the museum.

That's the first Phil's heard of this.

Well, she might not have told him, but it makes her sick to her stomach.

Phil rushes into the street and intercepts a cab headed for a couple on the corner. On the way uptown they listen to what sounds like a Haitian talk show. They stop in the video store and rent the one Pedro Almodóvar movie neither Phil nor Ellyn has seen. Tips is in bed by ten. They'll turn in a little after midnight.

"TO KNOW ME IS TO LOVE ME," Phil says, climbing on top of her and pretending to handcuff her wrists.

"I knew there was something I didn't like about that movie," she laughs.

"Watch and learn." He rattles off some of the farcical positions they saw the leading man keep his captive in, and asks her what her pleasure is. As if he doesn't know she likes it straight. No kinky sex, no fancy female drinks like whiskey sours or daiquiris. And she doesn't play head games.

"I want to just sleep, actually. I'm exhausted." Ellyn fluffs up her pillow, turns over.

Phil reaches across her, cups a breast in his palm, folds her body into his. She pulls away the moment she feels her nipple harden.

"May I remind you that your daughter is in the next room?"

"The door's closed, and she's asleep." He draws her back to him, clasps hard enough so she can't escape.

"It's a matter of principle," she says, letting herself relax in his warm arms. "Whenever the guy I'm dating has his children along, we take it slow." She promises they'll reopen the discussion after a few weeks, when Tips is more used to her presence. Thinking as she says this that maybe, maybe, she and Phil will somehow survive the city's pace and pressures. Hand in hand and all that. It's been a hell of a long time since she's felt so comfortable.

TC wakes in the middle of the night to the sound of furniture being moved. She jumps so hard the cushions almost fall through the sofa, and then she sits there in the dark chewing on the flesh around her fingers, terrified they're being robbed. Once things quiet down it takes her forever to get back to sleep. The next morning she discovers the twin beds in her bedroom pushed together.

"Hey, doing it in a single bed might be okay for Dad and RuthAnn, but I'll be damned if I'm going to stand for it," her sister says the next morning. Joan's apartment is being painted, so she and her current significant other come home for a few nights. With her relegated to the tiny guest room.

It never dawned on TC that her father and RuthAnn were "doing it" at all. They had twin beds because her mother had been so sick, she assumed they slept separately all night. And Ellyn was twelve at the time, a year older than Tips.

"In other words, you identify with kids," Phil says smugly.

"I wouldn't say *identify*. More like sympathize."

"We all appreciate your good intentions. But Tiffany was practically weaned on furniture being moved. Many nights we'd wheel her in here, crib and all; it was the only hope we had of getting back to sleep."

"Was I telling you about the furniture?"

"Sure."

"God! I must have had more to drink than I realized. I knew what I was thinking, but I didn't suspect I was saying all that out loud."

"Carried away by the memory."

"And then some."

"BET YOU CAN'T EAT just one," Ellyn calls on her way through the living room. Tips is sprawled on the floor in front of the TV, munching potato chips. How the hell do kids do it? They got back from brunch less than an hour ago, Tips barely touched her omelet, "borrowed" everyone's French fries, and here she is with potato chips.

"Bet *you* can't eat just one," Tips says with her mouth full.

Ellyn takes the largest one she can find; clamps her lips shut.

"You're going to turn blue!" Tips shouts. "Like when you hold your breath too long."

"No, I won't. I've waited half my life to prove this was a lousy commercial." Never thought she'd let a lover catch her looking so ridiculous.

Before she can get the last trace of salt off her tongue, the three of them are trading quips from various commercials. Tips' favorite is when Ellyn taunts "Hamster Brain" at her. They've all seen that one, but no one can remember what product it plugged.

"You deserve a break today," Tips sings as they head out for dinner. Off key.

"No way," Phil says. "No McDonald's, no Burger King, no Kentucky Fried. You won't be back in suburbia until tomorrow night." They go to the local Greek coffee shop.

That "tomorrow night" rings in Ellyn's ears, sounding more and more like a death knell.

PHIL LEAVES TO DRIVE his daughter back to Cherry Hill.

Not quite ready to go home to an empty apartment, Ellyn checks out the schedule at Loews, ends up taking in the latest Robin Williams film. Not nearly as impressive as his early work.

She walks uptown along Amsterdam Ave., glancing in bar after bar as she passes. It's a warm night, and the crowds have spilled out along the street. The usual sort of rowdy group she expects in these places that have pool tables in the back. Which is why she usually sticks to Columbus Ave., the Upper East Side, or the Village. She smiles, thinking how this latest "Mr. Goodbar" phase has been temporarily suspended. For a mildly attractive woman, with memorable red hair, even stopping in a bar to use the phone can lead God knows where. Take that night two months ago:

She shoved the quarter back in the slot, dialed the number yet again. Damn Sharon! Why the hell couldn't she live in a decent building, one with a nice buzzer system. That's the problem with befriending artists she's worked with – they tend to live in buildings locked at six on the dot. *No problem, just call from Broome St. Bar on the corner* and she'll toss keys down.

Nothing but a busy signal.

To top things off, this lanky blonde guy was nursing his drink at a nearby table, picking up the phone every time she put it down. "Pardon me, but I think we've been calling the same number," he said finally. A come-on so juvenile she had to laugh.

She couldn't help watching closely the next time he dialed. Two two eight, nine one nine seven. "You're calling Sharon?" She might as well be accusing him of calling Jupiter.

"Mark. Number 340, fourth floor?"

"Yes, but . . ." Suddenly she remembered Sharon's roommates. "Mark know you're coming?"

"I thought he did." Pushing his wire-rimmed glasses back up on the bridge of his nose.

"Same here."

"Phil Plattison." He cut the awkward silence with a clean, well-manicured hand. A firm, self-assured grip. She likes that in a man. "Can I buy you a drink while we're waiting? It looks as if we're in for a long night."

While not about to wait forever, she let herself relax over a glass of Chardonnay.

Ten or fifteen minutes, after she'd flipped her hair over one shoulder and was looking directly into his eyes every time she spoke, Mark and Sharon rushed in together. They just discovered their phone was on the fritz. They'd been upstairs getting angrier and angrier at these friends who didn't materialize.

As long as they'd met already . . .

Phil and Mark had been planning to head down to the Seaport, grab dinner at Gianni's, and check the rest of the scene. Nothing that couldn't be postponed. Sharon had made an Alfredo dish; easy enough to throw in a few more handfuls of pasta and take it a little easy on the sauce. "We're all connected, New York Telephone," Ellyn got them all singing as they climbed four flights of rickety stairs.

By the following weekend she and Phil were lovers.

June 2: Ellyn

There's a storm, or snowstorm, and they've all gone up to the roofs, but somehow she's managed to get herself swinging from a letter high up in a sign. She watches the fire trucks rescuing others, certain they'll rescue her too, but everyone tells her they won't – she's too high, even though the tall thin woman who tells her that is higher. She could jump into a snow drift like a mattress. But they tell her she'll be killed. She watches them rescuing others, watches other people walking on the ground. That tall thin woman in a pin-striped blouse could reach up and get her, or she could jump into her arms, but she won't even hold them out. Neither will the other woman. Her parents are around somewhere, and she thinks they're worried, but they're not helping either. She shouldn't have gone off like that.

CHAPTER TWO

THERE'S CAROL, DAWN, Illana, Phyllis, Marilyn . . . And these are the better ones, the ones who didn't try to impress him with their maternal instinct by continually asking how his daughter was. Tips never once asked about any of them, either. Now all of the sudden she's asking about Ellyn every time they speak.

Whenever there's a silence between him and Ellyn, she asks what Tips is up to. "Oh, marking time till school ends," he'll say. Or, "She's so bored I think she started on her Christmas list."

"Six months early?"

"Well, Christmas is always a big time for us." His eyes squint, his chin edges toward his nose – the better to smile with.

"I guess it would be for most kids."

"Hey, for me, too. Every year we walk along Fifth Avenue after Thanksgiving, looking at the store windows in their holiday best. I remember, the year she was two, Tips insisted she was too old for her stroller, and was determined to push it herself. She could barely see under the handlebars."

"Between Thanksgiving and Christmas, all Fifth Avenue ever meant to me was mobs of shoving people and stalled traffic." She talks about one year being up at Joan's and they decided to drive her back to the city, drive the kids past the tree at Rockefeller Center. "It took us over an hour to get from 59th St. to 50th St. Then, just as the kids could see the tip of the of an angel's wing, Mike saw an opening in the traffic and gunned it. He didn't even realize what he'd done till the kids started crying."

"He drove them back, I hope."

"Are you kidding?"

"I'd have taken Tips back. But driving's not a good way to see the decorations anyway. Making your way through the crowd's half the fun of Christmas." He goes on to talk about how Tips delights in making up stories about the window-people and how they're spending Christmas.

Ellyn props herself up on a pillow. Wants to hear more.

"The year she was four, Bergdorf's had a Christmas Past and Present window. In the Christmas Past scene she spotted the logs by the fireplace and the man warming his hands in front of the fire, and she told about how he'd been out cutting wood that morning so they could roast the turkey over the open fire, and how happy the children were to see little rag dolls in their stockings."

She snuggles against him. "Did anyone ever tell you what an incredible smile you have?"

His head shakes like a moderately wet dog's. He lets out half a sigh, yet the smile remains. "Those were incredible days. Remind me tomorrow, I'll show you that story."

"You have a copy?" The jolt of her own words makes her jump back slightly, away from him.

Phil continues as if he hasn't noticed. "We used to send out her stories instead of Christmas cards. Tips wrote them out herself."

"You're kidding."

"Cross my heart and hope to die." Making the cross with whatever's handiest.

Ah, the way to a man's heart.

"Tips has known the alphabet and been able to write her name since she was three," he tells her a few nights later, his eyes getting that same bubbly look Ellyn's come to love so much. "Printing, you know, huge block letters slanting down the page. And she could figure out how to spell words up to about five letters before she entered kindergarten – house, father, chair . . ."

"Father has six letters."

"I know, but it's a special word," Phil grins. More special than he'd ever dreamed it would be. He was there in the delivery room, holding Anita's hand as the head popped forth. Then the first thing Tips did was cry, and instinctively he reached out his arms. The nurse handed her to him, and the crying stopped. Holding his daughter's innocent, untouched flesh in his arms, still warm from her mother's body, is perhaps his most treasured memory.

This is going to be a very special family.

"She makes up stories from old photos, too," he tells Ellyn. "Especially since she's gotten older. She tells her story, and then wants to know how it *really* happened. The pictures of me as a child are her favorites. And my parents have hundreds, all carefully arranged in craft-show albums."

"Your parents sound like good people."

"They are. Or at least they try to be. Probably better at raising my daughter than they were raising me." No matter how good his parents are with Tips, it's not the childhood he would have chosen for her: lily-white schools, malls, Burger King, grandma as chauffeur, and a princess phone. He and Anita . . .

His arms slacken.

"Her current pride and joy is a picture of me as a six-year-old in a bathing suit, my belly button sticking out," he says, working up a smile again. "She made up a story about how we'd gotten to the beach at ten o'clock, and had gone in swimming, then I'd built this great big castle, and we'd all eaten tuna sandwiches sitting around it. After lunch I'd gone in swimming again, and while I was in the water a big wave came and wrecked the castle. Right after the picture was taken I sat down to build it again."

It's *The Arabian Nights* all over again: delight, expectation, enchantment.

THE CLOSING BELL RINGS at four, computers are shut down, and that's often when the hardest work begins. Phil's got a dinner meeting with clients in town from Chicago. Last night it was cocktails with prospective clients, two nights before that he left after dinner to go offer condolences to the children of a former client.

Not in the mood to fight the rush hour, Ellyn grabs a bite in midtown before catching the subway at about seven-thirty.

A little blond kid, maybe two years old, is seated across the aisle, hair in ringlets so you can't tell if it's a boy or a girl. Squirms in the seat. Smiles. Waves, a childish wave, not fully opening the fingers. The woman sitting next to Ellyn waves back. Kid smiles again. "I like you," he or she says, loudly.

"I like you, too," the woman answers.

Kid's smiling his/her head off. Turns to get the mother's approval. She's looking elsewhere, perhaps embarrassed but more likely not giving a damn so long as the kid's not whining or throwing a tantrum. Kid continues talking, shows the woman next to Ellyn his/her jacket, the buttons on his/her jacket, the drawstring on the bottom with the button that slides along it.

The woman makes some approving comment. The kid shows her his/her tricks again. She nods, smiles. At her feet is a huge pink shopping bag, the handle of an umbrella sticking out. It looked as if it might rain earlier today, but has cleared up now.

"I like that woman," kid offers in the mother's direction.

"I like you, too," the woman says. "I like you very much."

Woman's smiling as broadly as the kid is. Mother tries to suppress a smile. Woman across from them also smiles broadly. Ellyn takes it all in.

FATHER'S DAY WEEKEND. Phil spends Friday night at his parents'. Don't ask him why. Maybe to have a little more quiet father-daughter time. He knows, the minute they emerge from the tunnel, Tips will start bugging him about where Ellyn is and when are they going to see her. She's been sending him e-mail all week, but instead of the usual "I got an A- on my history paper!!!!!" or "Melissa's parents bought her this great SEGA game" it's been "Tell Ellyn I stood on the third rung of the jungle gym" or "I'm going to wash my hair tonight. Warn Ellyn." No matter how many XXXXXXXXs she ends her letters with, he doesn't know what to make of them.

They meet at the Museum of Television and Radio at ten o'clock Saturday morning. She gives Ellyn the sort of hug he used to wait all week for. Ellyn comments on how silky her hair feels.

"I was as mesmerized by television as you are by videos," she tells Tips as they walk in. "When I was your age I knew all the commercials by heart – I sometimes think I liked the commercials better than the programs."

"Me too. I used to pester my parents all the time to buy me the toys I saw on TV. The cereals, too. If I, like, hadn't seen it sing and dance, I refused to eat it."

TC's fists clench, her eyes water, she stamps her feet, making a scene in the long aisle of cereal boxes. The sugar pops contain a coloring set she wants, but they end up with the same stupid corn flakes as always.

"My stepmother used to insist that it made no sense to pay for sugar when we could add our own."

"Poor you."

"At least I had good friends."

She ushers them quickly through the first-floor exhibit, and then up to the library on the fourth floor.

"I remember one girl I was close to in fourth and fifth grade," she tells Tips while they're waiting for the elevator. "I'd sleep at her house on a Saturday night, and the next morning her father would make pancakes. He'd put our initials in the center of every pancake he gave us."

"Wow! Think you could make those, Dad?" Her ponytail's bobbing.

"Not unless I knew the secret," Phil says, casting a glance at Ellyn as he places an arm around Tips, drawing her close. Her head reaches to the middle of his chest now.

"I haven't spoken to that girl since high school," Ellyn tells them. "I think her parents moved to Florida."

"Fathers who make monogrammed pancakes always do," Phil comments, half smiling, half frowning.

Tips suggests that maybe they can call her.

Ellyn promises to see if her prop crew can figure it out. Finger to her lips to hush them, she sits them down before one of the terminals, presses Start Over then Advertising, and begins searching for the commercials she wants.

"I bought you alphabet soup, didn't I?" her stepmother screams, yanking TC's arm. But she hates alphabet soup almost as much as she hates corn flakes. RuthAnn pours it down the sink if she spends too much time spelling words. She never gets to finish.

Phil places an arm around Ellyn's shoulder. They turn their selections over to the librarian and head upstairs to one of the video alcoves.

They watch a commercial where Ajax turns into a white tornado and has the whole house spotless in no time. The one where the housewife's talking on the phone as she's working.

Tips says her grandmother would probably love that one. "She's always yelling when I drop crumbs or put a glass down on the coffee table without a coaster."

Quaker Puffed Rice, Madge soaking in Palmolive, Josephine the Plumber. It's nearly two o'clock before they can pull Tips away from the museum.

"Most days she's complaining she's hungry before noon," Phil comments.

Ellyn makes them watch one more before they leave. One of the last cigarette commercials on TV. This woman cuts a circle out of the Winston carton, puts it on the record player, and it plays the Winston melody: "Winston tastes good like a (thump thump) cigarette should."

"More about this over lunch," she promises. "I'm famished."

They walk over to The Sea Grill in Rockefeller Center. Get a window table facing a huge, empty courtyard. Tips gives them the rundown on all the Christmas trees she remembers seeing here. Ellyn retells the story of her brother-in-law gunning the car, her nieces and nephew going into a tantrum next to her in the back seat. Her leg is black and blue for the next week from one kid or another kicking her.

"I was here maybe two months ago, and people were still skating," Phil says. He suggests they all go ice-skating here next winter.

Once they've settled in and ordered, Ellyn finishes her Winston story. She tells about sneaking into the kitchen one morning after her sister and brother had gone to school, opening the cabinet under the sink, and pulling a spaghetti box out of the waste basket. "I took a pair of scissors from my sister's desk and cut out a funny-looking circle. Then I begged my sister to play it on the record player."

"You can't play a piece of cardboard," Tips laughs.

"Joan's words precisely. But you just saw them do that in the commercial, didn't you?" Lips open a bit, tongue pressing against her front teeth, Tips mulls it over. Phil puts his hand over his lips to politely mask his laugh. "What did you think it would play?" he asks finally.

"The spaghetti song, what else?"

"There is no spaghetti song!"

"How was I supposed to know?"

Only the food's arrival puts an end to Tips' attack of giggles.

Ellyn asks Tips if she remembers the first movie she ever saw.

"Mmmmmmm, *Bambi*?"

"Don't look at me," Phil warns.

"Probably Mommy took me."

"Well, I remember the first movie I ever saw," Ellyn tells them. "It was a few months after my mother died. Dad took all us kids to a Saturday matinee: *Willy McBean and His Magic Machine*, this stupid fantasy about a mad professor who invents a time machine and goes to visit Christopher Columbus, Buffalo Bill, King Arthur and the rest of them. I was bored stiff. Halfway through I asked Dad how to change the channel."

Phil's the one laughing this time.

"I'm not crazy about movies either," Tips confesses. "At least not in theaters. When you rent a film you can at least stop it if you, like, have to go to the bathroom, you know."

"I know," Phil laughs. "I remember the first time I saw a movie on a VCR. It was about twenty years ago, when VCRs were a rarity, and there weren't many rental places. A friend was house-sitting for this family and they had a VCR with a dozen or so movies. I came over on New Year's Eve with a bottle of champagne, and we watched the original version of *Camille*. I remember, we thought the people who owned that apartment had to be soooo rich."

"Sooo rich," Tips echoes, laughing. "When I was younger, I used to think people were, like, kidding me when they talked about how they'd grown up without even a television."

"Your children will probably feel the same way when you tell them you spent your first year of life without a VCR," her father tells her.

"Did I really?"

"Really."

BRIEF ENCOUNTER. THAT'S THE NAME of the movie Ellyn was trying to think of. One of those tearjerkers from the mid-1940s. Celia Johnson was nominated for several awards. And Tips' goodbye scene was every bit the equal of hers:

"I don't know what to say," she said as they were walking over to the garage, her sweaty palm hanging on for dear life.

"Promise I'll see you again. Soon." Sniffle, sniffle. "If we don't see each other for years I might be all grown up and not know you." The car was sitting at the exit, blocking anyone else from getting out. Ellyn pressed Tips' whole body against her in a hug and, still hugging, managed to walk her over to the open door. Phil went around to the driver's side. "I'll never be able to watch another commercial without thinking of you," Tips called through the open window as he drove off.

Ellyn blew a kiss.

She can picture Tips staring silently out the side window, angry at her father for spoiling their last few minutes together. Poor kid, she's probably seen her father with six or seven different women already; no wonder she doesn't trust her to be there next month.

Back at her own apartment, she turns on TNT, but finds herself rehashing the weekend instead of watching. They'll have to rent *Brief Encounter* one of these weekends; Tips would love it.

She pours herself a shot of brandy and turns in early. It's nearly midnight when she remembers she forgot to call and wish her father a happy Father's Day.

YOU CAN WEAR YOURSELF OUT following a child around. It's rejuvenating, though. Most Mondays she drags herself into the office an hour late; this week she's anxious to get started, and works non-stop all morning. In four hours she's come up with a dozen ideas for a pet food commercial which had been driving her crazy over the past month: a toddler is frightened by the dog jumping all over him, but rescued when mother sets the bowl of food down; a little girl sits at the table with a plate of steaming, fresh-baked cookies, watching her mother throw a Milkbone to the dog, and wants to know "How come you never give *me* biscuits?"

She's bouncing up and down like an eleven-year-old. Holding the pencil chopstick-like, she sketches a dog with long pointed ears like a rabbit's.

This has to be Tips' doing. TC never had a pet, and never wanted one. Her brother Geoff had a hamster once that he needed for a science experiment, but they gave him away after about two weeks. Aside from that, her friends' pets were trouble enough.

Five years old. Her friend's family invites her on a picnic with them. Joan walks her over, she rings the bell, and when they open the door for her the parakeet flies out. Her friend sits on the sofa crying. All she can think is *well, I guess that spoils the picnic.*

Speaking of friends . . . She writes a note about a man making breakfast, talking about his father making pancakes every weekend, putting each child's initials in the center. Now, he does the same for his children. Takes the monogrammed pancakes over to the table. Sits down. "Dad would have loved this." Maybe have him pour Log Cabin syrup over it, saying how this is family tradition also.

She names it "initials" and saves it under "Ideas\Food." That directory's so long it scrolls off the screen now. One of these days she'll have to make time to sort through it.

Not today. Rolling her chair back to reach the file cabinet behind her, she pulls the folder for another account. Within ten minutes she's leaning over the desk, taking frantic notes. She'd planned on seeing Phil tonight, but at six o'clock, still going strong, she calls and cancels.

CHAPTER THREE

SHE PLACES HUGE RED CROSSES on her calendar for every day Tips will be in the city. Fourth of July. Another weekend mid-July. And then, finally, August. What she wouldn't give to change her vacation schedule now, have her two weeks coincide with Phil's three. Had she only suspected . . .

She contents herself with one week coinciding. By August she's comfortable enough to break her not-with-junior-here dictum. Just straight sex, though; no fancy stuff.

No monogrammed pancakes yet, but Phil's developed a breakfast ritual almost as good. Getting eggs out of the refrigerator, he begins a litany of choices: "scrambled, over easy, sunny side up, poached, boiled, McMuffin, fried, pickled, baked, broiled, hundred-year-old, raw, painted blue and green." The possibilities become wilder and wilder as the list goes on. Even as he speaks he's cracking the eggs into the measuring bowl and adding a drop of milk, while Tips cracks up.

She always wants them scrambled.

They go to Jones Beach the first Sunday, Brighton Beach the second. Tiffany talks for two days about how weird Brighton Beach was. All those people talking Russian, they might as well have been in Moscow. And the ugliest bathing suits she'd ever seen in her life. She's not complaining, though; *enchanted* might be a better word. She e-mails her friend Melissa three different letters about it.

Ellyn takes off one Friday and they stop in the Met to see how the mummies are doing. Phil suggested a trip on the Circle Line, but Ellyn nixed that, not with a child along – more often than not a fight develops on board.

A radio Phil ordered arrives packed in bubble wrap; they divide it into thirds and spend the evening popping. Nights when she might have stayed late at the office she brings the work home, gets back to it after Tips is in bed. Thank God for laptops.

"We're working on a commercial for a new shampoo," Ellyn tells them over dinner (pepper steak; without onions, Tips hates onions). "Let me ask you – would you want to use this product if we said it brings out the blue highlights in your hair?"

"Ugh! Gross!" Tips makes a tragic face.

"You sure?"

"Yes! It's bad enough to have red highlights. Especially in the summer. What would they call you? Bluey?"

"Or sad-head."

"They'd probably think someone dipped your hair in an inkwell," Phil laughs.

His daughter explains they haven't used inkwells in ages and ages and ages.

"Okay then: Cry Baby!"

Cry baby! Cry baby! Tears streaming down her face, her Tastykake not only dropped but stepped on, TC wanders the playground at lunchtime, looking for her brother. Geoff and two friends jump her taunter on his way home from school. You call my sister that one more time and your life's worth nothing!

"Come on, guys, I need help," Ellyn says. "How about if we said this shampoo makes your ears curl?"

Tips bursts out in giggles, stray grains of rice popping out through gap between her two front teeth. "Seriously, what are you working on?"

"Like I said, a commercial for a new shampoo."

"You're not suggesting it, like, makes your ears curl, though, are you?"

"No. But it crossed my mind. I can't seem to come up with anything new to say."

"How about which triplet has the Toni?"

"God, Daddy! That's for a permanent, not a shampoo!"

"Men can't be expected to understand the difference." Ellyn grins in Phil's direction. "They have no idea what we women go through to make ourselves beautiful for them."

"*I* don't."

"You will, just wait," Phil and Ellyn say together.

Tips suggests they say it makes you feel as if pure white snow's falling on your hair, on account of that commercial they saw at the museum which compared shampoo to rain and showed a woman walking in the rain. "And snow's even softer than rain," she points out.

"No cheating," Ellyn chides. "We have to come up with something totally new this time." Phil might have taken her to PG movies, but obviously she hasn't seen *The Falcon and the Snowman* yet.

They bat around other ideas, none of them very useful. But, as Ellyn takes care to remind herself, useful wasn't the point of this. She smiles, recalling Tips in the supermarket yesterday. They picked up two cans of tuna, and Ellyn continued down the aisle while Tips ran back and found the Starkist cans. "Sorry, Charlie," she said, patting the picture of the fish.*That's called a mother's pride,* Joan would say if she heard this. *You'll understand it better when you have your own kids.* Her sister the world-famous amateur psychologist.

They go back to the Museum of Television and Radio, which quickly becomes Tips' most cherished place in the whole of New York City. Ellyn shows them the commercial, which was her favorite all through high school: the camera focuses on a high-school class. A girl passes a note, smiles sheepishly when the teacher intercepts it. "You, you're the one, growing up now, Mary Ryan," the offstage singer begins. You watch her fixing herself up, trying to get the boy of her dreams to at least acknowledge her existence. Finally, she gives up and stops at McDonald's on her way home. The boy comes in and sits beside her.

"This was your favorite, huh?" Phil grins.

"It made me everything I am today."

Making what he refers to as "the supreme sacrifice" to both of them, he stops in with them at McDonald's on the way home.

Phil takes Tips back to the museum himself, but without Ellyn around she's bored in less than an hour.

Ellyn takes her into the office.

"It was like walking onto some movie set," Tips tells her father. "These huge glass doors opened onto this waiting room which had this beautiful receptionist sitting behind a shiny round desk. Then we walked through this other set of doors into this room filled with easels and drafting boards. And the people there were even more gorgeous than the receptionist."

"Oh, yeah? Maybe I ought to pick you up at the office tomorrow night," Phil teases.

"Maybe I'll stay home tomorrow."

"But wait. You haven't heard it all yet. This other huge room next to it had the sort of cubby holes like they did in the Social Security office that time Grandma took me there, except every desk had at least two computers, and some had these monitors that were as big as movie screens. Bigger. Then this huge room was surrounded on all sides by offices with real doors, and Ellyn's was the third . . . no, the fourth one down."

"Fifth, but who's counting."

Between Tips and Ellyn, Phil gets the picture: Ellyn set her up at a drafting table with paper and various lead pencils. Catching her there with her head down on one arm, frantically moving an eraser back and forth, one of the artists brought her over to his table for an airbrush demonstration.

"I knew you could do that in PC Paint, but I never thought you could do it in the real world! Only then he explained that programs like PC Paint and Photoshop which is what he uses were based on the way people used to draw on paper to begin with."

When she was tired drawing Ellyn sat her down in a conference room with a VCR and videos of several commercials she's worked on.

"I watched this one tape that had nearly a hundred Perdue Chicken commercials. It was, like, weird. I cracked up every time I saw Frank Perdue's face staring straight at me. He got old right on camera."

"Hey, those commercials were spread over twenty years," Ellyn reminds her.

"I know, but it's still weird. He's weird. He says everything from *It takes a tough man to make a tender chicken* to *Should I raise turkeys?* and *My chickens fly more non-stops to New York than any other bird. I'm Frank. Try me.* There's even one where his father comes on and vouches for him."

"I'd vouch for you any day," Phil announces.

Tips picks up another chicken finger.

Ellyn can't seem to get enough of Tips' excitement. Joan was always so dour and uninterested, she was starting to feel like the only eleven-year-old in the world who didn't equate commercials with Santa Claus.

"When you were three years old, you used to pick up my briefcase when I came home and pretend to go off to work," Phil tells his daughter. "You'd go into the hall and close the door, only we'd have to leave it open a crack because you couldn't manage the doorknob on your own. Then when you came in again I'd have to kiss you good evening and ask how your day at the office had been."

Tips doesn't remember. "You remember my office, though, don't you? After Mommy went back to work I sometimes took you downtown with me. I had a computer and there were always a lot of numbers going across the screen? You used to sit on my lap and play with the keyboard. I think it was the first time you ever saw a computer."

"Even the one in the drugstore?"

"Let's say it's the first time you sat down at the keyboard."

Tips says she remembers his office, but there's not an ounce of recognition in her eyes. So he decides to take her there. Show her where he works, show her the World Financial Center plaza. There might even be some lunchtime event at the Winter Garden. If not, they'll take a trip to Staten Island on the ferry.

"When I was your age, where my father worked was the most mysterious and fascinating place in the world," Ellyn tells them, dreamy-eyed all of a sudden. The eyes come back to earth before the smile does. "When I was a teenager I made the mistake of asking my sister if she remembered anything about it. Leave it to Joan to spoil even that! She said she used to go to the office with Dad a lot, especially when Mom was pregnant with me. Then she went on about how boring it was."

"Nobody ever let her play with a typewriter?"

"You've got to be kidding!" She tosses her balled-up napkin down on the table, goes into the kitchen for the chocolate cake she and Tips picked up on the way home.

"One of the cheap ones!" RuthAnn calls as she runs to the rack of Barbie outfits in the drugstore. Geoff has Little League, Joan's at a friend's, her father's at the office. RuthAnn has no choice but to drag TC wherever. The display's right by the door, so she pesters and pesters.

She picks out a Candy Striper outfit, shows it to RuthAnn and RuthAnn nods. As they're ready to leave, RuthAnn notices she's already torn the cellophane bag open, and goes into a tirade about how disgustingly impulsive she is. "I'd decided to let you buy something more elaborate, but now you've already opened that one, so fine. But don't you come asking for another one, and don't let me catch you crying your friends have better."

TC stares at the red and white apron in her hand. It's the one she'd wanted.

On the way downtown the next morning, Phil reminds Tips how, if she'd been good and hadn't bothered him while he was trying to work, they'd made it a point to stop at the toy store on the way home.

"Umm . . . Is that when I bought the little people train? Or the stuffed dog that barked?"

He can't remember, either.

He flashes his credentials to the guard. "You need a special pass to get in here now," he tells his daughter. True, but unimpressive. He escorts her upstairs to his office. Introduces her to a few people. Sits her down at his desk, turns on his terminal and points out the stock symbols. He tells her what some of them stand for.

"I know. I've seen you do that from home, too. On your computer, I mean."

"Aha! So you were paying attention, after all. Except at home it's not in real time."

"What?!"

"Real time. That means the figures you see up there are changing on the screen the minute they change on the floor of the New York Stock Exchange. Every minute counts in this business. If a stock goes up ten cents everything changes. Watch."

He shows her some of the calculations and forecasting he can do.

Tips watches. Not very much to see.

"Watch it now," Phil says. He presses one key and, abracadabra, his screen's getting information from the floor of Nasdaq.

"Can it do long division?" she asks. "We have these computers in our math lab that can divide and multiply faster than you can blink your eye. We're not allowed to use them for tests, though. But you know what? Next year, in sixth grade, we're going to start learning how to, like, program them, too!"

The color drains from his face. His shoulders droop. He'd forgotten she doesn't even know about square roots yet.

"I'm sorry," she says, looking around the office for something she can get excited by. "I remember how I used to spin around in this chair." She kicks off the desk to start it spinning again.

He reaches out to stop it. "Nope. Different chair, they refurnished this whole place two years ago." He turns off the computer and switches off the lights. They head for the plaza, have lunch at an outdoor cafe ("Way better than the mall in Cherry Hill"). He takes her to the top of the World Trade Center, and then they head home. They'll save the ferry for some other time. Maybe with Ellyn.

"That's okay, Honey," he tells her, drawing her close with an arm on her shoulder almost as if he's guiding her along 79th Street. "You were always more impressed by your mother's job."

"MY GRANDPARENTS TOOK US ALL to Coney Island once," Ellyn says. "I must have been about six. The only ride I remember is the Merry-Go-Round." She's supposed to ride with her brother. The gates open, they pile on, TC climbs on the nearest horse, Geoff runs ahead trying to select the one he wants. All the horses end up taken, and he has to wait for the next ride. The music starts, she goes up and down a few times, and they pass where her family is. She spots Geoff standing there scowling at her, and bursts out crying.

"Not much fun?"

"About as much fun as anything else my family did together. Later Geoff got a black eye riding the bumper cars."

Tips promises Playland will be fun. "Scout's honor."

Phil dashes on and grabs them a whole flying saucer. They squeeze into the seats on the roller coaster and Ferris wheel. It's hot, and they run over to the water ride. Only two people can fit in these seats, no matter how they squeeze, and Tips won't let go of Ellyn's hand. Phil, who's already turned in a ticket, manages to find a seat to himself in another boat.

Water hits his face abruptly at the first dip. He has to laugh.

The whole day is more fun than Ellyn could ever have imagined. Best way in the world to have started her vacation. And Playland's so close to where her sister lives. She wonders if Joan's taken the kids here. Or is Joan still trapped by the memories, too?

TUESDAY FINDS THEM BACK at The Museum of Television and Radio. Thursday they trek out to the Museum of Broadcasting in Queens. Friday night; they've come home from seeing *Cats*. Tips is on the phone with her grandparents. All Ellyn can hear is Tips' side of the conversation.

"But I won't be by myself, I told you, *Ellyn's* here!"

"I know, I know. But Ellyn's different. Please."

"I'm not a baby anymore, you know." Tips' voice rises an octave.

"I can size people up for myself."

"Please."

"Please. Please please please please please."

Tips' chin could sweep the Persian rug and save having to vacuum. The moment she's not smiling her long, sweeping eyelashes dominate her face. "She wants to talk to you," she says, glaring at her father.

Phil goes into the bedroom to have a little privacy

Tips crash lands in the chair, swings her legs over the arm, and kicks off her sandals. Hard. She hates him she hates him she hates him. Why couldn't he have met Ellyn sooner?

All this is because of what's-her-name. The one he was dating the first summer after her mother died. The summer she stayed with her father all August. He took off work for three weeks, and they did a lot, but then the final week he had to go back to work and this woman was supposedly looking after her. The first day what's-her-name took her to the park, sat down on a bench, pulled out some stupid book, and told her to "Go play."

"Play what?" They hadn't brought along a friend or anything. She spun around, looking. Not a single kid she knew there. "Play what?"

The woman just waved her arms toward the swings and stuff.

She walked over to the jungle gym and sat on the first ladder rung. Carefully, holding tight, she squeezed herself in between two rungs. She leaned all the way back, grabbed hold and pulled herself up again. Then she lowered her arms to her sides, sat there.

It seemed like forever ago that she'd come to this playground with her mother. Mommy stood right behind her, told her to bend her knees and put one foot at a time on the next rung. You can do it, she said. And she did. She even climbed to the next bar, and leaned backwards, while her mother sat cross-legged in the center of the jungle gym, beaming up at her. When she got up really high, Mommy stood up and called for her to come down. What her mother meant to say was "climb down," but she didn't. She was facing the center and couldn't see where the bars were, so she jumped. Mommy reached out her arms to catch her, and she almost knocked her over. But Mommy didn't get mad or anything. She hugged her, and laughed.

Without her mother around, she was afraid to climb any higher. She sat down in the center of those bars, the same way her mother had, and watched the other kids climb. Finally what's-her-name came over and said it was time to go home.

She pretended not to notice, and the woman called again. "Go play," she mumbled. "Can't you see I'm playing?"

"Your father will be home soon. I have to change before we go out to dinner."

"Go read."

Finally the woman reached one arm in, caught hold, and pulled. If she'd been standing up, she'd have been able to run to the other side, out of reach, except she wasn't and she didn't. Her arm hurt for weeks and weeks, that's the only reason she ended up telling Grandma. Ever since then she's only been permitted to stay in New York for the three weeks her father's on vacation.

Even thinking about that day makes her want to puke. She hates him she hates him she hates him. She hates the women he's friends with. Every single one of them, including the ones she's never met.

"SORRY, KID," PHIL SAYS, coming back in the room with outstretched, empty palms. "I gave it my best shot, but Grandma and Grandpa insist you have to get home and start getting ready for school."

"School's not for two weeks yet!"

"Grandma wants to take you shopping for school clothes."

"I'll wear my old clothes. I'll wear pajamas if I have to."

"Don't be ridiculous." He suggests that, if Tips asks her, maybe Ellyn will take a ride with them on Sunday.

Ellyn cringes at the mention of her name.

Tips leaps off her upholstered perch. Bounces up and down like a four-year-old. "Will you? Please?"

"I'm not very good with families . . ." Phil should have had better sense than to ask in front of the child. Christ. "Your grandmother will probably hate me." Ellyn tries to laugh. Can't force it.

"No, she won't. She'll love you." Grandma and Grandpa will love Ellyn. They'll take one look at her and realize she can be trusted. They'll all have dinner, and then they'll say okay, you can go back to the city for one more week.

"Maybe if I'd known my own mother better it would have been different," Ellyn muses.

"I barely remember *my* mother but I'm okay with the mothers of my friends."

Yeah, Ellyn thinks. But you've at least got people who care about you. If Tips pushes too hard, all the chatty descriptions of "when I was a child" will turn into horror stories.

"Please. Please please please pretty please."

"Come on," Phil says, uncrossing his legs and taking his hand off the wall that's been supporting him. "If nothing else, we'll have a nice ride and an old-fashioned home-cooked meal." The way he's grinning, it's as if he's suggesting she give him a blow job while he's driving home. And who knows, if she did, they might both enjoy it. It's been a long time since the two of them have been alone; so long she'd almost forgotten.

These aren't Phil's parents, they're Tips' grandparents. The people Tips lives with.

"I've got this neat room," Tips says. She goes on to list all the things she wants Ellyn to see: her bike, her new bedspread, her stereo. . . She even goes off the deep end and says she'll play the piano for her, even though she hates that piano and knows she isn't very good, regardless what her grandparents tell her.

Okay, already.

It's way past her bedtime.

CHAPTER FOUR

AN OLIVE GREEN CALF-LENGTH skirt, a beige silk blouse with long sleeves, a scarf tied neatly at the neck, low-heeled brown pumps.

"Nope," Phil says. "Too corporate. You're not trying to impress them with a lavish presentation, you're taking a ride with us."

So what should she do, wear shorts? A bathing suit? Jeans? They end up stopping by Ellyn's apartment and rummaging through her closets. She models outfit after outfit.

Tips is wide-eyed. Wait till she tells Melissa about this! She can't picture Grandma wearing anything for dress except those tailored suits and pants suits, and it's always the slacks or skirt with a plain white or beige blouse and a matching jacket, she never mixes them up for laughs the way Ellyn's doing. She'd never have fun arranging and rearranging scarves and stuff.

"I used to love sitting in my mother's room and, like, watching her get dressed," Tips says. Maybe, if she spends another week in the city, her grandparents will give Ellyn money to buy her school clothes. They'd *have* to be better than the ones her grandmother chooses.

"I remember my mother sitting up in bed, brushing her hair," Ellyn says. "I was in nursery school, so I was home in the morning while the other kids were in school. If my mother wasn't feeling too bad, RuthAnn would let me come in and play on the floor of her bedroom. I had to be quiet as a teddy bear so I didn't disturb her."

"Disturb who – RuthAnn or your mother?"

"My mother. Actually, though, it's one of the few pleasant memories I have of RuthAnn."

"I knew there had to be at least one," Phil laughs.

Mother looks at the strands of hair that have collected in the bristles of her soft, silver-handled brush. "I sometimes think your father married me because of my long red hair," she says. No one speaks words such as "radiation" or "chemotherapy." Not in 1965. At least not when there are children within earshot.

When the brush is full, Mother balls the hairs up in her fingers and puts them in this little box she keeps in the drawer of the night table. She's talking as she brushes, explaining how pretty soon she'll have enough hair to fill the box. Then she'll take it to the hairdresser, and they'll make a hairpiece out of it.

Joan, Geoff, and RuthAnn laugh and say she's imagining things. She's not, though. That box of hair was probably a secret, between her and her mother. And if they can't find it then they must have accidentally thrown it out. Even now, whenever Ellyn passes a beauty parlor with hairpieces displayed in the window, she stops and looks, wondering which one Mother's hairpiece might have looked like. Sometimes she toys with the idea of buying one, keeping it in a box and pretending.

Tips would probably laugh, too.

Eleven-year-olds can be so cruel sometimes. Just like nine-year-olds.

"Gross," Joan calls it. Not only does she have to remove all the hair clogging the drain whenever she wants to take a bath, but she has to make sure the tub's okay for her sister and brother. She scoops up handful after handful of grungy, wet, tangled hair. Gross! There's a world of difference between a three-year-old and a five-year-old. Tips would have to remember so much more about her mother . . .

Tips picks up a rejected blouse and holds it under her chin to test the color.

"Can't tell that way," Ellyn laughs. "Try it on."

Tips puts it on over her tee-shirt.

The collar's wrong. Ellyn arranges a sheer blue scarf with red and bronze angels around Tips' neck. Puts her head next to Tips' shoulder as they look in the mirror.

Tips beams.

Ellyn imitates her beam. Can't quite duplicate the way the skin under Tips' left eye wrinkles as the cheeks push upward.

Tips cocks her head.

Ellyn cocks her head, first the same direction, then the opposite direction. They smile at each other. Tips' smile is slightly cockeyed, as if to balance that narrowed eye. Her freckles taper off around the chin.

Ellyn arranges Tips' scarf so it has that cowl front, thrown over one shoulder. Takes Tips' hair and tosses it over the same shoulder. That's the way she likes to dress sometimes. Tips stares and stares, mouth open, cheeks all dimpled up.

Meanwhile she herself is down to her bra and panties. "Perfect," Phil says. She whacks the seat of his pants with the skirt she's just picked up.

He gives a yell in mock pain.

Tips takes off the scarf and blouse, makes an awkward stab at folding them, ends up placing them neatly on the bed, goes back to watching. Ellyn tries on the next outfit, and the next. At last they decide on full-cut black rayon slacks (which hopefully won't get too creased sitting in the car) and a simple cotton print blouse she usually wears to the office, only tied in the front instead of tucked in. They're off.

"WHAT DO YOU SAY, TIPS? Should we stop at Molly?"

"Let's wait for Joyce."

"Huh?"

"Joyce is going the other direction, remember?"

"Oh, right. I mean, we could, you could, like . . . "

"We're getting close, kid. Molly or Richard?"

"It doesn't matter."

They stop at Molly. Molly Pitcher, that is. Phil explains that every rest area on the Turnpike's named after someone from the Garden State. The Joyce is for Joyce Kilmer.

"He was this really famous poet."

"She's wild about that guy having a woman's name."

"Stop at Joyce on the way back, okay?" She won't let up till they promise.

They use the restrooms, buy a Coke for Tips, take a quick look in the gift shop (Ellyn insists on buying his parents a box of candy), and are off again.

Ellyn spots the "Six Flags" sign a little further down the road. Great Adventure? She suggests they go there one of these weekends. If they liked Playland, they'll probably love this.

Phil and Tiffany exchange raised-eyebrow looks.

"The safari can be fun," Phil says. "Except they claim the animals are out in the wild and most of them aren't. They've got electric fences and attendants are consistently driving around the perimeters to make sure they don't really get near people. And the landscape looks nothing at all like their natural habitat."

"They've got monkeys that sometimes take a ride on top of a car, at least they say they do, but we didn't even get one."

Ellyn says she was thinking more of the rides.

"Maybe someday, when I'm bigger," Tips says.

"The rides are built for either babies or gorillas. Not very much in between. Even I got sick to my stomach on one of them," Phil tells her.

"Coney Island revisited?" Ellyn laughs.

"Complete with working class New Jersey mentality." Phil smiles that same wistful smile she saw that night on the balcony, when he pointed toward New Jersey as if it were Never-Never Land.

He pulls into the right lane as they near the Cherry Hill exit.

"Go one more stop! Please please please!"

He pulls back into his lane.

"I want to be sure you see the water tower," Tips tells Ellyn.

And there it is, right before the next exit, this huge white tower. *Welcome To Cherry Hill* is painted in bold red letters.

"They wrote that for you especially." She reaches over the seat to hug Ellyn.

"Okay now, for me especially, put that seatbelt back on," her father says.

"I know, I know."

"I usually let her go without it when we're in local traffic, but my mother has a fit."

"She says one fatal accident is all she can bear," Tips laughs.

Ellyn shudders.

Phil takes a few more detours, giving her the Grand Tour: one development after another, circa 1950s and early 1960s. Split levels, differing a bit in color and window placement, but obviously the precursors of prefab. Most have a few bricks around the front door. Every development's named for some wood or other, with a little cream colored sign as you enter giving its name and reminding you it's protected by the Cherry Hill Police Force. These developers never heard of a straight street, either; everything curves, winds back on itself, there's no discernible pattern. She could lose her mind here.

Tips urges him to show Ellyn her school, so they drive along a wooded area with sign pointing to a lake. At last they arrive at Carusi Junior School. There's a two-foot by two-foot pond in front. Past the building is a playground, complete with plastic slide and see-saw. No wonder Tips loves Central Park.

Tips asks if they want to get out and walk around. They both decline. Phil drives back on the other side of the school. Takes one turn then another. "And finally, Locustwood."

She's convinced he took her on this whole tour so the reality of his childhood home wouldn't seem quite as bad. It's the first area she's seen that isn't standardized. And it includes a few older, two-story houses, one of which they stop at. Nice white picket fence around the yard, like in an old Q-Tips commercial. Two-car garage. She's surprised a dog doesn't come running to greet them.

Instead Tips hops out and runs to greet her grandparents. Ellyn starts to get out, thinks better of it, and waits for Phil to come around and open the door for her. There are the introductions, the unloading of all Tips' new toys.

"Turn right at the top of the stairs, it's the first room you come to," Phil's voice calls from behind a stuffed panda.

Wow! The only way to describe this would be to say it's like walking into an ice cream parlor. The walls are cheery pink, the woodwork bright white. Against one wall is the small bed covered with a frilly pink sheet, with a friendly cluster of stuffed animals standing guard near the pillow. Yellow, white, blue, brown, black, green, and a purple Easter Bunny. A Snow White marionette hangs on the wall over the white headboard. A shelf under the window holds ceramic dolls representing various countries. Angel decals on the drawers of a white dresser with bright pink knobs. Then, and this is what's really incredible, there's a pink and white beach or patio umbrella opposite the bed, its fringe hanging down, a light globe placed in the center. It reaches out over the white desk with a computer desk beside it (the monitor has an angel frame around it). A huge, white, bear rug covering the wood floor. Undeniably the most perfect room in the world for a five-year-old.

Tips' energy propels them through the afternoon. Her descriptions of the Museum of Television and Radio not only leave Ellyn the opportunity to tell them about herself, they almost make it easy. And Phil's right, his mother is a good cook – brisket, gravy, mashed potatoes, cherry pie (Tips' favorite). Ellyn offers help with the dishes, and picks up plates without waiting for Mrs. Plattison (Barbara, she insists) to protest that she has a dishwasher and it's easier alone. The two women work together in the huge kitchen, as if they've been doing this for years.

"This brings back memories," Ellyn says.

"Doing dishes with your mother?"

"My older sister. She washed, I dried."

They have a dishwasher, too, but RuthAnn won't let the children anywhere near it.

Joan has her own dishwasher now.

Another woman would probably ask Barbara for her brisket recipe, Ellyn thinks. Knowing she'd never make it. She's cooked more in three weeks than she has in three years.

The minute she hears the dishwasher start, Tips comes in and drags her back to her room to see her New Kids on the Block poster, her stereo, her rock collection, her last year's school clothes. She puts on her computer and demonstrates every program. She finishes with the Barbie Dream House program which is her favorite: "It's been my favorite ever since you gave me that Barbie."

Ellyn's now on a first-name basis with a dozen dolls. Tips drags her into the closet, pushes her clothes aside, and shows her the picture of a house her father drew on the wall "when he was even younger than I am. Even

Grandma and Grandpa never saw it. Promise you won't tell?"

Well, she won't tell Grandma and Grandpa.

Phil and his father have watched the Phillies blow it in the ninth inning. The leftovers have been wrapped and refrigerated, the dishes have been taken out of the dishwasher and put back in the cupboard, the pots and pans washed, the table wiped off. And they're headed back to the city by seven o'clock.

It could have been worse.

"WANT TO STOP FOR A DRINK? There's a little bar I discovered about two miles from the highway," Phil says as they near the Trenton exits.

"Let's wait. I get tense with people drinking and driving. Besides, we promised we'd stop at Joyce."

"Do you want to?"

"No."

"Then we won't."

The past few weeks it's been Tips this and Tips that. Without her there's this all-inclusive silence. They fiddle with the radio and pick up some local college stations. They get back to the city, ditch the car, and head for the nearest bar. One sip and they burst out laughing.

"Poor Tips," Phil says in a perfect imitation of his daughter's melodrama. "She was hoping to come back with us."

"Think so?"

"Know so."

"It's probably just as well," Ellyn says, regretting her words a second later. She hasn't had as much to drink the past three weeks, and the liquor's affecting her more than usual.

"It's probably just as well," Phil agrees, flashing that grin again.

She slips off her sandal. There's a long tablecloth, the tables are close together, no one can see. She lets her foot ride up his leg. And up. And up. His grin deepens.

LABOR DAY. THEN ANOTHER QUICKIE near the end of September. "My parents think we're a steady twosome," Phil jokes for the thirty-fifth time.

It's her second visit to his parents' house, Phil's mother is in the bathroom downstairs and they tell her there's another upstairs. She starts up, comes to a sudden halt in front of her own face. High cheekbones. Eyes so intense and wide they almost counteract the smile. Carefully drawn eyebrows drowned out by freckles. A younger Phil beside her.

"Taken in the park outside City Hall: our wedding picture," Phil says, creeping up behind her. With him on the step below her, they're the same height. "Anita was two months pregnant, so her face is a little rounder there than it usually is. Was."

"Hey," she laughs, running one hand along the banister. "I've known a lot of guys who got women pregnant; most paid for the abortion then fled the scene."

"She'd been raised strict Catholic, and still had problems with the abortion issue. Besides, she wasn't some one-night stand. I adored Anita."

Ellyn sneaks one more look at the picture on her way down. Imagines Anita trying on outfit after outfit, settling finally on the gold silk suit and white lace blouse. Her own mother was probably married in a long white dress, but there are no pictures. The moment Mother was dead, RuthAnn cleaned house.

"How come you're not washing windows?" she teases, sitting back down in the living room. "After all, Columbus Day will be here before you know it." She goes on to explain her father and stepmother always made use of the long weekend to ready the house for winter – storm windows put in, summer clothes packed away, every room thoroughly cleaned. All three children helping.

September 30: Ellyn

She's with a group of people from some camp and they're driving up to Canada for the day. They take her car, with one of the guys (probably a counselor) driving, and just the two of them in the car. He could take his car, but he's got one of those wrecked cars he and his wife bought for $10 and fixed up, so he's not sure it would make it. Also this is the first she's hearing about his wife.

Boy, is she glad she's not driving this alone. The trip's almost completely uphill, and he's got the emergency brake on the entire time (she didn't know you could drive like that).

They make one stop and pick up another guy. He sits in back and isn't intrusive, but then at the next rest stop they pick up several people. She's squashed against the other side in the front, no longer with the driver's arm around her. Even though it's her car she no longer feels wanted, or special here. People look at the shows in the newspapers to try to plan what they'll do when they get to Canada. It seems the groups will be able to split up and do whatever they want. Apparently the matinees start late, so they still might have time to see one. But none interest her anymore. She tries to talk to one of the other guys she finds cute, but it's not the same. The first guy only used her to get the car. She's certain he's ruining it driving with the emergency brake on.

CHAPTER FIVE

TODAY'S THE DAY, FIRST day of the rest of her life, and if it keeps up like this she'll head for the Empire State Building and quietly jump. There's a nine a.m. meeting to present a new ad campaign, and the company nixes the whole package. They save the account, so far, but promise new copy within two weeks. She spends the afternoon brainstorming with her whole staff, and then is at the office until nearly eleven getting the preliminaries together. Stops for a grilled cheese sandwich on her way home, leaves half of it sitting there. At this hour, she's so far past hunger her stomach's in knots.

She tosses her purse onto the couch and its contents scatter. Thumps the answering machine on her way to the bathroom. Three calls, all from Phil.

His mother's going into the hospital, they discovered a blood clot in her neck and want to operate. He's leaving tomorrow morning to pick up Tiffany, bring her back to the city for a few days. Call.

Are you home yet?

Please call.

"You have no idea how good it is to hear your voice," he says, not missing a beat when the phone rings. "Take a ride to Jersey with me."

"I can't. All hell broke loose at work. That's where I've been all night."

"Please, Ellyn. Tips sounds really upset and it'll be easier if you're around."

"I've got two meetings scheduled." She promises to come over right after work, which, she warns him, might not be much before seven or eight. She'll make it as early as she can. She and her friend Bruce were planning to take in the new Sam Shepard play the next night – that all-important Friday-night date carried over from high school. But she'll cancel it. The child's more important right now. Besides, if Tips comes into the city now, she might not come Columbus Day, and there won't be another long weekend until Thanksgiving.

They've spoken to Phil's father by the time she gets to the apartment. The surgery went well. Mother's still in the Recovery Room. Tips hasn't appeared yet.

Over dinner Ellyn talks about the soap commercial they were shooting. They kept doing more takes, until finally the model screamed to get her a bar of Ivory; she has to wash this gunk off before she breaks out in a rash.

Phil asks if they can try to guess what soap it was.

Ellyn agrees to give them two guesses each.

Tips takes another half bite of food. Pushes vegetables around on her plate. Asks if she can please be excused.

Phil pledges to call her when it's time for dessert.

She says that's okay, she doesn't want any.

Ellyn tells Phil the soap commercial was done two years ago, by another agency. The exec joined their staff last year, and told that story one day when they met in front of the microwave. It's usually good for a laugh.

Phil tells Ellyn he moved the VCR into his daughter's bedroom. "She's been closeted in there all afternoon."

"I see my presence did a lot of good."

"Don't underestimate yourself. You at least got her to come up for air."

She'll stay in her room all night and all day Friday (to hear the sitter tell it). There's a brief exit for a strangely silent dinner, then back to her room. Which is, at the moment, just as well with Ellyn. She's brought home enough work to last the next twenty weekends.

The only other times Tips joins the human race are when the phone rings. Finally, on Saturday evening, there's the call from her grandfather she's been praying for. Grandma's sitting up in bed, eating solid food. Now that he's no longer as anxious as he thought he'd be, he doesn't see any reason Tiffany can't come home Sunday night. She can go back to school, eat at Melissa's, and he'll pick her up on his way home from the hospital.

With any luck, she'll be more relaxed in her own space.

Won't we all? Ellyn's dying to spend two or three hours in her own tub, immersed in a soothing bubble bath, maybe John Coltrane playing in the background, one of those hour-long solos where he's hitting ten notes at once. But she agrees to ride out to Cherry Hill with Phil and Tips.

Sunday morning. Or afternoon. It's raining out. Tips is in her room finally settling down with her homework, Ellyn and Phil are in the living room. Phil's buried under various sections of the *Times*. Ellyn sets her laptop up on his desk, goes over the notes from Friday's meetings yet again. Grasping at straws. If they get to Jersey about 7:30 they can see his mother for a few minutes, take his father out to dinner, settle Tips in, and head home. So they won't leave the city till after 5:00.

Phil's father calls. Crying. Don't bring Tiffany. He just got to the hospital, Mother's lying in bed, drooling. She's trying to talk but she's not making any sense. She won't sit up. He doesn't know what happened. She was doing so well. He'll call back when he knows more. The doctor's on his way.

Phil puts the receiver safely back in its cradle. Doesn't lift his head, doesn't turn around, doesn't move. Ellyn, as hesitant as she was that first day she met Tiffany, places a gentle arm on his shoulder.

"I'd hazard a guess she had a stroke," he says finally. But they wait an hour until his father calls back with the same word before even discussing it between themselves. Phil wants to drive out there. His father says no, wait. Wait.

Ellyn waits. Gives him quiet time to digest his father's words. "Tips needs to hear this from her father," she says finally.

Phil's jaw twitches a bit.

"Why don't you go talk to her?"

They hear the refrigerator cycle on in the kitchen.

"The longer you wait the harder it's going to be."

"I can't."

"Sure you can. You don't have to use the word stroke. Tell her Grandma's not as well as expected."

"Come with me."

"Come on, for God's sake. It's not as if this is the first time you've had to break bad news to her."

His eyes stare straight ahead. Hard. Dry.

Ellyn takes a step back. "What did you do when Anita died?"

"Poured myself a drink. No, strike that. First I called my parents, then I poured myself a drink. Then another drink."

"So who told Tips?"

"I guess my parents did."

"You don't know?"

"I was pretty out of it."

"It was her *mother*!"

"It was *my wife*!"

"Well, I'm not your wife! Nor your mother!"

No wonder Tips ended up living with his parents.

Ellyn sits down, crosses her legs, picks up a section of the paper. Puts the paper down.

Phil's rooted in the corner by the phone.

"Either you tell her this minute, or I'm going home. I've got better things to do than watch some lush fall apart again."

"Ellyn, please. Don't do this to Tips."

"I won't if you don't." She sorts through the stack of papers, picks up the Styles section. "After you talk to her I'll go in and see what I can do to comfort her," the bodiless voice behind the newsprint announces.

Poof! goes the happy family. She was too caught up in how different Phil was from her father to notice anything else. Daddy Dearest, indeed!

He shuffles down the hall like an old man.

Well, at least he's telling her. More than he did when her mother died.

RuthAnn takes Joan to shop for school clothes in early September, and insists she buy this navy blue pleated skirt and sweater, so they won't have to worry about her not having the proper clothes for the funeral. Then, of course, Mother lingers on until May.

The mercury will hit seventy later in the day. RuthAnn comes into their room, tells Joan she isn't going to school, gets the skirt and sweater out of the closet, checks to make sure it's clean. Picks out a wine dress for TC to wear. Its lace collar makes her neck itch.

In the kitchen their father, buttering his second slice of rye toast, confirms what Joan suspected.

PHIL'S BACK A FEW MINUTES LATER. "My loving daughter had two questions: will she still have to take piano lessons, and where will she go to school?"

"And your answers?"

"She doesn't have to take piano if she doesn't want to. And we'll have to see about school. Christ, she didn't even ask how Grandma's feeling."

Like father, like daughter.

"I'll go check on her."

Tips is lying face down on her bed, head buried in the pillows, crying soundlessly as only children can.

Ellyn sits beside her. Gently places a palm on her back.

Tips turns over, letting the cries escape now. "She's dead, isn't she?"

"No, she's not." Ellyn manages to sit her up, cuddles the feverish head against her breast. "But your grandmother's very sick."

"That's what they told me when my mother died."

Ellyn runs her fingers soothingly through Tips' hair. "I'd never lie to you, Tip Top."

Tips jerks herself loose. Glowers.

God, those eyes.

Ellyn places both palms on the mattress, rises enough to change position. Takes three deep breaths. "I'm trying to be honest with you, Tiffany. Your grandmother's sick, much sicker than anyone expected her to be."

"I know she's sick. That's why she, like, went in the hospital. They were supposed to make her better."

"Things don't always happen the way people plan. Even doctors don't always know everything. They operated on your grandmother, and for a few days she was better. Then she took a turn for the worse."

"How long till she's better?"

"I don't know," Ellyn says honestly. She reaches out an arm, pulls it back. "I don't think even the doctors know for sure. At the moment they're doing everything they can to make her comfortable."

Tiffany seems to accept that. Except she wants to call and talk to her grandmother. When Ellyn says she can't – can't call, can't visit – they have to start from square one again: Grandma's dead.

How do you explain she's alive, but can't speak, only drool? That even if Tiffany went to visit her, her grandmother probably wouldn't know who she was?

"I TOLD HER SHE COULD TALK to her grandfather later tonight. Maybe he can reassure her." She settles in back at the desk. Words from those commercials she and Tips had so much fun with fade in and out. Excedrin headaches number 39, 58, 62. The cough syrup they've been plugging lately, "recommended by Dr. Mom." Take Sominex tonight and sleep, peace and restful sleep, sleep, sleep (with the tablets moving along the musical notation). No, peace isn't the right word. Deep? Safe?

Grandma's far from safe. Tips has no "Mom." Ellyn wishes now she'd let Phil handle it.

Tiffany stays in her room the rest of the afternoon. Every now and then Phil or Ellyn passes the closed door and listens for a moment. No sounds of sobbing, no sound from the VCR, no computer beeps, just earth-shattering silence.

The Sunday *Times* is massive enough to keep Phil hidden. Ellyn looks over ideas she and her staff came up with months ago: nothing's salvageable. She and Phil haven't exchanged ten words in the past five hours. If it weren't for Tiffany, she wouldn't be here.

At eight o'clock they still haven't eaten. Phil wants to stay by the phone in case his father calls. Ellyn drags Tiffany over to Burger King. A bag lady sits down next to them. Walking home, Ellyn notices for the first time that the building next to Phil's has terraces also. It's a pre-war building; hell of a lot more character.

ONCE UPON A TIME there was a lady's head, ceramic, pink, Mother's favorite color and the color of the room TC shares with her sister. She has black hair, tied neatly back, and is always smiling – the kind of hair TC wishes she had and the kind of smile no one in real life ever had. That head takes flowers from her hands, and holds them. She starts out with rosebuds, then the roses get all brown, so TC and Geoff go over to the vacant lot near school and pick wildflowers. Father says Mother loves her, and the nurses always stop to see that she has enough water. It's almost as good as having a real person there, wide awake all night, watching over things.

Clearing the table after dinner Tuesday night, Ellyn suggests that Tiffany might want to send her grandmother flowers.

"I don't want to." The stock answer to everything she's suggested the past four days.

"Why not, Tips? Grandma loves flowers."

No response.

"Did I ever tell you about the time I bought her a giant sunflower for Mother's Day? It was almost as big as my face, and I carried it home barely able to see around it. I misjudged a curb, fell, and scraped my elbow. I walked into the kitchen to present her with my gift. Instead she saw blood running down my arm and shrieked."

Tips concentrates on making her tenth cat's cradle of the evening.

Ellyn says, if she wants, they can call 800 Flowers. Like those subway ads: "Secretary overwhelmed by 800 flowers!" Or they could go to the florist's and pick them out.

Phil suggests they could get a pretty vase. Maybe red, to match the red glass lamp Grandma loves so much.

"It would only get broken."

"Don't be ridiculous."

"It would! I mean, you just said Grandma's sick. If she's dizzy or nauseous, she'd, like, break it."

"In other words, we should never give you a balloon, because balloons get broken. Right?"

"That's different." Sulk. Sulk.

"I know it's different. I'm just trying to get you to see how childish you're being."

"Why can't we get her something else? I know what! We can get her a giant cookie from The Great American Chocolate Chip Cookie Company. You know, the place in the mall. And they decorate the cookies and everything."

"Honey, I don't think that's a good idea."

"Sure it is! You could pick it up tomorrow, on your way to visit." Then Grandma will call and say how wonderful it tastes, and what a great idea it was, and how she's glad they didn't send some smelly flowers like other people do.

"I don't think Grandma's feeling well enough to appreciate a cookie right now."

"But if she had a cookie it would help her feel better."

"Tell you what," Ellyn says. "Why don't you and your father send her the cookie, and I'll send her flowers? That way, she'll have both gifts." She gets her coat out of the closet. "Want to come with me to the flower shop?"

"DO-ON'T!" She tugs at Ellyn's sleeve.

"Tiffany, flowers cheer up a drab hospital room. They're what you're supposed to send sick people."

"They're what you send dead people!"

"Oh, Christ," Phil mutters. He reaches out to take his daughter in his arms.

Ellyn stands, one hand on the closet door, not knowing quite what to do with her arms or her legs, unwilling to let go.

No one holds TC.

That head holds flowers.

"OKAY," ELLYN SAYS, SITTING DOWN with paper and pencil. "We've got to plan exactly what we want this cookie to be."

Phil suggests a two-pound white chocolate chip.

"M & Ms," Tiffany insists. She wants it to be even more colorful than the cookie they bought her one time on her birthday. Her father and mother took her over to the mall and . . .

"M & Ms it is," Ellyn says. "Now, what should we say on it?"

"*Happy birthday?*" Phil jokes.

Ellyn suggests they walk over to the drugstore and look at the get-well cards.

No one seconds the motion.

"Okay, then we can just write *Get Well.*" (Ellyn).

"*Get Well Soon.*" (Phil).

"*Get well this minute.*" (Ellyn).

Grandma's one of those people who recovers really fast. For all they know, she might be better already.

"*Please Get Well.*" (Phil).

"*Eat Well, Get Well.*" (Ellyn)

"*Get The Swellest Ever.*" (Phil).

"That one, that one! Please!" Not that it's great, but it's the best so far, and at least her father thought of it.

Phil calls and orders the cookie. Sits his daughter down and, one arm around her, explains that flowers are appropriate for more than one occasion, and only people with hay fever need to be afraid of them. For other people, especially women, flowers mark important occasions. She'll wear a corsage to dances, carry a bouquet at her wedding. "And even before your wedding, you'll probably try to catch someone else's bouquet."

"And if I were afraid of flowers I'd duck!" Tips goes on to tell him about all the kids in her school who are afraid of being hit by kickballs. They're always the last ones picked for teams, and then stuck somewhere in the outfield where it doesn't matter much. "Nobody wants to play with them other times, either, you know?" Her face turns suddenly sad. She'll probably never see those kids again.

Phil presses her close.

Ellyn decides the flowers can wait till tomorrow. Or the next day.

"HALF THE GODDAMN TOWN sent flowers. More flowers than I've seen this side of the Brooklyn Botanical Garden," Phil says as he lies on his side, watching Ellyn undress. She has this disconcerting habit of sometimes taking off her clothes while staring straight ahead, a total lack of interest in what's going on or off. Also a signal he'd better not expect very much from her tonight.

"They filled the whole altar, I'll bet."

"And halfway down the aisles. My parents even thought to get this great big heart-shaped array of white flowers with pink roses in the center spelling out *Mother.*"

She could figure out how to spell words up to about five letters by the time she entered kindergarten – house, father, chair. Ellyn has this vision of Phil pointing out the bouquet and asking his daughter if she knows what that word spells. Her own father might have been that tactless. Had anyone cared enough to send such a bouquet. Had TC been a year or two older. Had their father paid a bit more attention to what his children were learning. Or doing.

"What's the matter, didn't anyone send flowers to your mother's funeral?" Phil teases, turning toward her as she gets in bed.

"How the hell should I remember? I was three years old!" Five-year-olds remember. Nine-year-olds remember.

How much does Joan remember?

Phil holds out a consoling arm as his lover climbs into the bed beside him.

Ellyn skirts around it. "My father lifted me up and told me to kiss my mother goodbye," she says, staring at the darkened ceiling fixture.

"Anita's parents wanted to take Tiffany up to see her mother's body in the casket, but she seemed frightened, so my mother led her over to the couch against the wall and they sat there."

"Lucky her!"

"I don't know if I'd call it lucky. You still saw this box being lowered into the ground . . ."

"I didn't go to the cemetery. Or the church. Only the Viewing, and it was past my bedtime so I was way overtired."

"None of the kids went to the funeral?"

"Joan did. Geoff had to go to school. They dropped me off at the babysitter's early."

"You didn't understand why?"

"All I knew was the kids I liked to play with were still at home."

"God."

"Geoff used to talk about how he looked out the window at school and saw the cars go by with their lights on and the police car leading them. He knew this was all for his mother, that they were taking her somewhere and his sister was with them. He felt left out."

"Yeah, I guess she would have."

"He."

"Who?"

"Geoff. My brother? Remember?"

"Sorry. I was thinking about Tiffany again. Had it been up to me, Tips wouldn't have gone to the funeral. But I guess I was too far gone to make much of a protest. My mother insisted she'd find it easier to accept her mother's death later if she went through the ritual with the rest of us, even if she didn't understand it."

"Did she understand?"

"I don't know. She was upset by all the people crying. But she was also disoriented by being in the strange house, strange town, all these places she'd never seen before. People she'd never met were coming over, saying petty, small-minded things like *God loves you* or *your mother's at peace now*. Leaving my mother with even more to explain."

"How the hell did she explain?"

"I don't know. I guess by holding her. Letting her cry. Telling her there's nothing wrong with crying."

Better than keeping things in your head, she supposes.

She moves over to the edge of the bed. Eyes plastered shut, she hears Phil's voice droning on in the distance, telling her something else about the funeral. No, about some other funeral. Something about being six years old and sitting in the car while his parents went inside. About it raining out. About associating rain and funerals ever since then. He mentions an aunt, a cousin.

TC is fighting to stay awake while, across the room, Joan's describing the burial in all its gory detail. Digging this hole, putting this box in it. It sounds like Mother's being planted. She keeps expecting to wake up one morning and see all these flowers in their yard.

A week after Mother's death RuthAnn fills the lady's head with stupid orange and white plastic flowers sticking out every direction. Then for a while Joan uses her as a pencil holder. She can't remember what happens after that. The lady herself probably forgets those soft pink rose buds she was born with. Her head is too cluttered with other things.

October 2: Ellyn

She's writing some copy for an ad on Dodge cars. She finds a car price and model guide in her doctor's office. This is going to be perfect. Only the doctor warns her that it's last year's guide, so it's not going to be up to date on specifics. She can either stick to general things, such as car bodies, or find this year's guide. She can also stop into Dodge agencies and pick up their literature. Only not all agencies carry all models – she'd have to go everywhere, and she doesn't have time. She'll have a few hours between meetings tonight. She can bring Phil's manual typewriter with her, because it's easier to carry, putting it in some kind of horn case with a round bottom and short neck. But what will he use? He can use her portable electric, she tells him, since he's carrying a big suitcase anyway, and it will fit with the other things. She supposes she could wait, though, and let him take his typewriter today. She does have a few weeks yet. It's just her nature to get everything done immediately.

CHAPTER SIX

PHIL AND ANITA PLANNED on sending their daughter to Walden. Which is now bankrupt. Public school's out of the question, even for a few months. Ellyn suggests Friends' Seminary.

"She doesn't need friends, she needs a safe place to learn. And no babble about some Higher Being."

"It has nothing to do with religion these days."

"A little might creep in. Jesus, Ellyn, you saw her reaction to the flowers. All we need is for someone to say something about God and have all the memories stirred up yet again."

Dalton, Phil's second choice, won't even consider accepting a child once the school year's underway. Neither will The Clarendon School. Ellyn discovers they could still get her into Riverdale Country School, but Phil insists Riverdale's too far away. And more than likely not good enough.

He calls Chapin, The Little Red School House, Birch Wathen, Calhoun, Corlears, Bank Street. Desperate for any leads he might get, he stops by a few places on his way to work, picks up brochures. Orders a sandwich for lunch and sits at his desk flipping through them, staring at the studious yet smiling girls and boys till he's managed to convince himself those dimples are air-brushed on. Or if not she'd never be happy there. And those Chapin uniforms – no way! He pushes the brochures aside, tosses the wrappings from lunch in the wastebasket, gets back to work.

One of the other brokers stops by his desk with papers to sign. Pokes around while he's signing. "Clarendon, huh? Isn't that the place . . ." He picks up the top brochure and thumbs through it while Phil recounts the past six days in ten words or less.

"Hey, I was right. Take a look at this."

In small bold type on page two is a list of the Board of Directors. Third name down is Marcus Anders. Sitting one flight above them at this very minute, playing god. The god of raises and bonuses.

"Think there's a chance?"

"Given your current state, I'd go for it. Once finding a school's off your mind you'll perform better – Anders is smart enough to realize that."

What the hell, he's worked hard all these years. No harm in trying.

PLAYGROUND, GYM, HOME ROOM, science lab, computer room, auditorium, study hall, library, what more do you want?

If they have to ask, they'll never listen. But what she mostly wants is for one group of those girls standing around talking to, like, open up and include her.

Fat chance! She's not even supposed to be here, it's what they call a "parent's tour." Which means they'll listen to Ellyn before they'll listen to her. The only reason they let her come at all is that they had no one to leave her with.

If those girls do start talking to her, she'll tell them right off that Ellyn's not her mother. She'll tell them her real mother's gorgeous, and she always wears her hair long, even when she's working, she never piles it up the top of her head the way Ellyn's done today. She'll tell them how her mother was driving her car out in California when she had a stroke, no, a heart attack, and right now she's in the hospital which she'll probably never leave, ever. She'll tell them Ellyn's this woman her father's hanging out with, for now, till they know for sure.

The sociology teacher steps out in the hall to talk with her father. He's young, and male. In Cherry Hill you don't have men teachers until high school, unless you luck out and get Mr. Rockham for seventh grade, which might not be all that lucky on account of she's heard he gives tons of homework.

The sociology teacher smiles at her.

They go into the principal's office. Only two extra chairs – her father takes one, Ellyn takes the other. She goes over and studies these stupid graduation photos on the wall while her father writes out a check. They'll expect her Monday morning, nine a.m., sharp. The doors open at 7:45, if they want to drop her off early. They try their best to accommodate working parents.

They stop for lunch at this fancy place with tablecloths and paintings of weird-looking women on the walls. Her father talks about the day they took her to register for kindergarten. "It was in May, and the kindergartners were playing in the schoolyard. Mommy pointed them out to you. Your mouth fell open. Finally you exclaimed, *they're so big*! You couldn't grasp the concept that you'd ever be like them."

Tiffany picks the lettuce off her tuna sandwich. She told them no lettuce, but no one listened! No one ever listens.

Ellyn asks if she's planned what she'll wear to school the first day, then suggests maybe they'll go shopping on Saturday, pick out some great outfit.

She doesn't need a new outfit – Grandma just bought her all these new things at Gap Kids. She doesn't want anything else. So what if she told them that? Ellyn would only go on and on about some wonderful clothes she's seen.

She blows bubbles through her straw. Some of her Coke spills.

THEY FINISH LUNCH, START walking back to the car, and then decide to take a detour through the park. With Phil's mother in the hospital, God knows how long it'll be before they get another chance to enjoy the city in the middle of the day. Tiffany wanders from swing to swing to swing, the only child over five in the playground, while Phil and Ellyn sit on a nearby bench, holding hands. They watch this guy pointing squirrels out so his dog can go chase them.

It's almost three by the time they're on their way back to the car. Wha . . . ? There are all these cars, double- and triple-parked up and down the block. Limos, Jags, Mercedes, BMWs. There wasn't a funeral parlor across the street, was there? Separately, silently, Ellyn and Phil are wishing they could get the deposit back. But even the car's locked in.

Oh. It's school letting out.

There probably aren't three parents in this crowd. There are au pairs, governesses, nannies, nursemaids, guardians. "I'll bet there's a mistress or two," Ellyn whispers. Phil smiles knowingly, looks closer at the women around him. Ellyn jokingly tugs his arm.

Simultaneously, they check their watches. "The earliest I can possibly get home would be 5:30, and even that's pressing it," Phil mumbles.

She reminds him how erratic her schedule can be.

She has this image of Tiffany hanging out in front of the school Monday afternoon. Or maybe even making it home, but then, of course, not being able to get inside. At least they caught it in time. Like the flu or pneumonia. He has the image of himself telling clients he has to leave before the closing bell, but they can read all the information in tomorrow's *Wall Street Journal.*

Having a child around, you know your neighbors. Phil makes four or five calls, rings a bell or two, and tracks down a woman on the tenth floor who has a college student who picks her kids up at school every day and takes care of them till six or seven, even does a bit of cleaning while she's at it. Turns out she has a friend who has a sister who needs the extra money.

She might have left out a step or two.

What's important to Phil is that Abbey seems clean-cut, caring and intelligent. And she can start on Monday.

Ellyn's impressed by the fact that Abbey goes to Parsons and wants to be a fashion designer. Now here's someone who should do her own modeling – she has that gamin look: delicate, flawless wide face, large blue eyes, thin dancer's body. Definitely a future Paulina. She can picture her five or ten years from now, showing up in all the Estée Lauder ads.

Tiffany just plain gapes. Her mother was pretty, Ellyn's pretty, but that's nothing compared to this. And Abbey's only twenty, which means she's only a little ways past being a teenager, they could be friends almost.

She wishes Abbey could take her shopping tomorrow.

SATURDAY MORNING: PHIL HAS BREAKFAST with them before heading off to New Jersey. As soon as the door closes behind him, Tiffany heads for her room. Ellyn clears the table and leaves the dishes in the sink to soak. Knocks on Tiffany's door. Three weeks last August, and this door wasn't closed three times.

"We said we'd go shopping, remember?"

"I remember." Tiffany's sprawled on the bed, barely looks up from the book she's reading.

Ellyn sits on the bed. "What's your favorite store in the whole city?"

"I don't know. Mostly, Grandma takes me to the mall."

God knows the number of times Ellyn's walked past some children's shop as she's wandered the city, looked in the windows thinking those clothes were so great they could almost make her wish she had a child. But she can't recall their names, or where they were.

"Want to go to the A & S Plaza? That's the closest thing to a mall we've got."

"It doesn't matter."

"How about Bergdorf's? That's where the people who really know fashion shop."

"Whatever."

Ellyn finishes the dishes, gets dressed, and they're off to Bergdorf's junior section.

Tiffany heads straight for a rack of jeans. "I said some great outfit," Ellyn laughs. "Maybe leggings with a big hand-knit sweater?"

"Most of the kids had jeans on."

"Jeans it is, then."

Tiffany takes a turtleneck and jeans into the dressing room. Comes out to show Ellyn. Oops. The turtleneck looks ridiculous on her flat chest. The jeans are cut for mature hips.

It's the first time Tiffany's laughed in ten days.

All of a sudden, Ellyn recalls those ads on the buses, the shapely woman in Guess jeans, no bra or blouse, sitting with her knee drawn up to cover her chest. Suggestive as all hell. Not to mention Brooke Shields.

So that's why she'd balked at the thought of jeans.

Tiffany goes back in to get changed, while Ellyn inquires as to where the teen or children's section is. No such animal, not here.

"You call it, kid – A & S or Bloomingdale's?"

"Umm . . . Bloomingdale's?" She used to go there with her mother sometimes.

They grab a cab to Bloomie's.

They walk around the floor, surveying their options. Tiffany selects a pair of Esprit jeans, and gravitates toward a table of stiff cotton pullovers; they look like sweatshirts turned inside out. $48. They're not worth $4.80. But if that's what she wants . . .

She wants a navy cotton turtleneck, even though there are some soft merino wool ones on the next table.

Don't make the mistake of the jeans again, she reminds herself.

Ellyn suggests Tif get a vest as well. They don't know what the weather's going to be on Monday and, what the hell, it's nice to have an extra, isn't it?

Tiffany flips through the rack, her eyes turned away from the vests, away from Ellyn. Picks out one with a black and white patchwork front made from antique materials, flecks of color here and there.

"Fantastic!" Ellyn says. "I couldn't have chosen better myself. That navy silk back makes it great with jeans, too."

They circle the floor one more time to be sure they haven't missed . . .

Wow! These looked like velvet pants the first time around. But they're not, they're jeans with thin velvet strips down the sides. "My sister Joan had a pair almost exactly like these. As a kid, I thought they were the most beautiful jeans in the world," Ellyn says, pulling out a pair with purple velvet, size 12. "Want to try them on?"

"I like the others better."

"These are dressier. Tell you what – try them on, and if they look good, I'll buy them for you. That way you can get both pair."

They look every bit as good as she expected. The stripe highlights Tiffany's long legs to perfection.

So there you have it, Ellyn thinks as they take the escalator down. Two pair of jeans, a turtleneck, a vest, and a pullover all of which, except for that one pair of jeans, could have come from The Gap on 86th St. Eight blocks from home.

Nothing's gone as planned today. When she first suggested they go shopping, she imagined a repeat performance of the fashion show in her apartment, the two of them taking outfits into the dressing rooms to try on, laughing as they mixed up crazy combinations.

They're not even on the same floor.

Phil won't be back from Cherry Hill for hours yet, so they head over to the Museum of Modern Art for lunch in the garden. Ellyn's hoping there might be a Calder show, or some information-age interactive exhibition Tiffany can get excited about.

No such luck. Ellyn takes her up to the permanent collection, parks her in front of a Picasso, a Klee, a Dali, a Pollock. In the gift shop next door, she flips through Magritte postcards until she finds his famous "False Mirror." She hands the card to Tiffany: "What's this remind you of?"

"I don't know," she mumbles. It's probably what her grandmother looks like now.

"CBS – Channel 2. Haven't you ever seen their logo? Look again. There's the eye in the center, the cheek curving under it and the eyelid on top, all three disjointed, floating in space."

Tiffany shrugs.

"Imagine it colorless, behind a grey grid."

Tiffany's giving her that head cocked, *you must be crazy* look she's seen in other kids.

"Anyway, this is where it probably came from." She takes the card out of Tiffany's hands and puts it back in the bin. Maybe they should have gone to the A & S Plaza, after all. At least Tiffany would have been in familiar surroundings. This was probably the wrong day for culture shock.

Still, it's so hard to fathom: TC would have adored a day like this.

Joan would have hated it.

It's not even four o'clock yet.

Home sweet home. Or rather, Phil's. Goes to show how much time she's spending here.

Tiffany goes to her room, closes the door. She takes the clothes out of their bags, stares at them. Those velvet jeans would look a lot better if they had holes, right about . . . here. She picks up her scissors. Puts them down. They're kindergarten scissors; she'd probably break them.

IT'S NOT EXACTLY A CONSCIOUS decision, but she finds herself staying later and later at the office those nights Phil takes off for Cherry Hill. Once home, she busies herself in the kitchen making dinner. Tiffany has homework, watches some TV, then retreats to her room for whatever else an eleven-year-old does behind closed doors most of the night. Weekends seem to drag on forever.

They'd planned on having so much fun together. Even after Phil's mother had the stroke she'd hoped . . .

TC's ecstatic at anyone spending time with her. Joan shrugs people off. Joan's not three, she's nine. And she remembers. *Remember when* . . . , TC would say, and make up something just to have Joan, maybe, give her own remember.

Ellyn stares across the table at the silent child.

"Your school's having a Halloween party, isn't it?" she asks one night when the three of them are eating together.

"I don't know."

"It said in the newsletter they are," Phil points out.

Ellyn asks Tiffany what she wants to go as.

"It doesn't matter."

"Yes, it does. Think of the most outlandish thing you can, and we'll work on getting a costume together."

"A ballerina?"

Too easy, Ellyn explains. What makes or breaks a costume is the ability to create an overall effect by mixing disparate elements, like in some of those commercials they saw at the museum.

"What did you used to go as?"

Ellyn gulps. "A princess, most years. One year Joan made me wings and I went as an angel."

"I thought you said creative." Phil nearly drops the plate he's drying.

"Hey, I had no choice. And no money."

"And your mother was dead and your stepmother couldn't have cared less," father and daughter continue in unison.

"What can I say? You guys bring out the best in me."

"I went as Uncle Sam one year," Phil says.

"Like in that hot dog commercial?"

"Exactly like in that hot dog commercial. They even pasted on a cotton beard. Grandma's got a picture around somewhere."

"Come on," Ellyn interrupts. "No more stalling. This isn't about what we used to go as, it's about finding you a costume for this year."

"I said, a ballerina."

"And Ellyn said you can think of something better."

"Umm . . . Maybe . . . a poodle ballerina?"

They watched dancing dogs on television last night. An old Ed Sullivan rerun.

"Did I ever tell you about Grandma's costume?" Phil asks, hoping to keep his daughter out in the open a bit longer.

One year he came home from Trick or Treating with a candy apple he got from one of their neighbors, Mrs. Alison. He loved candy apples, and his mother decided to go get him another one. She dressed up in this pair of overalls his father used for working on the car, put on this generic half-mask, and went to Mrs. Alison's, plus a few other houses on the block. Mrs. Alison recognized her right away, but one of the other neighbors didn't. So she came home and changed into a pair of his father's pajamas, and went out again. *Boy, they're getting bigger every year*, the neighbor said this time. His mother changed into a suit and tie, and went out again. This time she couldn't keep a straight face.

"I can just picture RuthAnn doing that," Ellyn jokes, looking upward as if she were at this moment a little girl holding RuthAnn's hand, being hurried along while she's trying to tell her something important.

"Actually, I think my mother was feeling a bit left out," Phil says. "When I was four or five, she used to take me around to all the neighbors."

"Grandma always does that! I hate it when Grandma does that!" Or she used to hate it. Last year she didn't even want to go out Trick or Treating because Grandma insisted on all but holding her hand like a two-year-old. And now look what's happened.

Tiffany heads off for her room, alone.

On Saturday Ellyn takes her to buy a leotard. She chooses the first one she lays her hand on: black, no frills. But at least she's interested.

"Now for the poodle part," Ellyn says as they're walking home. "I asked the art director in my office for some ideas, and he pointed out that Persian lamb fur resembles poodle fur. There's this flea market down on 77th and Columbus tomorrow where we should be able to get cheap stoles – we'll wrap one around your chest and another around your hips, and we'll get you some imitation Persian lamb earmuffs. How's that sound?"

"Okay, I guess. Anything you want."

But then the next day, Tips volunteers the information that she used to take ballet classes. "I mean when I was still living in New York."

"You couldn't find ballet classes in Cherry Hill?"

"I guess we could have. But my grandparents, like, wanted me to do different things. Piano and stuff. They said if I had other interests they wouldn't always make me think of my mother taking me to ballet classes, you know."

Ellyn puts her arm around Tips' shoulder. Gently. Tiffany's been pulling away from her more often than not these days. "Would you rather skip the poodle and just go as a ballerina?" she asks, softly.

Tiffany either doesn't hear or pretends not to hear.

THE END OF HER POODLE STOLE flaps against Ellyn's face, smelling mustier than ever in the small, crowded elevator.

On their way to the subway they run into a father Phil knows from the neighborhood, holding a skeleton by one hand, a dog's leash in the other. The skeleton puffs out his chest and makes a scary face at Tiffany. Tips barks back at him, which starts the dog barking. She lifts up her mask and crouches down. "It's me, Buster, you know me, come on."

"I had a skeleton costume when I was three or four," Phil says as they're walking again. "They were pajamas, actually. And they glowed in the dark." Tiffany pulls away, looks away. He tells Ellyn the rest of the story, how the first time he wore them to bed he woke up in the middle of the night and thought he was seeing his own bones. How terrified he was.

Two teenage boys, their faces covered with white paint, run past them with a quarter-inch clearance, shopping bags dangling from their arms. Trick or treat.

Adolescents used to go out collecting for UNICEF.

Another group of teenagers runs across the street, shouting, pounding on the windows of stores, rattling gates, dashing back across Broadway right before the light changes. Brakes squeal, car horns scream their heads off. God knows what it'll be like at the Halloween parade.

Ellyn turns to watch a mother crouching down, readjusting the masks of Wonder Woman and The Bionic Man. She finds that nurturing pose more haunting than anything else tonight.

THE PARADE WAS MORE FUN than she's had in weeks. Costumes even better than Ellyn could think up. Two people dressed as garbage. A bunch of guys going as a "NYC car" – except only the part that's supposed to hold the wheels on and the sign saying "No Radio" remained. She can't picture people in Cherry Hill understanding that one.

Not a single skeleton. But even if there'd been skeletons, she wouldn't have been afraid of them. Even if their bones glowed. She hasn't been afraid of skeletons for years and years. Not since she first lived with Grandma and Grandpa and thought the skeleton was going to eat her alive. He'd come to the window in the middle of the night, night after night, and she was so scared she wet the bed, night after night.

Grandpa looked out the window, then Grandma looked – they looked both ways like you're supposed to before you cross the street. But they never saw the skeleton, and she'd have to plead and plead for them to leave the light on so he wouldn't come back. Finally one night they ran in fast and forgot to put the light on. That's when they saw him.

Grandpa rushed to the window. "I've got his number now."

She buried her head under the covers.

"Watch, honey. Want to see him get fatter?"

She peeked out only long enough to see that his bones had gotten fatter than a hippopotamus. Fatter than an elephant.

Grandma sat down on the bed and took her in her arms. "It's only the streetlights shining through the Venetian blind," she said. "Look at the wall. I'll bet Grandpa can make him turn into a blaze of light."

"I can do anything. Watch!"

He pulled the blind up, quickly. Then he made the skeleton come back. He called her over to the window to do it herself.

Again they left the light on, in case the skeleton came back. The next day they took down the blinds, went to the mall and bought shades for her room. And that was the end of the skeleton. No more bones reflected on the wall. No more wet beds.

"We were at our wits' end," her grandparents laughed, telling her the story later, and again later. "We were on the verge of taking you to a psychiatrist."

She almost wishes now they had.

At Clarendon, her new school, shrinks are *in.* Her very first day at school she heard one girl in her class telling another that she couldn't come over right after school to work on the science project, but she'd drop by after her shrink appointment. Tiffany shot a glance in the girl's direction: she didn't look crazy. Then in the lunchroom last week, two older girls at the table behind her were discussing a classmate suspended for selling dope. It was all *my shrink said this, my shrink said that.* All around her kids are saying *my shrink said* in the same way kids at her old school always say *my mother said.*

When she told Grandma about kids saying *my mother said* all the time, she suggested responding with *my grandmother said.* Except it sounded all wrong. If she told her grandmother about everyone saying *my shrink said*, it would be even worse. Grandma would be horrified that parents would send kids for therapy, and even more horrified that they were permitted to talk about it. She'd probably be accused of lying. *Besides*, Grandma would say, *the word is psychiatrist, or psychologist.*

No, she wouldn't. Grandma probably wouldn't say anything. She overheard her father tell Ellyn about how Grandma has all this trouble speaking.

SHE SHIFTS AROUND IN BED, holds the rabbit up so he catches the light coming in the window. She watches the shadow his long pointy ears make – first on the quilt then, if she struggles to get out of the way and holds it up a bit higher, on the wall.

Her father took her to see a performance at the museum last year, a sort of puppet show, only a great one. You couldn't see the people at all; you only saw the shadows on this white screen. And afterward the people came out and they showed the kids these flat metal puppets they'd been moving. On the screen they looked real.

She puts the rabbit on the pillow, folds her hands together, catching the light. She holds her two index fingers straight out, to make a bird's beak. Open, close, open, close.

"Look at the birdy." She makes the rabbit lunge toward the shadow, the way she's seen cats do. Then she explains all about shadow figures, and how there isn't any bird, he just thinks there is.

"Right now Grandma's probably a shadow of the Grandma we know," she tells the rabbit. "That's why we can't see her." She lies back down, watches the headlights of passing cars making the room dark, then light, then dark again. She wishes it were still just the light, playing new tricks on them.

A LOT OF RESTAURANTS IN CHERRY HILL, like the diner and the Friendly's, use these place mats that are filled with follow the dots and word games and mazes. But her father takes her to places where they cover the whole table with a sheet of paper and then put a jar of crayons in the center instead of plastic flowers. They've always been her most favorite places.

She reaches for a yellow crayon, draws a soft curve for the woman's breasts, then a lot of small lines to show her waist tucked in, the way Abbey showed her. She picks up a red crayon and draws the sweep of her skirt in another curve. Then she draws a little girl holding her hand. A tree beside them. A tall building. A funny-looking figure floating in air. Ellyn thinks immediately of Chagall.

Phil asks who it is.

"I don't know."

"It looks like an angel to me," Ellyn offers.

"Or a kite," Phil suggests.

Tiffany draws a line to trace the kite or angel to the little girl's hand. With a quiet shudder, Phil recalls families he and Anita used to see at the mall: mothers holding one child by the arm, with a toddler trailing behind, a leash-like apparatus tied to one wrist. They'd always sworn they'd never let that happen.

Anita's long gone. His daughter's spent the past six years in Cherry Hill.

Phil says it looks like a jump rope, and the angel looks like someone who jumped so high he touched the clouds with his fingers.

Tiffany agrees: it's a jump rope. The woman's turning one end and the girl's waiting her turn to jump.

"Who's turning the other end?"

Tiffany doesn't answer. She's busy filling in the grass and flowers. They've noticed, in the past month, how much more meticulous her drawings have become.

"How about Grandpa?"

"I don't think so. Grandpa gets out of breath when he pushes me on the swing and stuff."

"How about me?" Ellyn asks.

All of a sudden this is one of her pretend-this-stranger-isn't-here nights.

Her father suggests she draw Grandma.

Tiffany picks up a black crayon and begins to draw a woman at the other end of the rope. The other figures have bright yellow, green and red clothes, but this one is black – black eyes, black hair, black lips.

"That doesn't look like Grandma to me." Phil suggests a bright red apron, or maybe a colorful scarf.

"It's Grandma." Tiffany fills in the outlines of her skirt and blouse.

THAT'S THE MOST GODAWFUL DRAWING I've ever seen, Ellyn wants to tell her. Four years old, five years old, six years old, TC runs over to show RuthAnn a new drawing and RuthAnn says it's a terrible picture. Sometimes she points out a tree is lopsided, or a house looks all wrong.

"I told her it was stupid, but she wouldn't listen to me," Joan says. Maybe once, maybe a million zillion times. It all runs together.

By the time she enters kindergarten, she decides heads are the most difficult thing in the world to get to look right, so all her figures are ghosts or torsos. Long before she's eleven years old, she stops showing pictures to her sister, her stepmother, or anyone else.

Ellyn bites her lip. Phil should have had better sense than to suggest she draw her grandmother. She would have been fine if he could have left her alone.

Tiffany puts the crayon down and waits for comments. Phil tells her how much he likes the little girl and the first woman she drew. Ellyn praises the flowers she's drawn at the woman's feet. Comments on how well her figures blend into the landscape. If she takes another bite of food she's not going to be able to hold it down.

She reminds herself again not to take it out on the child. Don't become RuthAnn just because Tiffany isn't the wide-eyed little girl she was last summer. Besides, it's Phil she's angry at.

She supposes their lovemaking will be invigorating again tonight. Sometimes it's when they're angriest at each other that sex is best – all that tension building up, and releasing. Just don't let that hostility translate into her relationship with Tiffany. Don't don't don't don't.

Don't.

CHAPTER SEVEN

"ONE FATAL ACCIDENT IS ALL Grandma can bear." Tossed off like any other flip comment last summer. These days Tiffany fastens her seat belt every time she gets in the car. Then she'll want to see, hear, or say something, so she'll open it and lean forward. Sit back and fasten it again. Click, click, click, click the whole trip.

It's driving Ellyn batshit. "You don't need a seat belt," she says finally. "We're only going across town."

"It's safer this way."

"What kind of car are we riding in?"

"Volvo."

"Remember those Volvo commercials we saw at the museum? They all talked about how safe Volvos are."

She doesn't remember.

"Sure you do, they were on the same tape as Josephine the Plumber and Madge Soaking in Palmolive."

"I just told you: I don't remember."

Phil reminds her about the Volvo commercial on TV the other night, "The one with the little boy drawing pictures for his brother, saying, *this is Mommy's car, this is the only car we're allowed to ride in.*"

Ellyn mentions another one that's on a lot now, "where this little girl says *My Daddy loves me so much he bought a Volvo.*"

"Did you write those?" Tiffany asks with the same excitement Ellyn witnessed last summer. So surprising these days.

"No, but I wish I did. They're honest commercials, too. Volvos are the safest cars on the road."

"That's right," Phil adds. "Grandma and Grandpa bought this car for us, because they wanted to be sure and protect us." It was two weeks after the other car was totaled. He put up what he got from the insurance, his parents footed the rest. "Even if we did have an accident, usually people don't get hurt in a Volvo."

"What kind of car was Mommy driving?"

He takes a deep breath. "A Honda," he says. "A brown one. You know, one of those little cars; it's supposed to be a station wagon, only the back's tiny."

Ellyn watches as her lover's hands tighten on the steering wheel. This is how accidents happen.

JESSICA. SHE REALLY HOPED and prayed it would be Jessica. And it is. Jessica's the first girl at school to invite her over after school. Or not really "invite her over," more like "you want to hang out?" Like there's nothing much to do and nobody's watching me so we can do whatever we want.

She asks Abbey, and Abbey says it's okay with her if her father says it's okay, but they have to call him. And Jessica stands there leaning against the wall like what the hell am I doing with this baby and her father says not today ask about tomorrow, and Jessica just sort of flips her head and says how about next Monday, and her father says yes and she tells Jessica yes and Jessica says see you tomorrow and she has to go wait for the bus with Abbey. At least Abbey gives her a knowing glance like I understand how you feel little girl but that doesn't help much.

"Grandma let me go over to Melissa's all the time without planning it weeks in advance," she tells her father before she says hello. Then she pouts all through dinner and dinner the next night. Except really she's too excited about next Monday to pout for long. She wears her junkiest jeans all weekend to make sure they'll be good and grungy by Monday. Almost as good as Jessica's.

Phil assumed. Ellyn assumed. Abbey assumed. If they'd told Grandma, Grandma would have assumed. Even Tiffany assumed that she'd go over to Jessica's apartment after school on Monday. But when Jessica said "hang out" she meant hang out around the school, around the neighborhood, wherever.

Wow!

They walk a few blocks just to get away from the school grounds. They pass this Catholic school and make fun of the kids in their stupid uniforms who have to carry all their books home every night (Jessica tossed her backpack to this woman who was picking her brother up). Jessica leans against a building and pulls out a pack of gum. Only one stick left. Jessica looks at it, then looks at Tiffany, then tosses it down on the ground. "It's stale anyway. Let's go get some more."

Tiffany follows her into one of those indoor newsstands that has candy and stuff. Tiffany picks up a pack of spearmint, thinking she ought to buy it and offer Jessica some, while Jessica rummages around. "This candy looks like its been here since Easter," she tells Tiffany so loudly Tif would be embarrassed if this were anyone but Jessica or Di or Lara or one of the other really neat girls in her class.

Tif puts the gum down, follows Jessica outside, then around the corner. Jessica pulls a pack of gum out of her pocket. Then another pack. Then a chocolate bar, a pack of M & Ms, and a Reese's Peanut Butter Cup.

Wow!

They head over to this playground on York Ave., where this group of high school boys are playing basketball and sort of hang around watching them while pretending not to be watching them, choosing which one's cutest, which is ickiest. At 5:30 they go hang out around the lobby of Jessica's building on account of her father's picking her up there.

IT'S A THANKSGIVING TO RIVAL those of their worst nightmares. Phil gets a speeding ticket before they're to the Elizabeth exit. The third he's gotten since his mother's stroke.

"Damn Jersey cops," he mutters, trying to pull back in lane through an unbreakable stream of traffic. "If my license wasn't from New York, I'd have lost it by now."

Tiffany whines the entire trip; she's going all this way and not even permitted to see her grandmother. She doesn't want to spend the day with Melissa.

"You've been pleading with me to take you there."

"That was ages ago."

"It was six weeks ago."

"What are we supposed to do, play Clue? Or Pictionary?" Tiffany asks in a sarcastic tone neither Phil nor Ellyn has ever noticed in her before. "Too bad it's not Saturday morning, or we could sit on the floor and watch PeeWee's Playhouse."

"PeeWee's Playhouse isn't on anymore," Ellyn reminds her.

Tiffany bites her bottom lip: that was the whole point, Dummy.

Ellyn's starting to wish she'd taken Tiffany up to Mamaroneck. Her sister invited them: "the more the merrier." Ellyn recalls Joan saying those same words to the mother of some kid who was over playing, and to the couple down the block whose air conditioner broke in the middle of a heat wave.

Too late now.

The hospital dining room resembles a school cafeteria, sophomoric pictures of turkeys on paper tablecloths, cornucopia centerpieces filled with half-spoiled fruit. Phil's mother is one among many men and women wheeled in so they can drool mashed sweet potatoes down bony chins and make one-handed stabs at turkey so dry you could choke on it. Christ. Turkey roll would have been better.

There's no doubt in her mind they'd have been better off in Mamaroneck. At least on holidays her family's pretty much muzzled. And a lot of distractions help. Geoff, wife and son in tow, drove up from Philly last night.

Her nieces and nephews are probably out in the yard on the swing set. The adults are evenly spaced around the living room. The Parade was blasting in the background earlier; by now it's the football game. If Joan's in the room, she's guarding the remote with her life, flipping channels every time there's a commercial.

Her father and RuthAnn are arriving, late as usual. RuthAnn, reeking of perfume, is carrying the Boston cream pie she buys for every holiday at the same bakery where she bought cupcakes for their birthdays when TC was growing up. Day-old cupcakes TC took to school and shared with her classmates. Three kinds of icing.

She can see Tiffany now, insisting on sitting next to her father instead of at the far end of the table with the other children. Mike, dutiful host and husband that he is, carves the turkey. Joan fills up plates and passes them down the table. Tiffany catches sight of the brown giblets in the stuffing, says she doesn't want any of that.

Ellyn whispers to leave it on her plate, quite possibly alienating her for the rest of the decade.

RuthAnn startles everyone by rising to Tiffany's defense. "If she doesn't want stuffing she shouldn't be forced to have it on her plate."

Ellyn, Joan, and Geoff exchange bitter glances.

While Joan's taking the stuffing off Tiffany's plate one of her kids, probably Ricky, says he doesn't want any, either. Both parents glare at him, RuthAnn looks the other way, and Joan plops down an extra large helping.

Because she's a guest, Tiffany's given the wishbone. She probably chooses RuthAnn to break it with.

THE ORDEAL'S OVER. PHIL'S MOTHER is back in her room, helped into bed. Phil got a wet cloth from the bathroom and cleaned up her face. She's anxious to sleep for a while. All they have to do now is drag his father, who wants nothing more than to sit beside his wife, over to pick up Tiffany so the four of them can go to The Olive Garden for a second dinner. This one's complete with canned Italian music, green carpeting, plastic plants. The overcooked spaghetti has a peculiar aftertaste. They'll be stuck in traffic for the next four hours.

"Grandpa barely ate," Tiffany whines. She sounds even more like a five-year-old than she did this morning.

"He ate enough to sustain him," Phil says.

It's a miracle he got anything down, considering that his granddaughter's presence made him that much more aware of how sick his wife is,

Ellyn thinks. Score another point for having gone up to Joan's.

"People don't need to eat big meals all the time, it's nothing but a bad habit we get into," Phil continues, sensing his daughter still unconvinced. "You don't remember what a terrible eater you used to be, do you?"

"I was not!"

"Were too!"

"When?"

"When you were two-and-a-half. Right after Mommy returned to work. I swear, I've never seen anyone clamp her lips as tightly as you did. I had to work as hard getting cereal down you as I did on my college term papers."

"Then it was probably on account of you, like, bought the wrong cereal."

"I bought the same one Mommy bought."

"Then how comes I didn't starve to death?"

"Because Mr. Brown came to visit."

Tiffany's freckles pop out. "Mr. Brown," she laughs. "I'd almost forgotten Mr. Brown."

She tells Ellyn about a book she had, "One of those picture books, you know." *Here Comes Mr. Brown.* About kids who used to play ball on this vacant lot next to Mr. Brown's house, only Mr. Brown always chased them away. They began calling out when they saw him coming, and the kids would hide. "Then they caught on and realized they could call out Mr. Brown was coming when a guy was about to catch a fly ball, or if the team was losing."

"You thought it was the funniest book you'd ever read. And, lucky for me, you opened your mouth when you laughed. Instead of wearing us both out fighting over breakfast, one morning I tried calling out *Here comes Mr. Brown*, as I guided the spoon to your mouth like a baseball."

"Didn't you start calling out other names?"

"You bet I did. I had to. After a few spoonfuls you got wise to Mr. Brown. I called out Mrs. Brown was coming. Then I began calling out the names of people you knew, television personalities . . . "

"You used to make up names, too, right?" Tiffany laughs.

"Yep."

"I thought so. You used to tell me they were the names of people you worked with, but I never believed you."

"What, no Arabella Purpleheart, no Scooter the Hooter?"

"I knew they weren't real." Tiffany beams. Undoes her seatbelt and reaches forward to hug her father.

"You ate most of your cereal, though." They spend the next three hours reminiscing: past Thanksgivings, Halloweens, Christmases, Easters.

Foods, costumes, presents, more food. From there they move on to listing favorite and least favorite restaurants.

"Chinatown Ice Cream Parlor," Phil says. Favorite. Least favorite: Burger King.

Tiffany says her favorite is that place in Chinatown where she tried to use chopsticks and her least favorite's the Olive Garden. For right now, anyway. "And you know what my favorite food is? Gerber's junior sweet potatoes! Or it was up to about a year ago."

She would have adored dinner at the hospital, Ellyn thinks.

Phil bets he can guess what her least favorite food is.

"What?"

"Bread cut into quarters."

"I remember that one! I hated Grandma after that night."

"Anita's mother," Phil hastens to add.

"I don't have to see her anymore, but she sends me money for Christmas and my birthday and stuff."

"And warns her not to waste it on toys," Phil laughs. He gives an abbreviated version of the bread incident: Anita's parents were visiting from Georgia, their one and only trip to New York. Tips was in the learning-to-run stage, and loving her freedom. In this new, big room, she didn't want to be bothered with eating.

On one of her trips back to the table for attention, Anita buttered a slice of bread and handed it to her. "Grandma" scowled, called Tiffany back, and showed her how nice young ladies never take a whole slice, they cut it in quarters.

"And after she did that I wouldn't touch it!"

"Go ahead and laugh. But Mommy and I spent the next ten minutes trying to get you to stop howling. Everyone in the restaurant was staring at us."

"I wish it had been her who'd gotten sick."

"Don't say that." Phil's chin drops. He reaches his arm back to meet his daughter's. "You might not love her, but you wouldn't want to wish that sickness on anyone. No matter what else she is, she's still your grandmother. And she loves you, in her own way."

Only Ellyn's so-called maturity kept her from wishing aloud it had been RuthAnn instead of Phil's mother.

Now they're talking about food mishaps. His mother pouring boiling water over tunafish to make her think it was chicken. Him telling her a particular bread wasn't pumpernickel but was "dark rye" because she'd decided she didn't like pumpernickel.

Ellyn closes her eyes, takes their words in. It's the same melodic tone of voice she remembers from when Phil first shared memories of Tips making up stories about Christmas models. The smile she bets few women could refuse. To hear him talking right now, one would think him the perfect father. Certainly not the kind of man who would be too drunk to tell his daughter her mother died. Who would ship her off to his parents in the same town he'd felt stifled by. Who would be all but incapable of telling her about her grandmother's stroke.

Appearances are deceptive.

"HEY, LOOK, GALAXY'S OPEN," Phil says as he puts on his blinker and waits for the light to change. They pull into the garage and walk back over to Broadway.

In the city, coffee shops are about the only thing, other than fine restaurants that are booked weeks in advance, open on Thanksgiving. Ellyn remembers a few years ago, she was supposed to go skiing in Vermont with a group of friends, and they got caught in a blizzard. They turned back, ended up eating in a coffee shop and then going to see *The Bostonians*. The theater was almost empty. Two little old ladies walked out tsk-tsking half way through.

His arm resting lightly on his daughter's shoulder, Phil guides her through the glass doors. So what if they've already eaten? Always room for milkshakes. Chocolate, black and white, diet Coke.

"If I didn't know you better, I'd suspect you of trying to fatten me up so no other guy will want me," Ellyn laughs.

Phil flashes a mischievous grin at her.

Anita taught phys ed.

"We'll always want you," Tiffany says.

She feels her lips curling sharply upward. Wonders if there will ever again be three weeks in a row when Tiffany will be glad she's with them. At the moment she'd settle for three days in a row.

Who would have suspected, last spring, when she was bristling at the prospect of meeting Phil's daughter, that hearing an eleven-year-old say "we'll always want you" would mean more to her than anything a guy's ever said?

Phil hasn't said anything.

He can't get Arabella Purpleheart off his mind, he'll tell Ellyn later. "All of the sudden she was gone, along with Mr. Brown and all our other favorites. I woke up one Saturday and had to fix myself a silent breakfast. No crayons to push aside, no stuffed rabbits sitting in the high chair being spoon-fed. Tips was in New Jersey, the refrigerator was filled with beer, wine, milk that was probably sour, salami, moldy cheese, and a loaf of stale bread."

He tells about calling his parents, taking a quick shower, hopping in the car, picking up Tips and bringing her to the city for the rest of the weekend. Then another weekend. And yet another. "She spent most of the time sitting in front of the television; new dolls she hadn't bothered introducing me to were propped up beside her.

"All of the sudden one Saturday we were sitting at the kitchen table and I heard Tips whispering *here comes Grandma* as she moved the spoon of Sugar Frosted Flakes to her lips," Phil continues. He called *here comes Grandpa* with the next spoon. And she responded by calling out people with his spoonfuls – friends at school, teachers and kids he'd never heard of. Excited as only children can be, she called three names to his one. *Here comes Susie, here comes Marcie, here comes Melissa*!

Here comes Miss Piggy!

Here comes Tommy, here comes Danny, here comes Mommy!

"Tips' mouth fell open. I put my arms around her hot neck, trying to hold it steady as it throbbed with each sob. I told her it was okay to remember. That remembering all the good times was how we'd keep Mommy with us." He lifted her up, carried her out to the living room, and they sat there hugging for what seemed like the rest of the weekend. And the weekend after that, and again two weekends later.

So there you have it. No apologies, no fancy footwork, no big excursions or expensive presents. Just opening your mouth and taking food in.

December 2: Tiffany

She's away with her parents, or just her mother, and she's working incredibly hard on an essay for school. So hard that when Mom tells her she's thinking of going to Detroit for a few days before going home, she says she doesn't want to go.

Now she realizes the deadline has passed, but doesn't even know when the deadline was; since she's not used to doing schoolwork and her grades have slipped, that's why she's been working so hard on this. She starts stomping around the house screaming.

Her mother doesn't understand the change that's come over her.

A young man knocks on the door and her mother lets him in.

"Please come and meet him," she pleads. "He's my best student."

She enters the kitchen and screams that her book is gone. Her mother hands it to her, then she sees it's the wrong book, though it has the same pale blue cover. There it is. She's still stomping around, in the bedroom now. The student, who's turned into a girl with black hair and a stupid bouffant hairdo like they wore years ago, peers in behind her mother.

"Look what they've done," she screams, pointing to the pictures over the bed, where the glass is cracked in several places. "I loved these pictures," she screams. "I've spent years collecting them. You've got to them make them stop."

Her mother holds a picture and mumbles, "She was my best student."

"And look at these." She holds up a handful of old family photos in which the smiles have been carefully enlarged with scissors. There's also an old illustrated storybook, where her mother and she are the main characters . . . "This is irreplaceable," she screams.

CHAPTER EIGHT

"MACY'S, WE'RE A PART OF your life," Ellyn sings. Tiffany doesn't condescend to join her.

With any luck, shopping for a bed jacket will help prepare Tiffany for the sight of a grandmother not yet recovered. Or so she thought last night. The cab bucks midtown traffic, the radio blasts pidgin Haitian, and she's starting to reconsider.

Straining to make conversation, she asks Tiffany what her grandmother's favorite color is.

"Blue. I think. No, blue was my mother's favorite color. Grandma always wears these dark outfits – brown, grey, dark green. Hard to think of any of them as her 'favorite.' White, I guess. She says it goes with everything."

Same colors RuthAnn wore.

White. As in those dreaded hospital gowns her mother wore. Shows all the food stains. She suggests maybe something more colorful, "cheerful."

Tiffany runs down a list of the brightest colors she can think of: "red, green, blue, yellow, orange, pink, purple, turquoise, chartreuse, magenta . . . "

"Teal blue."

"That doesn't count. They have to be one-word colors. Lavender, gold, tan, ruby . . . "

"Scotch plaid."

Tips cracks up. The rest of the ride is spent dreaming up crazy colors, combining two, three, and four words into one. They walk through the revolving doors giggling.

When they get to the lingerie floor, Tiffany's immediately drawn to the nylon robes with lace trim. Not wanting to point out how scratchy lace is and how sensitive her grandmother's skin will be, especially after the first operation on her neck, Ellyn mentions that it's getting colder and colder out, so maybe they should look at the heavier ones.

Tips runs toward velvet, holding various robes up to her cheeks to test their softness. "Please don't squeeze the Charmin," Ellyn quips, glancing around, hoping there aren't any salespeople watching. There aren't.

At last Tips decides on a soft, off white brushed cotton with peach lace trim at the pockets but not at the neck.

RuthAnn wouldn't be caught dead in this.

Nice, deep pockets. While they're waiting for the cashier, Ellyn talks about how her brother-in-law keeps everything in his bathrobe pockets. He goes for a screwdriver to fix a kitchen towel rack and puts it in his pocket. A month later no one can find the screwdriver, and they'll check his robe. Same thing with a new credit card or coupons he clips from the newspaper. "One time they even discovered my niece's report card in his bathrobe pocket. She had to bring it back signed on Monday morning, and got hysterical when they couldn't find it." Of course, it wasn't her brother-in-law. And the report card's bull . . .

"I wish that would happen to my report card."

"They'd only find it sooner or later," Ellyn reminds her.

"I guess."

Ellyn signs the credit card slip. Starts out with the bag swinging from her hand. Realizes this is no way to walk into a hospital room.

"Do you think we should get it gift wrapped, or would you rather wrap it yourself?"

"I'm, like, not very good," Tips begins.

"I could help if you want. We could stop at the Hallmark shop and pick out a great paper, maybe get a little stuffed animal to put in the bow." They'd buy more paper than they need. The two of them would spread out on the living room rug and they'd wrap it again and again until every corner was perfect. Then they'd take the extra paper and cut out little figures or flowers, she'd teach Tips about origami and collage, maybe Tips would even want to make Christmas cards. It would get them doing things together again, without even realizing it, they'd be back to casual, uninhibited fun . . .

"Let's get it gift wrapped," Tiffany decides.

"WHEN MY SISTER AND BROTHER were even younger than you are, they visited my mother in the hospital," Ellyn tells Tips.

"What about you?"

"I was too young."

"Even for your mother?"

"Even for my mother. You had to be over six. And the patient had to have a private room."

It's nothing more than a closet, to hear Joan tell it.

"Every time my mother went in the hospital, Joan and Geoff would plead with Dad to get a private room. He always said we couldn't afford it."

"I thought you said they visited her?"

"They did. There was one time when all the semi-private rooms were filled. So she ended up in a private room for the same price."

That can't be right, can it?

It's what she tells the child.

Joan describes the TV high in the air, and how when Mother can't sleep late at night she puts it on, low, and the nurses come in and watch old movies with her when they're not doing anything else. "When Geoff and I get there after school, they all come in to say hello to us."

If I were there I'd share my cookies with the nurses, TC thinks. And I'd be extra careful not to spill the juice they give me.

Ten days later the nurses stop by to say hello to the children. And it's a good thing, too, because no one else says a word. Mother lies there not moving at all; she won't even look at them. That night, their father tells them, private room or no, there will be no more visits.

TC, on the floor of Mother's empty bedroom, draws a picture of a room narrow as a closet, with a bed, and a TV high up in the air, so high a bird's flying next to it. She gives it to her sister to take to Mother, but Joan, in a tantrum about not being permitted back in the hospital, tears it up and throws it in the garbage.

GRANDMA HASN'T SEEN HER in two months, and she's grown a lot since then. Once she sees how big she is she'll say okay, she can come back and stay in the house with Grandpa.

"I didn't mean what I said last August," she imagines herself telling him the first night. "Honest. I love New York City and my father and my new school, but there's no place on earth I'd rather be than Cherry Hill. I want to live here with you and Grandma, for ever and ever." Even if she chokes on the words she'll force herself to say them. And she'll try her best to be happy there, really, she will.

If she hadn't gotten so upset last August, screaming about how much she hated Cherry Hill, how much she wanted to come and live with her father and Ellyn, Grandma probably wouldn't have gotten sick. It's all her fault.

But she'll make up for it.

Every day after school she'll ride her bike to the hospital. She's eleven-and-a-half, so they're sure to let her in. And Grandma probably has a private room. A pink-colored private room with a great big, comfortable bed. There'll be plenty of room for the two of them. They'll lie back in the bed with a zillion pillows behind them and watch *General Hospital*, like they sometimes do at home. Grandma can fill her in on all the episodes she missed, on account of Abbey doesn't like her to watch it, and sometimes she gets home too late besides. The nurses will give her lollipops, the way they do at the doctor's office; or used to when she was younger. It won't matter at all that Grandma has trouble talking; they won't have to talk. They'll just be together.

Besides, Grandma will be so happy to see her that she'll get better in no time and be ready to come home. She envisions herself bringing Grandma breakfast in bed every morning. Running home from school to help take care of her. On those days when Grandma's not feeling well, she'll bring her homework into the bedroom, sprawl on the floor and read her social studies or history book, being quiet quiet quiet as she reads.

Except the bedroom's upstairs, and she's not an idiot. She heard her father talking with Grandpa about managing the stairs. Talking about installing a second handrail on the other side, so she has something to grip with her left hand when she goes down. She remembers Grandpa explaining how important it is to have someone walking behind Grandma on the way up, in front of he on the way down. Just in case she gets dizzy or something.

These words will ring in her ears until she croaks.

Grandma can come stay here! "With a Jennifer sofa bed there's always a place to stay!"

No, a sofa bed would have to be in the living room and her father and Ellyn sit around there until pretty late, and Grandma would probably want to go to sleep earlier.

Grandma and Grandpa can have her room. Maybe they'll put a cot for her in her father's room, the way they used to when she was little and they'd stay in a hotel.

No, wait. Her father and Ellyn could take the sofa bed, Grandma and Grandpa could take her parents' room . . . she means her father's room. And she'll keep her own room. Perfect.

PHIL GETS OFF THE TURNPIKE two exits before Cherry Hill. After being silent most of the drive, he launches once again into his description of Grandma walking very slowly and painfully. He reminds Tiffany that she can't use her right arm, and her speech is slurred. "There's one more thing you ought to be prepared for."

Even Ellyn wonders what now.

"Grandma had a stroke. You know, I explained about what a stroke is, how there's a brief period when oxygen has trouble getting to the brain, and the body reacts. Well, people who have had strokes tend to cry a lot. They'll burst out in tears over anything – if the television's turned to the wrong channel, if wind blows the curtains, if there's too much gravy on the mashed potatoes."

Tiffany isn't laughing at his sick joke.

"What I want you to understand is that the tears don't mean she's sad or upset or anything. Crying's only a physical response."

The car continues spinning its wheels.

She saw people crying, and that upset her . . . Children learn by watching what others do. *Holding her. Letting her cry.* No, Ellyn thinks, you don't have to understand. But if it's all in your head it means you're crazy.

"That's why Grandma made me take piano, you know?" Tiffany says finally. "Cause she saw me crying to myself a lot of times, and she thought it would help take my mind off things. It didn't though."

"Well, we're not going to make Grandma take piano," Phil laughs.

"Is she afraid of falling? Everyone cries when they fall down. And if she's walking funny, the way you said, then maybe she's, like, crying because she's afraid of falling."

"It's not that clear-cut." Ellyn turns around to face the child. "What your father's trying to explain is you'll probably see her crying, but there's not a real reason for it. The tears are a symptom of her illness. Like when you have chicken pox you always want to scratch."

When she had chicken pox she got better in ten days.

They pull into the rehabilitation center parking lot. The car goes over those bumps they put in the road to slow you down. "Sleeping policemen," Phil calls them.

"A lot of women cry," Ellyn continues. "I read somewhere that one out of four women who've been drinking end up crying."

"I've dated my share of those," Phil laughs. "I always thought it was something I'd said or done. Now you're telling me it was nothing more than statistics!"

"Simple feminine logic."

They follow Tiffany's glance to a sign on the side of the building announcing wheel chair races next weekend.

"I know you might get upset seeing how thin Grandma is, or how slowly she gets around, but I want you act as grown up as you possibly can," Phil says, taking his daughter's hand as they walk toward the entrance. "Do us one favor, will you? Try not to cry."

Tiffany pulls away.

Christ, Ellyn thinks, stepping back and putting an arm around her. She's only eleven years old.

Joan and Geoff at least had each other.

"Your father's not saying don't cry ever," she says, easing Tiffany forward. "You can cry all you want later, when we're alone with you and can comfort you. But it's for the best if your grandmother doesn't see you cry."

"Right," Phil adds. "It would upset her."

"OH MY GOD," they hear a man call out from the gym on the first floor. "You work so hard to get here, then all you want to do is go home." It's not a scream, just a deep, resonant voice in excruciating pain that carries well.

"IT'S DEAR," GRANDMA SAYS when she sees the bed jacket.

That's not what she meant to say. She said "it's" then groped for the word she wanted. "Dear," when it came, was her means of addressing her granddaughter.

Tiffany tries to guess at the missing word. It's *pretty*, dear. It's *soft*, dear. It's *warm*, dear . . . But this isn't another dumb guessing game. They warned her Grandma might cry, they warned her the words might be slurred. No one said she might not know the words. No one said she wouldn't even be able to open the box herself.

Then Grandpa has to take the cast or brace or whatever it is off her arm before she even puts the robe on. What's nice about the robe is it pretty much covers the brace. What's nice about the brace is it hides how thin and red and creepy her arm looks.

Splint – that's the word. One of the girls in her class last year wore a splint when her ankle got twisted.

She pleaded and pleaded to see Grandma; now she wants to run away. Instead she describes every single robe or bed jacket they looked at, and when she gets past the ones she remembers she starts making some up: the purple-blue robe with the bright yellow hearts, the chartreuse robe with little red men running along the bottom. Except Grandma cries instead of laughing the way she's supposed to. She uses her good arm to pull the bed jacket closer around her. She's glad now they bought a soft one.

She goes on to chatter about her new school, and the neat jeans and stuff all the kids wear.

"What's that on your face?" Grandma interrupts.

It's so quiet you can hear a wheelchair creaking three rooms away. Grandma asks her to come closer, and points to a pimple on her cheek.

Tiffany rubs her hand across her face, finds it. "I'm getting acne!" she screams.

"It's one pimple!" her father laughs. Even from her sickbed, his mother has better eyes than the four of them put together.

Ellyn pledges to get her the best cleansing cream on the market.

Tiffany tells her grandmother about two new t-shirts she bought to wear to school.

"I'll never get to see them." Grandma starts to cry again.

"Sure you will, Mom," Phil says. He clasps her hand for a minute. Then he starts talking about recent trends in the stock market, assures his parents he's keeping close watch over their portfolio. "The minute Motorola goes above $100, we'll take the money and run," he promises. He also talks about two other communications stocks he's watching closely. Either might be a good place for Motorola profits. Since his mother's been in the hospital he's gotten power of attorney. For the first time in his life, his father doesn't want to be bothered.

Now that she's not part of the conversation, Tiffany lets her eyes walk themselves around the room. There are two beds, after all. The other woman, who looked younger than Ellyn, came in wobbling between these two canes, got something from a drawer, and went out again. Every patient she's seen walking here has a cane or crutches or one of those three-sided metal things on wheels. And Grandma can't even manage her wheelchair by herself. She has to get someone to push her, even into the bathroom that stinks of Lysol.

Guests have to use the small bathrooms on the first floor. Which are almost as bad.

She supposes this lets out the possibility of Grandma and Grandpa coming to live with them, even after she's feeling better. Grandma wouldn't want to stay in the apartment all day. And it's so windy she can't even make it down 78th St. sometimes without walking backwards.

"THANKS FOR BEING HERE," Phil says, placing his arm around Ellyn as they head for the car. Such a simple gesture, and suddenly she's glad she came.

"I don't mean this to sound unfeeling, but in one sense seeing her was inspiring. I wish the people I work with took half that much care with words."

Tiffany's wandering in front of them, wearing *Don't Touch* or *Danger Keep Out* placards. She hasn't cried yet.

Eleven's probably too old to cry. Even at nine, Joan never cries, at least not where anyone might notice her. Instead she makes up stories about how great it is.

Phil looks exhausted. "Why don't you drive until we get back on the Turnpike, and I'll take it from there?" Ellyn suggests. "You're more familiar with the local roads."

"That's okay, I'll be fine."

"Come on. It'll be fun."

"You've never found driving fun before."

What the hell?

"Sorry." Phil shakes his head. "Anita used to complain all the time about the long drive to and from work," he says by way of explanation. "Sorry."

SORRY. IT'S THE LAST WORD Phil and Ellyn will exchange over the next three hours. He drives all the way. Knows the turnpike so well by now he could drive it with his eyes closed. The far-right button on his radio's set to 1610, so he can quickly get traffic information and road conditions (when he runs into congestion he sometimes ends up taking alternate routes through towns he's never even heard of).

They stop at Bob's Big Boy for dinner. Returning to the car, Ellyn silently crawls in back. Tiffany gets in front beside her father. Who wants her, anyway? Ellyn taking her to buy that stupid robe. Standing in Grandma's room not saying a word, as if she was a retard or something.

She and her father can't find much to talk about either.

"Bedtime. You've got school tomorrow," Phil announces almost the moment they've walked in the door. It's not even 8:30 yet, but she knows better than to complain tonight.

He goes in to kiss her good night, comes back to the living room. Ellyn's not there. He finds her half undressed in the bedroom. "A little early for us to turn in, don't you think?"

"No, as a matter of fact it's too late. Way too late." She slips into a different turtleneck, puts on a deco pin he knows is one of her favorites.

"Going out?"

"Yes."

"Where?"

"Out. Just out."

"Today's been murder on all of us." He goes over to put his arm around her. She moves away. "Please don't do this."

"You don't know what I'm doing. I'm not even sure myself."

"What if Tiffany wakes up and discovers you're not here? What am I supposed to tell her?"

Ellyn blots her lipstick. "Tell her her mother's dead." She heads back to the living room. Slams the door behind her.

"Your mother's dead," he whispers.

TIFFANY TWISTS THE RABBIT'S LONG EAR around her finger like a ring. One thing about Grandma and Grandpa, they both came all the way upstairs to kiss her good night, every single night, for as long as she can remember. Or at least as long as she's lived with them, which is pretty much the same thing. But Grandma didn't kiss her hello or goodbye today, either. And the way Grandma was slobbering all over the place, she doesn't even think she'd want to kiss her.

She should at least be glad her father came in to kiss her. He doesn't always. It usually depends on what woman he's with. There was Carol, Dawn, Phyllis, her mother . . . She ticks off their names on her fingers, pausing for a moment to remember each one. Dawn used to kiss her father right while they were walking along the street. Phyllis only kissed him when she thought no one was looking.

Carol, Dawn, Phyllis . . . how many can she name?

This game's as boring as Ellyn's stupid commercials.

Ellyn didn't say good night, that's all. It's no big deal. Seeing Grandma probably upset her, too, only she didn't let it show because she didn't want to set a bad example. She saw Melissa's parents do that when their dog got run over by a UPS truck.

She wishes she'd fallen asleep right away, or turned on MTV, or put on her Michael Jackson tape and turned it up loud. Too late now to pretend she didn't hear the door slam.

She wonders if her father's next girlfriend will be someone she's met already. Jill was always fun. A lot more fun than Ellyn, that's for sure. The more she thinks about Ellyn, the more she wants to cry. Or maybe she's getting as bad as her grandmother, crying for no reason at all.

Maybe she can go back home and stay with Melissa's parents until her grandmother's better. Her father won't want her here, not without Ellyn. He'll tell her it's too dangerous for her to be by herself in New York City, and Abbey can only work so many hours. He'll remind her of all those nights he has to work late.

He's right about New York City being a little creepy. Sometimes more than a little. The other day she and Abbey were walking to the bus stop, and this high school boy got there right as the bus pulled off. He was so angry he kicked the glass around the bus stop sign, and smashed or shattered it. If they'd been standing there they would have been cut bad.

She has to go somewhere.

Barbara, Di, Kevin, Rick, Jessica . . . How many of the kids in her class can she remember? They're the ones she can count on being there tomorrow. Kelly, David, Evan, Laura – no, her name's Lara – Janet, Paul, Neil.

There's no Ellyn, not even Ellen spelled normally. There's a girl named Annie, which is about the closest there is to Anita, but she doesn't like her very much.

No Anita at her old school, either.

No one's ever going to take her mother's place. They might try, but she's never ever going to let them. Not in a zillion million trillion years. Not in a century.

And she couldn't care less what the next one's name is.

CHAPTER NINE

Monday mornin', Monday mornin' couldn't guarantee
That Monday evenin' you would still be here with me . . .

The Mamas & The Papas

NOT MONDAY, SUNDAY. "TIPS USED TO think Sunday was the bestest day of the week," Phil told her once. She can hear him now, bragging about those little mother-daughter outings – to the park, Baskin Robbins, the Burger King four blocks away. One more working Mom trying to assuage her guilt.

Why the hell couldn't he have sat back and let them enjoy themselves? No, not mister perfect father, he had to use it as a way to teach and discipline: "*If you want to go with Mommy Sunday you'll finish that sandwich*" or turn off the TV when you're told to or go to bed or wash your hands or whatever. Another of his innocent games, like making up stories about photos or mannequins.

Of course, he said, they'd never have canceled those outings, no matter how bad she'd been. Anita would have been crushed.

Right, and Tiffany would never grow up and prefer to be with her friends. She and Anita would go on those Sunday outings forever. Anita would never die. Christ, he made her death sound like a harmless epilogue to his little tale: "Tips kept asking why Mommy wasn't taking her out. We told her again and again that Mommy was gone. She asked if maybe next Sunday? Or the Sunday after? Three Sundays from now?"

She can just picture Tips as a five-year-old, putting all her toys away, helping set the table (napkins folded crooked, on the wrong side of the plates), learning to tie her shoes, trying in all the ways she can think of to be so good Mommy would come back and they'd go somewhere together. No matter how much love she's given later, she'll probably never feel she's good enough.

Sunday, Sunday,
How could you leave
and not take me . . .

Simple. You tell him where to kiss and walk out. This is one "Mama" who needs a stiff drink.

She gets ten steps into Dublin House. Notices the Jerseyites haven't exited yet. Some punk saunters over, holding his beer bottle near his crotch, pointed out and up.

Enough already! She'll go home and fix her own drink.

The apartment looks as neglected as a three-year-old. Still, it's good to be back in a place that has sculpted woodwork and plaster walls instead of vertical blinds and central air. You could move Phil's building lock, stock, and barrel over to the east seventies and it would feel right at home.

She pours a double shot of rum into a glass of flat Coke. Rubs her fingers across her neck, trying to work through the tension. Mother's sitting up in bed, combing her hair, wearing a quilted pink bed jacket. She steered Tiffany toward the warm ones. Soft. Comfortable. Exactly what she's been looking for all this time. In every man she's slept with.

An hour ago Phil reached out to hold her and she walked away. Hold too close and they die on you.

Mother's dead. Father lifts her up so she can kiss Mother goodbye. It feels so cold. Old enough to go to the viewing, but not to the cemetery. She'll never see the end of it.

"YOU WANT TO HANG OUT?" Tiffany asks Lara Tuesday afternoon. Thinking Abbey can do whatever she damn well pleases. Only Lara can't.

"KISS MOMMY GOODBYE," ELLYN SAYS, pressing a bright red pig against her cheek.

Not soft enough. She picks up, in turn, a giraffe, a dinosaur, a koala bear. On the shelf above her head is an assortment of "pregnant pandas," each with its tag explaining that Chinese pandas are an endangered species. You unzip the belly and there's a little panda sitting inside. Or you can buy one with twins or triplets. Also recommended for teaching kids about pregnancy.

Just what Tiffany needs!

She's doing as well as can be expected, considering, Phil said this morning. Considering what? Considering she finally saw her grandmother? Considering all of the sudden you're not around? Considering she has an English test tomorrow?

Considering Phil didn't call her. Considering there's no way she can justify having called him.

Three nights alone and she suddenly can't seem to sleep straight.

Phil had to get back to work. They agree to dinner.

She unearths a fuzzy lamb. A turtle. "KISS Mommy goodbye!" she orders, holding the back of Miss Piggy's neck and squeezing so hard her face becomes distorted.

She throws Miss Piggy back in the bin, goes back to weeding out animals. You'd think F.A.O. Schwartz would have a larger assortment. They do, actually, if you're willing to spend over $100. If she's going to pay that much she might as well chuck it all, buy one of these for herself and say to hell with the whole sex and obligation bit.

It's not "sex and obligation." It's Tiffany and Phil (or vice versa).

Walking out the other night took care of the obligation part.

Even sex only seems to be one component.

Maybe it's letting herself be kissed for once. Without being held up and ordered.

Digging deeper into the bin, she unearths a shaggy albino cat, complete with pink eyes and nose, a pink ribbon on its neck. That'll do.

She's halfway to the cashier before she turns back. Tiffany's too old for stuffed animals. Remembering her promise to pick up something better than Noxema for the budding acne, she walks over to Cosmetics Plus. Picks out a small gift set of colognes as well.

RuthAnn would love this: Tiffany perches on the sofa, folds the wrapping paper neatly, says thank you very much, chews with her mouth closed, barely looks up from the plate. The moment dinner's over she asks to please be excused, goes to her room, shuts the door.

Phil picks the gift box off the sofa, balances it in one hand as if testing its weight, puts it on the coffee table. "If you're planning to leave, leave now," he says, still staring at the box. "Tiffany's suffered enough already. I don't want her going through all this a second time."

"Going through all *what* a second time, my leaving or her mother's death? Are you even aware there's a difference?"

"There's a difference, all right. Anita didn't choose to die."

"That's the only difference you see, isn't it?"

Silence.

– Who's taller, Anita or me?

– Whose hair is longer?

– Redder?

– What size shoe did she wear?

– What size shoe do I wear?

– What about bra size?

– What's her favorite color?

– My favorite color?

"Anita was taller. She cut her hair two weeks before her death. Seven and a half, blue, how the hell do I know?!"

"Name one thing you see in me aside from the physical resemblance! One!"

Her head's pounding.

– What the hell's my favorite food?

– My favorite song?

– Movie?

– Commercial?

– What's my middle initial?

– What was my mother's first name?

"You've got to give it time," Phil says. "It's always one aspect which immediately attracts you to a person, then slowly you learn more about them."

"Was Anita the same in bed, too? Was sex with her as physical?"

"Sex was *more* physical."

"Great! I spend three sleepless nights longing for the heat of your body, our legs in that crazy pretzel twist, and you tell me I'm not physical."

"Look who's calling the kettle black! Talk about only seeing the physical!"

"I didn't say that was all I saw in you!"

"Neither did I!"

"You say it a hundred times a night!"

"You're the one who physically walked through that door, you know."

"You never saw I was here to begin with!"

"How the hell do you know what I saw?"

"What do you see?!"

Phil's chest deflates. "Someone very beautiful," he says softly. "And very vulnerable."

She turns away. Gasps. Buries her head in her hands.

Phil puts an arm around her, leads her over to the sofa. Doesn't let go. "Don't tell me you're one of those criers we laughed about," he teases finally.

She pulls away. Wipes her tears on her sleeve.

He takes out his handkerchief. Pats her eyes dry. Pushes her hair back off her shoulders. Kisses once on each eyebrow.

She presses against him. Kneads his thin, tense shoulders with those magic fingers. Works her way down the chest, gets his shirt unbuttoned.

"I've got you now," he whispers.

They hug all the way to the bedroom. Phil brakes within inches of the bed. "We probably should wait . . . Tiffany . . . "

For the first time in four days, Ellyn doesn't have to force a smile. A month ago Phil wouldn't have even remembered his daughter at a moment like this.

So okay, maybe her presence goes beyond the physical.

Tiffany's in bed by 9:30.

"I GOT TALKING WITH THIS NEW broker at my office," Phil says as he and Ellyn tackle the dishes the following Tuesday. "He moved here from Chicago six weeks ago. Looking for a place to sublet until he gets to know the city better, has time to settle in at work."

Ellyn feels a sudden cramp in her stomach. She hopes what's coming next isn't what she thinks is coming next.

It is. For the next twenty minutes Phil spouts off the reasons she shouldn't think twice about subletting her apartment and moving in with them. She can save over a thousand a month (maybe even topping it off with a little extra). She's spent so little time there in the last two months. Gas, electric, Christmas gifts for the super, doormen, mailmen, porters. Now that he's got the extra school expenses, plus Abbey's wages, he wouldn't exactly mind it if she paid her own way at restaurants and the like, and not that she wouldn't anyway, but he'd feel better about taking it if he knew other things weren't costing her as much. "Besides, if you're not willing to at least try living together, what's the point?"

"The point is you're getting ahead of yourself. He might not even like my place."

"I thought maybe we'd invite him for dinner Thursday. Then walk over to your place and let him take a look. I can cook up that chicken paprika dish tomorrow night, all we'll have to do is heat it up."

And bring it to the table on a silver platter, like the Baptist's head.

Her pulse rate's probably up to 150.

But who knows? Maybe there won't be as much tension in this relationship if there isn't the added pressure of darting back and forth, picking up her mail, running a dust cloth over things, making sure the timers are still turning lights on and off, that no one's broken in, and still getting over here so they can have dinner before Tiffany dies of unbelievable starvation. And no matter how many blouses, skirts, necklaces, pins, books or whatever she brings with her, it always seems the one thing she needs is back at her own place.

She envisions her closet filled with suits, ties on her scarf rack, the *Wall Street Journal* spread out where her printer is at the moment.

It's just what Dave's looking for.

CLOTHES, JEWELRY, BOOKS, KNICK-KNACKS, bubble bath, cosmetics, correspondence and folders from work, laptop, desktop, printer, fax, two cartons of paper, photo albums, two cameras, hair dryer, makeup mirror, Nordic Track whatever (one of the handles bends in transit), decorative glassware, linens, artwork, CDs, tapes. Thank God she doesn't have a record collection. And, of course, the furniture stays.

Phil teases that they probably should have alerted the super, maybe used the service elevator. Like you do for "real" moves. Asks if RuthAnn had this much stuff.

"It was a big house," Ellyn mumbles. Though obviously not big enough to keep her mother's clothes or photos.

Clothes, jewelry, books, photos, tapes, stereo, camera, posters, art box, walkman, Mickey Mouse clock, rock collection, stamp collection, bicycle . . .

He puts a stop to the bicycle. Convinces Tiffany she'll have outgrown her summer clothes long before it's warm enough to wear them. Makes her choose between the rocks and the stamps. They take her city computer to Cherry Hill and clone the drive, to be certain she'll have everything she needs.

They spend one rainy night shopping for another dresser, find one at Conran's, then discover it's the floor model, and have to squeeze the thing into the open trunk of a cab. They bring in another dresser from New Jersey. Phil suggests Ellyn store some of the glassware, linens, and knick-knacks at his parents' house.

She opts instead for her sister's attic.

Ellyn brings in the first box. Then Mike, hugging his sister-in-law with one arm and grabbing his coat with the other, goes out to help her carry in the rest. Six-year-old Ricky follows them outside, and Ellyn asks him to carry a box of linens.

"The least Phil could have done was drive up with you," Joan says the moment they sit down.

"It was enough to lend me the car and help me load up."

"Come off it. The first time a date fails to hold a door open for you you kiss him goodbye."

"Give the guy a break, Joan. He's driving back and forth to Cherry Hill two or three times a week. And Tiffany needs a night alone with him."

"Since when do you care what a child needs?"

"Will you at least wait till you meet them? You'll love them."

While Joan goes out to the kitchen to put the coffee on, Ellyn fills Mike in on how much Tiffany reminds her of Joan as a ten- or eleven-year-old: sharp and sullen. When she's angry her eyes take on an intensity you wouldn't have deemed possible.

"Admit it, you're anxious to meet them," Ellyn laughs as the three of them sit around the table. "It's almost as if you're not going to believe they exist until I bring them to the house."

"Oh, I believe they exist, all right. What I don't believe is how involved you are with them." Joan stares at her sister. When Ellyn first came in, Joan assumed that loading and unloading the car after a full day at work had been a strain, that Ellyn's arms loosely dangling at her sides and her shoulders visible below her hairline were signs of fatigue. Now she seems more natural. Casual.

Robin calls in from the living room, asking if they can have some cake, too. Joan says no, that they had dessert with dinner.

"You don't want it anyway, Rob. It's fattening," Ellyn says, tilting her chair back. "A year from now you'll be going out with boys and snacking on yogurt."

"There's this boy in her class she's already got her eyes on," her younger sister announces.

Ellyn goes into the living room to find out more about this heart-throb. Joan catches her sneaking a piece of cake to Ricky.

"If he's considerate enough to help carry boxes, it's the least I can do," Ellyn laughs, blushing.

Joan's starting to believe. "What happened to all that freedom you're always harping about?"

"It's still there. Freedom means I'm free to choose this, too."

"You've never been one to assume responsibility for others before."

"I never had the chance before. I was the baby, remember?"

"God, don't start." As if Ellyn's five or six. Pleading for an ice cream cone.

SHE'S NOT SUBLETTING HER APARTMENT, she's subletting her sanity. The more belongings either she or Tiffany move in, the more aware she becomes of how much of a mess Phil's place is. Last August the clutter seemed temporary, and she was having too much fun to let it bother her. It's different now: Tiffany's papers and books are spread out on the floor; pencils, cassettes, cookies, straws, and combs turn up wedged between sofa cushions, glasses of soda rest precariously on the edge of any flat surface. This place is a veritable minefield, with no space to call her own.

No, strike that. The chair at the far end of the dining room table, near the window: that one's hers. It's the chair that was serving as the stage of an elaborate marionette theater the first day she met Tiffany. Prior to that, of course, it had been Anita's.

SHE'S NOT ABOUT TO CONTINUE DOING HIS DIRTY WORK. She's not a maid, housekeeper, servant, domestic, cleaning woman, or whatever they're called these days. If Phil expects his little troika to survive more than the first month, then he'd damn well better get someone in. Cooking, washing up after dinner, things they'd be doing together anyway – that's one thing. Picking up after a child is another.

Fine with him. Else's been coming to clean for two years now, every other Tuesday; he trusts her, she's looking for more work. He increases her schedule to every week then, shaking his head over fingerprints on the refrigerator door, twice a week.

Friday's unfortunately not one of Else's days. But they've invited friends for dinner, so Ellyn wants to at least straighten up a bit. She pesters Tiffany to make her bed, goes into the room to check, walks over to the window and straightens out the shade.

What the . . . ? The shade's bent near the top, there's something preventing it from lying flat. Then she spots Barbie hanging there, the cord tied around her punked-out, bright green hair. Ellyn stands on a chair and frees what's left of her.

She sits on the bed for a moment to compose herself, wrinkling the spread again. Gripping Barbie by what was once her hair, she carries her out to the living room. Tiffany's curled up on the sofa with a book and a bag of potato chips, leaving crumbs.

"What's this is supposed to be?" She drops the doll between Tiffany and the book.

"Barbie."

"The Barbie I gave you, right?"

"Prob'ly."

Ellyn yanks the book out of her hands, inquires first as to whether Tiffany knows where she found her, then as to how she might have gotten there. The answers are exactly as she might have expected. What she didn't expect was Tiffany's nonchalant attitude.

"I don't believe this!"

"And I don't believe how upset you're getting! Di and Lara, these two girls at school, do it, like, all the time."

"Torture Barbies?"

"Di sometimes calls it torture. I call it enjoying myself."

Tiffany tries to pick up her book again. Ellyn holds it out of reach.

Torture.

"But why?"

"I told you: it's fun."

"How would you feel if someone did this to you?"

Tiffany sits upright. Lets her eyes stare hard into Ellyn's. "I know exactly what it feels like."

Ellyn drops the book in her lap, accidentally hitting Barbie in the face. She doesn't know what else to do with it.

LARA'S STAYING AT HER MOTHER'S this week. She ends up inviting Tiffany over, since it's sort of on her way home anyway. "My mother has never, not ever in, like, her whole life, lived anywhere she didn't have a view of the Museum of Natural History. When my parents first split my father talked about how he could finally breathe again. He really hated that museum."

"Me too. Once you're, like, older than six or seven it's really boring."

"Our apartment on Park Ave.'s way, way better. My room there's twice the size of this. You should see it. And I have my own dressing room. It used to be a playroom."

"This" is almost as big as their living room. Tiffany looks around. "My mother used to have a friend who lived on 81st St." She starts to tell Lara about them all going over to watch them blow up balloons for the Macy's parade, then decides that's really immature. The sort of thing Melissa would be excited by. Or Ellyn.

"Do your grandparents live here, too?"

"They moved to Sarasota. That's how we got this apartment. We used to have a small one in the building two doors down, but my father said he'd file for divorce if they didn't find something bigger, so my mother laid this trip on her parents about how they'd been talking about leaving the city so, you know."

"They're divorced anyway."

"Yeah, well, that was before I was born. My birth was, like, supposed to make everything fine again."

"I guess it didn't, huh?"

"I like it better this way. Besides, I almost never have to see my grandparents. And they're even more out of it than my mother is."

"My mother's parents are pretty awful, too. They live in Georgia."

"I didn't think anyone really lived in Georgia! What do they live in Georgia for?"

"I don't know. Maybe because it's the only place in the world they'll let an old witch like my grandmother teach Sunday school."

"Oh Gawd, church!"

"Everyone in Georgia goes to church. Even the pet poodles. My mother couldn't wait to get out of there."

"I'll bet. Wanna watch MTV?"

"Sure."

They join Abbey in the living room. There's a 23" surround-sound TV. MTV sounds, like, fab. But Lara turns it off as soon as *Real World* comes on. As far as she's concerned, *Real World* has, like, absolutely nothing to do with reality.

December 22: Tiffany

The teacher's giving Carvel ice cream cakes to a group of people. She knows there's one for her, and starts looking at the smaller boxes, but hers is one of the largest and has an elegant gold unicorn pictured on it. She opens the box to find a lot of little red boxes inside. Do they really take their cakes apart, instead of giving them complete, like you see in the display cases? And why did they make the unicorn with chocolate ice cream, when vanilla's much closer to gold? She calls the store and finds out there's been a mistake. Someone else ordered two dozen chocolate soldiers, and they accidentally got into her box.

CHAPTER TEN

"INGLE ELLS, INGLE ELLS," Tiffany's voice rings out from the back seat.

"That's *Jingle Bells*, honey," her grandfather corrects.

"No it's not, it's Ingle Ells," she laughs. "What would Christmas be without the J & B?"

Phil reaches back to clasp Ellyn's hand. He reminds his father she works in advertising.

"Someone in Ellyn's office wrote that commercial!" Tiffany announces.

Ellyn gives a nervous laugh.

Phil points out the window to a lawn with a cute Santa in western garb.

TC's head turns. Taking the kids around to see the Christmas lights doesn't even cross her father's mind. She should be grateful they even have a Christmas tree, let alone presents under it.

The car pulls into the garage. The door closes behind it. His father and Tiffany go upstairs to bed. Church is over for yet another year.

Phil pours a Scotch for himself, a brandy for Ellyn. "Ingle Ells," he laughs. "I wish Anita's parents could have been around to hear that."

"I'm not sure your father was exactly pleased."

"He'll get over it." But he also makes a mental note to warn Tiffany not to start singing in front of his mother.

"Would you believe it, that church has had the same minister for as long as I can remember. And his sermons are as boring now as they were then."

"Don't talk to me about sermons," Ellyn laughs. She tells him about going through a typical collegiate stage of reading *The Seven Storey Mountain* and envying the spirituality Merton found in the Catholic Church. It all came to a dead end the Christmas a white-haired priest grabbed hold of the pulpit and began loudly and aggressively declaiming the tenth anniversary of Roe Vs. Wade. *Suppose Mary had been able to obtain an abortion*? he bellowed. *What would have happened then*? "I leaned toward my friend and whispered we might have all been better off." That was the last time she set foot in a church, except for a wedding here and there. Which proved equally jolting.

Phil gets more ice for his drink. Sits down and takes stock of the living room. "My parents bought this house when I was seven, and every year since then they've had a Christmas tree. Right there, in the corner near the stairs.

With the presents spreading out along the staircase wall."

It was fifty degrees out two days ago. Doesn't feel like Christmas.

He speaks of various Christmases in this house. The year he was nine and his aunt sent him four white dress shirts with a note about how he might not want these but he's a big boy now and needs them. The Christmas they bought his first watch, and had to make two extra holes in the strap because his wrists were so small. Last year, when Tips got her ears pierced and he gave her these little rhinestone earrings from Fortunoff.

"My mother's wedding ring came from Fortunoff," Ellyn tells him. "She used to talk about it sometimes. How she tried on every ring they had, for the sheer thrill of feeling them on her finger. Most were way more than they could afford, though. They settled on a half-karat diamond which had a slight, barely detectable flaw."

Oh. In these strange yet familiar surroundings, she finally hears her own words.

"God."

"So small you could hardly see it."

He reaches out, cradles her in his arms. Feels her shaking. Rocks slowly, back, forth, back, forth. After minutes, or maybe hours, she's the one who pulls free.

He gets up, refreshes both drinks. Stops and looks through the boxes of presents ready to take to the hospital. "Looking for anything special?"

"Just checking there isn't a present here with teddy bear paper that says *Daddy* in purple crayon." He goes on to talk of Tiffany's first Christmas living here. So many presents you could barely walk. He stayed up later than the others that night, too. He walked over to the tree and silently read off the packages: Tiffany, Phil, Tips, Tiffany, Mom, Tips, Tips, Grandpa, Tiffany, Tips, Tips, Grandma, Tiffany, Tiffany . . . "Then I got to the teddy bear wrapping and stopped short. I expected my parents would buy presents for Tiffany to give me, but it looked too frivolous for my mother's tastes. I was right, it contained a scarf one of my girlfriends had taken Tiffany to shop for."

"Damn! I knew I had to be forgetting something!"

"Thanks but no thanks. You have no idea how much trouble that present caused. Tips' teacher even called my parents in for a conference." The class had been learning how to write thank-you notes. One girl thanked her aunt for sending *The Cat in the Hat*, said she could read it very well, and was teaching her younger sister to read. A boy thanked his cousin for the fire truck, saying it was better than the one his parents bought him. Then his darling daughter: "Tips thanked her other grandparents for the check they sent her. She told them she used it to pay back money she'd borrowed from one of my girlfriends, who took her to the store and helped her pick out a scarf. Then she ended by saying her real mommy would have chosen a better one."

Ellyn's in stitches. His parents hadn't found it nearly as amusing.

She thinks about the first stories he regaled her with, where Tips explains what the mannequins are doing for Christmas. These days, when they've caught sight of some display or other, Tiffany doesn't even want to look, let alone imagine what their lives are like. The most she'll say is *I need, I want* or *I don't want.*

That's the way it's been lately; every time she plans a fun outing – for the three of them, or just Tiffany and herself – something goes wrong. Take her to Toy Park, ask for her help in picking out toys for her nieces and nephews, and all Tiffany can say is that this or that toy's "stupid." They go down to Chinatown, Tiffany orders General Tso's Chicken and hogs the whole plate, not offering them a taste and not wanting anything to do with the (probably "stupid") dishes they order.

Phil finishes off the Scotch and they pull out the sofa bed. "Oh, I almost forgot this," he smiles, handing her an expertly wrapped package. "This is one I thought best to give you while we're alone."

A black lace negligee. Sheer. Sexy. The last thing in the world she's in the mood to wear at his parents' house.

IT TAKES TWO TRIPS to carry everything upstairs.

Seated on the edge of the bed, a green ribbon threaded intricately through her braid, the first present Tiffany opens is the one from her grandmother. She pulls out a little knitted sweater, bright blue. Holds it at arm's length.

"It's for your doll," her grandmother says. "You know, the little orphan one, your favorite. Inez?"

"Isabel." She lets the sweater drop on the bed, looks frantically at the others for help, gets none. "Grandma," she whines, "I haven't played with Isabel for years!"

"Don't be silly. I saw you the other day . . . " she breaks off mid-sentence, crying.

"She bought it in the gift shop downstairs. It's one of those things the volunteers make," Grandpa offers. "For charity, you know."

"Maybe it'll fit one of your other baby dolls," Grandma says.

"I'm in sixth grade! You don't even remember how old I am, do you?"

"We remember how old you are, all right," Phil's father barely has a grip on his anger. "You're eleven. Old enough to at least be able to keep your shoes tied. Didn't we teach you better sense than that?"

"It's the style," Tiffany says, wrinkling all her freckles and giving her braid a flip.

Ellyn gulps. It's the style. She hung around the school a few times after dropping Tiffany off, wanting to see for herself. Frayed jeans, jeans with great big holes in them, untied sneakers. For church last night they forced her into a skirt she outgrew a year ago.

"Your grandmother used to stay up nights shortening or lengthening your skirts half an inch. Everything had to be perfect." Phil's father's voice is cracking by the end.

Perfect. The first of many New Year's resolutions.

Phil's mother finally breaks the silence. "Blue's your school color, isn't it?"

"I don't even go to that school anymore!" Tiffany throws up her arms in frustration.

"Cut the histrionics," Phil says, yanking his daughter aside.

"I used to have this teddy bear named Jacob," Ellyn chimes in. "I even took him to college with me." Tiffany won't look at her.

Only the prospect of all the unopened boxes with her name on them keeps Tiffany standing quietly at the bedside. It's a good thing the names are there, too, 'cause her grandmother would probably give everything to the wrong person.

Her grandparents also get her one of those murder mystery jigsaw puzzles and a bottle of bubble bath. From her father she gets a Swatch, a great backpack, two pairs of earrings, and the new Jackson Family bio she might have even bought herself except all the stores were sold out.

She chooses the gold earrings with tiny amber drops and puts them on only cause they expect her to. Now what? Ellyn reaches in her purse to get her compact, only Grandma says wait, she has a mirror. They wait. She can't remember where it is. Looks around the room. Phil asks if she means the mirror in the bathroom. No, wait. There's one here. She remembers now, it's in the tray table. Lift the lid.

Tiffany goes over. Lifts. Yuck. It looks as if someone spit food all over it. There are smudges right where her ears should be.

"You still haven't opened the gift from me," Ellyn says, placing an arm on Tiffany's shoulder, turning her back to the bed and closing up the tray table in one seamless motion.

The Keith Haring sweatshirt she wanted! Thanks! Except it's hard to get excited now. Christmas is ruined.

Reluctantly, Tiffany helps her grandmother open the present she and her father bought – a brown shawl they found at the WBAI Crafts Fair that's even softer than that bathrobe, and hand made, too. She's already been warned not to mention they chose this because it's easy to slip over her shoulders, she won't have to use her right arm and she won't keep trying to put her right arm in the left sleeve and then waste the next twenty minutes trying to get it adjusted right. But she wants to blurt it out now, accidentally for spite.

They bought Phil's father a trench coat – one of those thin ones that comes with its own pouch and folds up till it's about the size of an anthill. Phil and Tiffany give Ellyn a blue and beige silk scarf. Ellyn gives Phil the leather attaché case he fell in love with at Sharper Image last summer – a memento of the night he never made it to the Seaport. Phil also gets a check from his parents, who give Ellyn a gift-boxed marmalade assortment.

They call an aide in to help Phil's mother clean up a bit and dress. You used to be able to take family out for a few hours on holidays, maybe to a family dinner, maybe to a restaurant, but they stopped that policy two years ago. Too many people were abusing the process, coming back late, and often drunk.

So they head for the dining room. The tables were covered this morning with white plastic cloths that have small green Christmas trees and red ornaments drawn on them. It probably looked festive a few hours ago, but by now there are bits of congealed food all over the place and all these torn wet spots where drinks probably spilled. Phil's father drives to the deli to pick up a chicken they ordered. It takes ten minutes to clean off a spot where they can put it down. An aide helped, and now the area stinks from too much cleaning fluid.

Making the excuse that he doesn't want to get caught in traffic driving back to the city, Phil manages to get them out of there by 3:30. He plays with the radio, trying to find something other than news or Christmas elevator music. When he recognizes the first bars of "Grandma Got Run Over By A Reindeer," he shuts it off.

"People try their best to find the right presents, but it doesn't always work," he tells his daughter.

Sure they do. He told her the same thing when Jessie gave her the stupid mermaid watch! This isn't some girlfriend; this is her grandmother.

"Do you remember the first Christmas I took you to buy a present for Mommy?"

"No."

"Well, I do. You were three years old. We went to look in Bloomingdale's, except this guy was selling jewelry on the street out in front.

You spotted this great big Santa Claus pin, and that's what you wanted to buy her."

"I didn't though, did I?" little-miss-know-it-all quips.

"Only because I refused to let you, and I was the one with the money."

"Grandma's not three years old."

"No, she's not," Phil says calmly. "But she's in pain right now, and sometimes living in the past is easier than facing things in the present. She was a lot happier a few years ago, when she was in good health and you were playing with Isabel."

Tiffany turns to look out the window. Next thing you know, he's going to tell the whole world how she started sucking her thumb again after her mother died.

Ten long minutes later, Ellyn glances around to check on how she's doing. Catches sight of all the presents stacked up beside her in the back seat. "My nieces and nephews are probably sitting beside equally high piles," she laughs, reaching over to steady a box about to topple. "If I'd gone to Joan's I'd be opening the Liz Claiborne blouse from my father and RuthAnn about now."

"How come Liz Claiborne?" Tiffany asks.

"It's cheap, and a name she recognizes, so she figures she can't go wrong."

Phil says Liz Claiborne's a big name at the malls. Reminds his daughter about her second Christmas in New Jersey. They'd planned on going to see the New York windows, but it snowed heavily all weekend. He managed to drive out to Cherry Hill, and they went to see the decorations in the Mall instead.

"Most of the stores weren't decorated, they just had Christmas balls or crepe paper snowmen in the window, only Sears and Hallmark had big displays." Tiffany goes on to laugh about how junky they looked, not only the clothes but the mannequins: they didn't have good wigs or anything. There was one with this dyed red hair, another had on this stupid blouse with green bows on it. "I made up this story about how their fathers or their husbands lost their jobs so they weren't doing much for Christmas this year."

"There was one display where you said they were caught in a blizzard in Alaska, and all their gifts were home waiting for them."

"I would have said the North Pole, except I'd, like, lost faith in Santa Claus."

"How about the rest of your family?" Phil asks Ellyn, shifting lanes to pass an elderly couple driving 40 mph. "What presents are they likely to come up with?"

"I don't know. They've probably already mailed me some innocuous little things – costume jewelry, gloves, a wallet."

"Jars of marmalade."

"At least it's high-quality marmalade."

Tiffany asks how come her family didn't mail the presents in time for Christmas, like she did with their stuff.

"Because they didn't trust I wouldn't change my mind at the last minute and go up there," Ellyn laughs.

"Even though you promised to come with us?"

"Other years I've shown up there after saying I wouldn't."

TC dutifully brings her small, boring presents to school for Show and Tell the first day back. By fourth grade she begins lying about other presents too big to carry.

Jacob's gone. For five years he sat atop her refrigerator, disguised as a polar bear. Then she gave him to her nephew three Christmases ago. But her brother's son had a right to him. Actually Mother gave the bear to Geoff.

After Mother dies, Geoff leaves him lying around all sorts of places, including the living room. If RuthAnn sees him, she's liable to throw him out. So TC comes to his rescue. Treats him the way her friends treat their dolls.

No Tiny Tears, no Betsy Wetsy, Cabbage Patch hasn't even made it to the drawing board yet. Babies are boring: they don't do anything, and you always have to be afraid of dropping them. When she's eight or nine her father and RuthAnn splurge and buy her the biggest Christmas present ever – one of those three-foot-high walking dolls. God, what a disaster.

"Still thinking about those presents?" Phil asks, catching sight of her idiotic smile.

"Zooming in on one from way back when."

"Oh-oh. What did she do this time?"

"Tried to give me a good Christmas, actually. She and my father bought me this doll I'd seen on TV. You hold her arm and she's supposed to walk beside you. Except I could never get her to walk right. After a day or two I gave up and went back to dressing up my Barbies."

"That's not funny, it's pathetic," Phil says.

"Not when you hear the end," Ellyn laughs. "My junior year of college I was in this seminar on the history of children's television. And they played the tape of my walking doll commercial, then ran it back slow motion to show how she doesn't *walk just like you*, you have to stand behind her, holding her up and pushing her forward. And here I'd spent all these years assuming it was all my fault she wouldn't walk right."

Phil pats her hand, but has a hard time containing his laughter.
"Isn't that, like, lying?" Tiffany asks.
"Commercials lie all the time," Ellyn answers.

SEVEN FIFTEEN. HER FATHER and RuthAnn have probably gotten as far as the tollbooths on the Whitestone, RuthAnn's sighing and remarking that they're halfway home. Had Ellyn spent the holiday with her family this is about the time when she and Joan would be comparing their blouses, maybe trading. The only difference between them would be color, and RuthAnn still tries to push Joan into wearing brighter colors, the same as she did when Joan was ten, eleven, twelve.

"I always think it's best to get them the same, to be sure there's no competition. And no one can accuse me of playing favorites," Joan says, a perfect imitation of RuthAnn's slightly nasal voice.

"Of course when they were little I bought them different things, the girls were so far apart in age, but I spent the same amount of money for each of them," Ellyn answers. And the sisters collapse in laughter.

Easy to poke fun from a distance, she supposes. Accustomed to the comfort of Phil's car, she manages to forget how inconvenient Metro North can be. And God forbid Joan or Mike should drive over to the station to pick her up. They're too busy making eggnog.

"No one can accuse me of playing favorites . . . ," she silently repeats, suddenly finding even RuthAnn's words reassuring.

Who the hell's she kidding? RuthAnn probably hasn't spent a cent on her yet. All the stores will be having sales the day after Christmas; why buy now when she won't even be joining them for the holiday? If Ellyn knows her stepmother, she's spent the past week trashing her.

"Someday I'll understand," TC used to console herself. She envisioned her father sitting in the kitchen late at night, talking with each child in turn, maybe a year before they graduated high school. The first thing he'd say is he wishes he'd kept his mouth shut. He'd been just rambling on. His wife was sick; his second cousin came to help out. RuthAnn even had two years of nursing school before she decided college life wasn't for her.

"I couldn't have been more appreciative. I used to tease RuthAnn that, if your mother didn't recover, maybe I ought to marry her." Head cocked toward the ceiling with its harsh fluorescent light, he'd go on to explain the warmth the three of them shared back then, before the word cancer had been spoken, when there was no doubt in anyone's mind: his wife would recover.

He'd recount how, as time went by, the joke became more and more serious. Somewhere along the line it turned into a promise. Without apologizing or asking for forgiveness, he'd make sure each child, in turn, understood why he thought RuthAnn's presence would make things easier for the whole family.

"Besides," he'd say. "It wasn't as if I could easily find someone else. I had three children. Dating's only for people with no responsibilities." He'd pause then. Give TC or whomever time to reflect on Friday night movies, Saturday drives to the beach or the skating rink, pool parties, pizza parlors.

"Grandma warned against it," he'd continue, shaking his head. He'd explain that his mother was never on the best of terms with her cousins – or so she said after he and RuthAnn were married. The marriage solidified the rift; to their dying days the two branches of cousins didn't speak. "RuthAnn's mother's side of the family muttered something about how she should have married another man and had children of her own. *Real* children, grandchildren to give her parents a little joy." And he'd shake his head again. Father and daughter, glasses of hot milk in hand, would silently climb the stairs to their bedrooms.

Enough said.

CHAPTER ELEVEN

SHE LIES ON THE COT in the nurse's office, barely holding back tears. Her Keith Haring sweatshirt is wet where the nurse tried to wash it out after she puked all over herself. The room is spinning around her. She told them this would happen. All during breakfast she complained her stomach hurt. Her father poured himself another cup of coffee and insisted she had grasshoppers in her stomach because this was the first day back after Christmas break.

Since Grandma's been in the hospital, she's been stuck with an old rabbit to talk to.

Well, the rabbit can't come and get her, that's for sure. And they won't let you sign yourself out and walk home, the way they sometimes did at her old school. When Jessica got sick last month, her au pair picked her up. All the au pair does all day is sit around by the phone in case Jessica or her brother needs her. Abbey won't even carry her backpack.

She closes her eyes and imagines her father walking through the door, his tie draped around his neck, his shirt unbuttoned at the collar. She hopes he doesn't take her into his office to get dizzy watching numbers go across a screen. If it came down to that, she'd rather just lie here. Except she really hopes they don't leave her to lie here and lie here and lie here, the way they've left her grandmother to lie there in New Jersey. She wants to die before she gets that sick, the way her mother did.

If she's sick for a long time, she bets no one buys her a fluffy bed jacket or sends her flowers. She hates flowers, anyway. She told them not to send her to school today! It'll serve them right if she ends up in the hospital, too.

HE DOESN'T EVEN HAVE time to watch the numbers himself. The Dow's gained twelve points already, then lost two. This coming Friday's a triple-witching day. He's been getting frantic calls all morning. Put. Buy. Hold off until Wednesday. Why the hell did you recommend that option? No way he can leave now.

Ellyn, on the other hand, is just about to order a sandwich and go over notes from this morning's meeting. Easy enough to take this home with her.

Phil mumbles thanks and he'll make it up to her and gets off the phone as quickly as he can. An institutional client's on hold.

She begins packing up her briefcase.

Kramer vs. Kramer was a piece of shit, Phil told her once. No guy in his right mind lets his job go to hell like that. Besides, Anita's death couldn't have happened at a worse time: Boesky'd been indicted, Drexel was on the verge of collapse, Salomon Brothers had begun laying off its top people. One false move and there'd be a hundred guys with as much experience as he had ready to position their gold-plated coffee mugs on the corner of his desk, bringing a skeptical but loyal clientele with them.

Ellyn could argue that point, actually Kramer had been one of her favorites, but what the hell – she can think of worse ways to be spending an afternoon. Assuming she makes it out of this cab alive. Drivers like this could make her swear off cabs forever. She clings to the door handle, holds her breath, while he zooms up Third, races lights, leans on the horn, curses in what sounds like some Indian dialect, turns onto 83rd, pushes it to make the light at Lex, jams on the brake two inches away from the barricade. Barricade?

The street's a playground during lunch break.

At least it gives her a half-block walk to learn how to breathe again. After stooping to pick up a ball rolling toward her and tossing it back to a girl who's about to cry, she hurries in the doors, stops and asks the first kid she sees where the nurse's office is, and continues on down the hall. She introduces herself, realizing as she says her name that two forms of ID won't mean anything when it comes to releasing a sick child. Unless they can track down the principal . . .

The nurse places a gentle hand on Sleeping Beauty's shoulder. Tiffany opens her eyes. Ellyn! The last person in the world she would ever have expected. Most times, Ellyn doesn't even go to visit Grandma.

Quick with the thanks, Ellyn promises to get Tiffany straight home, changed, and into bed. She helps her get her coat on. Walks her slowly toward Park Ave., catches a cab. This time, at least, they have a driver who not only speaks English, but maneuvers in traffic as if there are human beings in those other cars. If he was as bad as the last guy, maybe she'd work up courage to ask him to please take it easy, she has a sick child here. Joan did that for her once, when she'd picked her up at the gynecologist's after he'd taken a biopsy. It had made her feel cared for.

HER HANDS ARE SHAKING SO MUCH they almost drop the tape. *Doggystyle* by Snoop Doggy Dog.

"You *said* you didn't have it," Di says, hand on one hip, head inclined so it really looks like she's disgusted. It's not a stance Tif's familiar with, but she saw Di fall into it when she went to challenge the teacher about the C+ on her English test. Like, *why in hell did I bother?*

"Oh-I-don't-have-it!"

"You *said* you loved it."

"Are you kidding? Of course I love it!"

"It's an old tape, anyway. I've played it so many times it's all but worn out. Besides, I've got the CD now."

"Thanks." Tif stares at the tape, at her hand, at the school building in front of her. "Di . . . do you, like, ever play this when your father's around?"

"My father's never around."

"Well then, your mother?"

"Sure."

"I mean, she doesn't get upset or anything? The language, you know . . . Mothafucka. Bitch. Pussy. Nigga." And that's just the words she remembers from that one time she and Di and Lara and Evan and a couple other kids were hanging out listening to it.

"You really think your mother – I mean your father, sorry – is gonna stand outside your door listening to the words? Turn it up loud, crank up the bass, they won't hear a thing but the rhythms and they'll be so ecstatic when you turn it down that they still won't be listening. I promise."

Tif puts the tape in her backpack.

Grandma would have listened, she knows that much. Melissa would be grounded for years if she showed up with a tape like this. She doesn't even think Melissa would understand it, let alone want to hear it again and again and again and again and again. The more she thinks of Grandma, the more she thinks of Melissa, the more she wants to run home right now and play it really, really loud and leave her door open and everything. But she knows she won't.

"I NEVER GET TO DO ANYTHING!"

"You do a hell of a lot more than I did at your age!"

"I thought you wanted me to make friends here."

"Not the sort of friends who have unsupervised all-night birthday parties!"

"Jessica's parents trust her!"

"So her father told me. He also goes away for weeks and leaves his kids with a sitter."

"The word is *au pair*, not sitter. And one night isn't weeks and weeks."

"Let me tell you, kid – this has nothing to do with age. I don't trust anyone," he says, modulating his fury by falling into the slow southern drawl

Anita worked so hard to get rid of. "Especially as far as you're concerned."

"All we're going to do is rent a few movies and sit around with popcorn watching them. What's wrong with that?"

"Tiffany, I don't want to discuss it. Case closed."

"The happier your grandmother is, the harder she works to get better," Ellyn tries to reason.

"And seeing me makes her so happy she just cries and cries," Tiffany says in a voice used for reading storybooks to toddlers.

Phil slaps her face.

If he hadn't, Ellyn damn well might have.

"That's child abuse, you know!" Holding her cheek. Slowly edging away from him.

"That's enough!"

"I've got a right to be happy, too!"

"All you ever think about is yourself!"

"That's what Grandma and Grandpa used to say about you!"

Phil's face reddens. His fists clench, unclench, then clench again. "You will go to your room this instant, young lady! And you will not come out until you're ready to apologize. Meanwhile, aside from visits to Grandma, consider yourself grounded for the next month. And I don't care how many parties you miss!"

A flick of her proud little head, and Tiffany's stomping off to her room. She slams the door behind her. Puts her earphones on. Finds her Madonna tape. One of the movies Jessica's renting is Madonna's *Truth or Dare* video. They're not supposed to be seeing it since it has an R rating, but Jessica convinced her parents it couldn't be that bad if she supposedly sings happy birthday to her father and it's her birthday party.

Now she'll have to wait till she's eighteen to see it, unless she can get Abbey to rent it. Abbey knows her mother died when she was five, and Madonna's mother died when she was five, so, like, maybe . . .

She turns the volume up.

Ellyn's in the kitchen, waiting for the water to get hot so she can start on the dishes. "I've got this really neat room," Tiffany said last summer. That room was nothing compared to what she has here. It makes the Room Plus commercials look like they were filmed in the Projects.

TC in a third-floor room right under the roof with a sloping ceiling and tiny casement window: hot in summer, cold in winter. She and Joan share it. Two beds, bookshelves, one old desk, and one clock radio Joan bought with her babysitting money and won't let her sister touch. Oh, yeah, and a clothes hamper. The stairs creak whenever anyone's approaching.

She doesn't hear Phil come in. He reaches over, turns the faucet off, tells her to leave the dishes be: his daughter will do them after she apologizes. Ellyn picks her watch off the counter and straps it back on: 7:30.

9:15. Phil's been at the computer all night, calling up one stock history after another, jotting down figures, tapping the end of his pencil against the desk. Ellyn's flipped through five different magazines, staring at the ads and trying to keep track of market trends. The tension filling the air smells like sour tomato sauce.

"I've had enough of this! What she needs is a good old-fashioned spanking." Phil scrapes his chair back, shuts off the computer, storms off down the hall.

"That doesn't solve anything, and you know it." Ellyn grabs his arm. "You and Anita used to swear you'd never hit your daughter. Or so you told me."

He pulls away. "That was a long time ago. A belt's what she understands now, and it's what she deserves."

"No child deserves that."

Three years old. She spills milk on her new dress, and RuthAnn has her down on the cold kitchen floor in no time flat, whacking with the back of a spatula.

"No child deserves that."

"Tell that to my mother." Phil steps around her. She hears the door open, then slam. There's indiscernible shouting, then a child's high-pitched shrieks.

Crying over spilt milk. Precious milk. You don't have it to give, so you take out your resentment on The Child who spills it. Not a goddamned thing she can do about it.

Phil walks back into the room, threading his belt through its loops again, a self-satisfied expression on his face the likes of which she's never seen before. Tiffany follows, red-eyed, sniffling. "My father says I have to apologize to you for ruining your evening," she says, pausing in front of Ellyn on her way into the kitchen. Speechless, Ellyn stares at the child, then the father. Anita's turning over in her grave. Mother's dead and buried.

In silence the dishes are washed, dried, put away. Tiffany all but tiptoes back to her room.

"Let me at least go say good night to her." Ellyn gets up slowly, half expecting Phil to stop her. He doesn't.

"YOUR FATHER LOVES YOU, no matter what you think," she offers.

"I hate him." Mumbled. Wrapped up in the down comforter, her face turned toward the wall, Tiffany could be a four-year-old.

"Don't say that." Ellyn sits down, runs her fingers along Tiffany's back. "It's hard for your father, too, you know. Your grandmother practically raised you over the past few years, and he feels guilty about that."

"That's his problem, not mine!"

"How do you think it makes him feel when you don't even want to see her now?"

"I don't know, and I don't care. I've hated him ever since my mother died! He doesn't even want me here."

"Yes, he does. He wants you very, very badly. But he's also not used to your being here, so he isn't sure what to do. And he'll make mistakes sometimes."

"Right. He's, like, going to walk in the door right now, tell me he's sorry, and say I can go to the party."

"No, he's not. There will be other parties, and I agree with him: visiting your grandmother's more important right now. I'm not saying it was the best idea to spank you, but you've got to realize you pretty much pushed him into it. And he gave you plenty of time to come out and apologize."

"I hate him."

"You know, I remember one time when my father spanked me," Ellyn continues, talking to Tiffany's back. "I was in fifth grade, and absolutely hated my teacher. My grades were slipping, and one night my father decided it was his duty to help me study. He must have spent two hours going over my math homework with me. As he was walking out of the room I announced that I didn't understand it one bit better, I hated math, hated school, and was not about to spend any more time on this stupid homework. He spun around, dragged me out of the chair, got me over to the bed, and let me have it."

Hey, your move, kid, she wants to say.

Tiffany's wondering if Ellyn's father pulled her jeans down, then her panties, and spanked her bare ass. Bet you ten to one he didn't. She's never been so embarrassed in her life. It's, like, he couldn't even leave her a drop of dignity. Not one!

"I threw the math book at the door the second he left," Ellyn continues. "Its binding ripped and I had to buy a new one out of my allowance."

Tiffany refuses to even look at her.

TC turned her back on RuthAnn once. Once. Every Saturday morning she was supposed to help with the housework. RuthAnn was giving precise instructions on how much Pledge to spray and which furniture was to be dusted first. As if she hadn't heard this a thousand times already. Two or three sentences into the lecture she walked over to the far corner and started working. The sooner she finished, the sooner she could go out and play.

RuthAnn warned her to pay attention when she was being spoken to. She didn't turn around. Or didn't turn around fast enough. The next thing she knew RuthAnn was dragging her into the bathroom, where a cake of soap would be shoved in her mouth. RuthAnn poured cup after cup of hot water into her foaming mouth before she let her go. Back to dusting.

Christ, the stories Ellyn could tell this kid.

"Both my father and RuthAnn spanked us a lot, but that time with the math homework stands out," she continues. "I wasn't behaving so bratty because I hated school, or hated math, or hated my teacher. It was my father I was angry at. Here was this man who'd been pretty distant most of my childhood suddenly thinking he could step in, spend two hours playing father, and have me do whatever he wanted. No matter what the consequences, I couldn't let him get away with that."

"But he got away with it, didn't he?" She finally turns around, lifts herself up on an elbow. "Just because they're bigger, some fathers think they can push you around!"

"Your father's not pushing you around, he's trying to do what's in everyone's best interests." She forces her voice to remain calm.

"I kept screaming I was sorry, but he wouldn't stop."

"I know." RuthAnn used to threaten to buy a cat-o-nine-tails.

"You don't know anything! Besides, you're the one who hates your father."

"I don't hate my father. I get angry at him sometimes, but I try to stay on good terms with him."

"You hardly ever see him."

"That doesn't mean I don't love him." She was in her early twenties before she understood anger and love could co-exist. What does she expect from the child?

While Ellyn's thinking of a way to explain that things aren't always black or white, Tiffany seizes one more chance at getting to that party: "So if I, like, don't go to see my grandmother this once, why does everyone assume I don't love her?"

Ellyn reminds her no one, ever, accused her of not loving her grandmother. Small comfort, emphasized by Tiffany's harsh silence.

She turns to face the wall again. It calls to mind the figure lying on the cot in the nurse's office: small, helpless, defeated.

Ellyn gets up, walks over to the door, turns around. "I don't think the party means that much to you," she offers, deciding to call Tiffany's bluff. "I think you got started and then had too much pride to back down."

She's as stubborn as her father is.

One hand on the doorknob, she blows an unreciprocated kiss, then walks across the hall to the bedroom she and Phil share. All of a sudden she's exhausted.

"Your father loves you no matter what," she repeats, slipping on the black lace negligee Phil gave her for Christmas. It's true: Phil not only loves, but needs his daughter right now. And he needs me, too, she whispers. Reminding herself for the umpteenth time that she needs them as well. Both of them.

HAPPY BIRTHDAY TO YOU, you belong in the zoo, you look like a monkey, and you act like one too. Then they form a line and paddle you. All this for a few stupid gifts? It's not worth it.

She's not Nancy's friend, anyway; she doesn't understand why she's even invited until she gets to the pizza place and sees all the kids in her first-grade class there. All the girls, anyway.

This pizza's yucky. So is this restaurant. They have three tables pushed together, and three balloons tied to the back of every chair. The kids eat pizza and drink Coke. Then plates are pushed aside, and they bring out a chocolate cake. Most of the kids look on jealously as the gifts are opened. She just keeps eating, trying not to get chocolate all over her.

She wanted Grandma to at least walk in with her, hand the gift to Nancy, tell her happy birthday. Grandma told her she was acting like a baby. *All you have to do is be friendly, and they'll be friendly back.*

"I went to a party for a real monkey once," she tells the girl sitting beside her. Addie, her name is. The girl's, not the monkey's. "This woman, Carolyn, who lives in our building – I mean the building where I used to live – has a pet monkey. Carolyn gave a birthday party for the monkey, and she invited me."

Addie whispers something to the girl on the other side, who bursts out laughing.

"How old was the monkey, dear?" Nancy's mother asks.

"Four, I think. No, *I* was four. The monkey . . . " It doesn't matter. Anyway, Nancy's mother's looking off in the other direction.

Her own mother went to the monkey's party with her. They sat around a little table and had juice and fruit and granola bars, on account of Carolyn insisted monkeys only ate healthy things. Aside from that it was like when she and her friends give a party for their dolls, with chocolate milk and cookies. Did. Her old friends. She'll never have any friends here.

After lunch they're going to a matinee at the movies, but the theater's all the way on the other side of the mall. Holding hands, they all begin skipping along the walkway, Nancy's older sister and her friend in the lead. They chant as they walk:

Step on a crack
break your mother's back.
Step on a line
break your father's spine.

She's pushing as hard as the rest of them, trying to get the next person to step on a crack or line. Then all of a sudden she stops short. She'd been pushed from behind while she was pushing sideways and lost her balance. She stands motionless on the line, tears streaming down her cheeks. What if her father broke his spine and died like her mother did?

"You'd have kept on living with your grandparents, that's all," the eleven-year-old tells the dumb six-year-old. No big deal. And they wouldn't have been able to send her off like this, even if Grandma and Grandpa were both sick. So what if her father loves her? That still doesn't mean he wants her here.

THEY DRIVE OUT TO SEE Grandma Friday night, stay over, see her Saturday, and again for a few minutes Sunday morning. Before eleven o'clock they're on their way back to the city.

"How comes we're not, like, staying late and taking Grandpa out to dinner?" Tiffany asks.

"We took him out last night," Phil answers.

"Actually, this is my fault," Ellyn laughs. "I have to be home by three to watch the Super Bowl."

"Football?!"

"Not football; the Super Bowl." She goes on to explain that this is the biggest day of the year for advertising agencies. Most expensive air time in the business, with sponsors introducing their best and bravest. Two people at her office spend a full year just working on Super Bowl commercials. The thing flops, you can kiss the account goodbye. "Now I'm anxious to see what the other guys have come up with."

"You could've watched it in Grandma's room."

"We could have put the TV on, but I have to concentrate. Other people around would be too much of a distraction."

"It's comparable to us insisting you can't do your homework and listen to music at the same time," Phil laughs.

Grandma isn't homework.

Now Ellyn's playing palsy-walsy again, talking about how as a kid she watched the Super Bowl mainly to see the commercials, but at the same time learned a lot about football. She's talking about how once she got to high school it spelled instant success on dates: "Almost as good as being a cheerleader."

"Know what else? If you'd been watching the Super Bowl last year you'd have seen Madonna's Pepsi commercial."

"Lara's got it on tape. I've seen it." So there.

Phil asks what the big deal was with that commercial, and Ellyn explains that Madonna's *Like a Prayer* video came out right after that. Pepsi got spooked by the controversy and pulled the ad.

Tiffany kicks the back of the seat until her father tells her not to. She knew he would. Don't this, don't that, don't this, don't that: there are so many things they tell her not to do these days, she can't keep track of them all. She pleads to go to one birthday party, and what does she get? Spanked. Ellyn wants some dopey television show and the whole world has to rearrange their schedules for her.

The second they get home she goes into her bedroom and turns on the stereo. Ellyn throws a bag of popcorn in the microwave. Ten minutes before the pre-game shows begin, she knocks on Tiffany's door. "Want to come watch with us?"

"Not really."

"Come on. Rumor is one of the sportscasters gets hit in the head with a ball as he's plugging McDonald's." Had she suspected Tiffany would act this way, she'd have let the two of them go alone to Cherry Hill. God knows, she could have used a break from this.

She glances at her watch: five minutes to. "Final call. If you don't come now, you'll probably miss the first Bud Bowl. Plus your father and I will eat all the popcorn."

"I'd only be a distraction," Tiffany mumbles, almost, but not quite, loud enough to hear.

February 9: Phil

They live next to a red brick building that they think is a barn. It has one large stained glass window. They assume the building's on their property, and dig a pond behind it. Now his parents come and discover it's a schoolhouse, and they don't own it. His mother laughs: he moved away from home because he hated living next to a school, the children always woke him. He says this barn's not in use, but they go up to the door and find the schoolmaster there, setting up. He tells them it might not be used this year, they might use the larger building next to it, but it was used all last year. Now he recalls going for walks and seeing all the kids lined up. He sometimes wondered what they were doing there, but they never woke him.

But if that's a school, then where are his four acres? The schoolmaster points to a small area around the house, then to blue blocks buried in the high grass, saying they're the property line. Can't be: he's certain the realtor drove past the barn to show the dividing line. All it says on the lease is "next to so-and-so," and he says that's him. Does that mean the pond's not theirs? No, he says the boundary curves around and includes that. But look at all his grass they've been paying the kid to mow. Their property has almost no grass, only an awful blue pavement.

CHAPTER TWELVE

THERE'S NEARLY A MONTH OF PLANNING before they spring her. Meetings with the social worker, the physical therapist, the occupational therapist, the medical team. How will washing be handled? What about cooking? Did they remember to install grab bars next to the toilet (no, the towel rack will *not* be enough)? Will there be neighbors checking up on her during the day? All the area rugs are put in storage (too easy to trip on), the bathmat is replaced by one of those no-skid rubber mats you find mostly in tubs. The house seems just an extension of the hospital now.

They stop just short of test-driving the route home to make sure there are no potholes or sharp turns.

Physical therapists will be working with her at home for at least two weeks, to see how she functions in her normal environment, so there are meetings with them as well. Everyone says they just want her to be safe. They don't want her falling and breaking her hip and ending up back in the hospital in even worse shape than she's in now.

Ellyn and Phil take off work Friday, take Tiffany out of school, and are there to surprise her when she hobbles in. As soon as his father leaves to pick her up they hang a banner Tiffany spent the past week coloring: *Welcome Home Grandma.*

For the tenth time, Phil tells them about the banner he made as a seven-year-old to welcome his parents home from a cruise. It hung in that very spot: *Welcome Home Momy and Daddy*! For the twentieth time, he chokes up, goes on and on about how he'd give anything now to change that around, have "Mommy" be spelled correctly. Give Grandma one more moment of happiness.

These days the lap-desk for her wheelchair has an alphabet chart pasted on top: she's supposed to point to the letters if people can't understand her.

Ellyn and Tiffany drive over to the mall to pick up a giant cookie.

His mother's the happiest he's seen her in years. It's as if she's so glad to be home she's oblivious to how poorly she's getting around. The whole day is vintage Three Stooges.

They hear a shriek from the bathroom, rush in, and see her leaning over the toilet bowl, staring. She tried to comb her hair, the comb flipped out of her hand, landed dead center. Phil reaches in and fishes it out, throws it in the wastebasket. They'll buy a new one later. Meanwhile, keep the lid down on the toilet seat.

The next time she goes to the bathroom she has to call her husband in to help her pull up the underpants she's somehow managed to tangle.

Phil looks the other way: his daughter's cringing.

He and Ellyn make spaghetti and meatballs for dinner, only with ziti rather than spaghetti, and the meatballs are more or less bite size. His mother ends up picking up the last few with her fingers, but at least she gets them down. And she doesn't tip over the water glass like she kept doing on those little tables in the dining room where they couldn't get the wheelchair up close. Ellyn and Tiffany take the dishes out to the kitchen. Phil and his parents stretch out in the living room. They watch the 6:00 news, then the opening of some game show. Probably *Jeopardy*.

This is just like it was in the rehab center, except her Hispanic roommate had the TV on 24 hours day. Low, but they could still hear it.

"Want to get the rest of the things out of the car?" Gordon asks his son.

"What things?"

Phil freezes, half in, half out of his chair, the way his mother's been taught to do, gripping the chair's solid base or arms until she's certain she's got her footing.

"Tiffany's things!?"

"We didn't bring her things."

"Why not?"

All he has to do is look around him. That's why not.

"Give us some time to think about it."

"There's nothing to think about. All we have to do is notify the school."

Phil refuses to discuss this at the moment. Insists they give it a few days to see how his mother adjusts to being home. Promises they'll drive back without Tiffany on Tuesday, no, Wednesday night (Ellyn's got a late meeting Tuesday). They'll talk then.

His parents should be turning in soon anyway. They're sleeping on the sofa bed in the living room, so he and Ellyn say good night and head upstairs when Tiffany does.

Settled in bed (the only comfortable place to sit in the room), they watch some made-for-TV movie until neither of them can stand it any longer, turn off the TV and read for an hour, then put the news on.

"They want her back," he tells Ellyn during a commercial for some luxury car, so quiet you'd think there's no one else on the road.

"Now that my mother's home, they're taking it for granted she will move back here. They were expecting us to bring all her belongings with us this weekend."

No one in their right mind would believe this.

It's not a question of belief, it's a question of need.

"IT'S A QUESTION OF TRUST, of responsibility," Phil's father says. "A child Tiffany's age needs constant supervision, especially in New York City. And you have to work."

Phil points out that Tiffany's in school most of the day.

Ellyn reminds them that Abbey picks her up and stays until one of them gets home.

They go back and forth about nutrition, her bike, news stories of shootings, knifings, kids having their lunch money stolen, the high tuition costs. Finally, staring directly into his son's eyes, Gordon gets around to what's been on his mind all along: "Neither your mother nor I trust you to provide the proper environment. After all, you gave her up once."

"So did you!"

"We let her go back to live with you because I was sick." Phil's mother grasps the arms of the chair and stands up for emphasis. "I'm better now."

"I let you take her in six years ago because *I* was sick. I'm better now, too."

"Drunkenness is not sickness!"

"The hell it isn't!"

"It's the middle of the school year," Ellyn says in a conciliatory tone. "Tiffany's had a hard enough time adjusting to a new school once this year. To make her go through a reverse adjustment, after only a few months, is . . . Well, it's unnecessary."

Phil's father insists it's not a new school. These are the same kids she's been in classes with for years.

"Right," Phil says. "You should have heard her tonight. All the way here she was threatening to slit her wrists if we left her at Melissa's for more than two hours."

"Melissa's her best friend!"

"*Was* her best friend!"

"Give her three days in school here and they'll be best friends again," his mother insists. She goes on to talk about how "adaptable" children are. "Everything's a crisis for them. But go get a Kleenex to dry their eyes and they've already moved on to the next crisis."

"I suspect she's past the Kleenex stage," Ellyn mumbles. "Look, both Phil and I . . . "

"You're nothing but a stranger!" Gordon shouts.

"Not to Tiffany!" Her face turns redder than the rouge she gave up wearing two years ago.

"And not to me."

Phil's words are drowned out by his father's: "We appreciate everything you've done for Tiffany over the past few months, but there's no guarantee you'll be around tomorrow."

"No guarantee I won't."

"My son goes through women as quickly as liquor. Or haven't you noticed yet?"

"What do you think I am, a Kelly Girl?"

"As soon as the bottle's dry we'll have seen the last of you."

"I'm hardly in this for the thrill of it," Ellyn says, enunciating every word. As if it makes a difference. Phil's sitting beside her on the fucking sofa, head down, legs wide apart, arms limply clasped genital-level. For Christmas he gives her a skimpy negligee. In the eyes of the beholder . . . If he were to defend anyone, it would probably be his dead wife.

She threads her fingers up and under her hair, pushing it off the front of her shoulders. Perches on the edge of the sofa. "You want to know about strangers? I'll tell you about them. If you're home sick they'll leave the medicine bottle by your bedside and run off to the Great Books discussion group at the library. You crash your bike into a wall, fall and scrape your knee on a rusty nail, but they're too busy gossiping on the phone to even look up when you walk in crying. And you can't go on the class field trip because they never bothered reading the permissions form you brought home, let alone signing it."

She finger-combs her hair again the second the words stop. Mother taking care with the thin, loose strands. She leans back to feel Phil's arm possessively around her. Jerks forward. "My father never stopped to think children might have different needs than near-invalids." She pauses, makes eye contact with her eerily silenced accusers. "Maybe that's why I've worked hard to establish a good rapport with Tiffany."

"And tell me, did your father ever marry this 'stranger'?" Phil's father sneers.

"As a matter of fact, he did. Almost as soon as my mother died."

"And are you and my son planning on getting married?"

"Someday, maybe," Phil begins.

"But in answer to your question: No. Not in the foreseeable future,"

Ellyn finishes.

"In other words, you and my son are planning to continue shacking up, and expect us to feel comfortable leaving our granddaughter with you."

"Come off it!" Phil leaps up in one quick motion. "Marriage is nothing more than a word to children!"

"What the hell do you know about children?"

"I at least remember how old my daughter is! I knew better than to give her dolls' clothes for Christmas!"

Phil's mother begins sobbing. Gordon runs to get her a glass of water. She's already shaking.

"Don't," Ellyn whispers. "Keep this up and she's bound to have a relapse." Though she hasn't the faintest idea why the hell she cares.

Anyway, it doesn't matter what she says. He starts in again the moment his mother's settled. Pacing, talking a mile a minute, he can't resist describing how much her grandmother's physical presence upsets Tiffany. Exaggerating, of course.

Now Phil's into a monologue about half the children in Tiffany's school living with single parents or step-parents. There's not the stigma attached to broken homes there had been when he was growing up. "What matters is how the adults treat each other, how stable their home life is."

"That might be the case with the people you associate with, but it certainly isn't here in Cherry Hill," Phil's father proclaims.

Counting on his fingers like a five-year-old, Phil ticks off the list of people he went to high school with who have been divorced, remarried, and sometimes divorced a second time.

"I think my father realized he'd made a mistake when he married my stepmother," Ellyn adds. "But he was stuck. And if you ask me, being saddled with three kids only made RuthAnn more resentful."

If only she'd once, just once, said this to her father. The two of them in the kitchen late at night, everyone else asleep. If he didn't initiate the conversation she'd bring it up herself, ask him what he thought he'd gain by marrying RuthAnn. He'd make a feeble attempt at explaining, go to put his arm around her, and she'd back away. Then she'd pour the steaming milk over his head.

Phil and his father square off in a "discussion" about what a "stable home life" means.

It means trying to hold your head up on a bucking bronco, she wants to tell them. But, before she can get a word in, Phil's mother screams at everyone to stop. She can't take any more of this. Loud, strong, sure of herself.

Until she bursts out crying.

Everyone promises to give it more thought.

"One more thing I wish you'd consider," Ellyn says. "Eleven's a hard age – you're not a child, but you're also not even an adolescent yet. If you're in a situation where there's illness or death, you're forced to grow up too quickly. Even if you don't mean to be imposing that on Tiffany, I think she'd assume more responsibilities than she can handle." And resent every damn one of them. Just like Joan did. And move in with her boyfriend the day after high school graduation, desperate to get away.

"I'm not dead yet!" Barbara screams. This time she's inconsolable.

So there! Ellyn takes a step back, drinking in an unexpected pleasure.

Phil's right behind her.

TIFFANY SITS PRIMLY ON THE SOFA. Melissa's got to be the only sixth-grader in the world who has to go to bed at nine o'clock sharp, even though she has a friend over.

Her father and Ellyn promised they'd pick her up by nine. It's almost 9:30, and they aren't here yet. Maybe they aren't coming. They refused to let her go over to Grandpa's and Grandma's, which means they're talking about her. Probably trying to decide what to do with her.

Melissa's mother comes in to see if she wants milk and cookies or some nice hot chocolate.

She says no, she's fine, thank you, her father will be here any minute. She starts fooling around with a transformer that's lying on the coffee table, so Melissa's mother won't stand there feeling she has to make conversation. Right now it's a robot, but you can make it a sports car.

Her father and Ellyn are probably at this very moment trying to convince her grandparents to take her back, even though Grandma's sick and can't even eat scrambled eggs without getting them all over herself. Grandpa's probably pointing to Ellyn and saying see, you can keep her with you now; Ellyn can be like a mother. And Ellyn's trying to explain that she doesn't want that on account of her own mother died when she was only three. And now they're all involved in a discussion about what else they can do with her and it's probably going to go on and on and on, and she'll end up having to spend the night here and Melissa's parents will make her go to school with Melissa tomorrow.

Years ago, when they were in, like, first grade, she and Melissa were walking home from school and Melissa was bragging about her parents telling her that her being adopted meant she could be anything she wanted.

In first grade it meant she looked different and not many kids wanted to play with her.

She still looks different. And partly it's her own fault. When she got here tonight she took one look at that dopey ponytail Melissa's been wearing since second grade and decided they'd better work on her hair. Abbey's been teaching her all these great new styles.

It's thinner than any hair she's ever seen. She fixed it in a French braid, but it'll be all undone by morning and Melissa won't be able to fix it on her own. And even if she got it done in the morning, it'd be out by lunchtime. It would have helped if they'd used a conditioner, but there wasn't a bottle of conditioner in the whole house. Melissa wanted them to go over to the mall with her mother and buy some, but she didn't want to be seen with someone who looks so childish, even in Cherry Hill. Melissa still wears pink and white argyle socks and sneakers that have these bells tied on the laces!

There isn't a can of hair spray in the whole house, either.

God, she hopes they're not sending her back to live with Grandma and Grandpa. She doesn't know what she'd do if she had to go to sixth grade here. It would be like going back to kindergarten.

When she was in kindergarten for real her mother was still alive. Everywhere she looked, there were people who wanted her.

She shifts the transformer from hand to hand. Folds the trunk of the car over once, and then again. She raises the fenders until they're arms, folds the engine down to let his head out. Separates the legs as if he's walking. Turns it back to a car. Robot. Car. Robot. Car. She used to believe these things were magic. If the robot-person could pop out from under the car it meant he'd been hiding there all along. And if this little plastic thing could do that, then so could her mother. All you had to do was know the secret.

Melissa's mother puts a plate of cookies in front of her, in case she wants them. "My brother's three-year-old must have left that here last weekend," she comments, seeing the transformer half robot-half car.

Tiffany drops it in her lap, reaches for a cookie. It's not polite to talk with your mouth full.

Her mother won't come back; her father doesn't want her. There's nothing much left to believe in. She throws the transformer, trying to hit the pillow on the chair across the room. Bull's eye. That's the best she can hope for.

SO HERE THEY ARE, the happy couple, picking up the child and heading home. She forces a smile in response to Phil's arm around her. "I think we did it," she says, for want of anything else to tell the bastard.

"Correction: *we* didn't do it, *you* did. If my parents give up this ridiculous custody battle, it's all because of you."

"There's no guarantee I'll be around tomorrow."

"I know, I know," he laughs. "You're nothing but a stranger. C'mere stranger!" He bends to kiss her, winds up with lips stiff from hair spray.

"Maybe I should make it easy on everyone and leave now," Ellyn says, her voice loud enough that his parents just might hear. The longer she stays, the harder it's going to be to break away.

Phil sighs, shakes his head, opens the door for her, steps in front and forces a hug on her before she gets in. "Look," he says over the hum of the engine, "I'm sorry I couldn't be more constructive in the dialogue tonight."

"Constructive!?"

"You seemed the only person there saying anything sensible. Christ, they pushed every one of my buttons, and I reacted exactly the same way I did when I was fifteen or sixteen. I couldn't stop myself."

"I don't have a whole history with them." Looking out her window.

"We'll have to change that." Phil reaches an arm out around her.

If Ellyn slid over any further she'd be out the door. "We'll have to change a lot of things," she says. "A hell of a lot of things. Like your parents calling me a gold-digging hussy."

"They were attacking me, not you. Let's face it, I've been through a lot of girlfriends over the past four years."

"Tell me just one thing. No, two things. If Anita had been there, would your parents have dared talk to her that way? And if they had, would you have risen to her defense?"

"Anita would never have had nerve to stand up to my parents like that. I was frankly too stunned to say anything. And proud, too." For the rest of the seemingly endless five-block drive to Melissa's he talks non-stop about how he knew RuthAnn had been insensitive but never understood she'd been so very insensitive, and how in a way he didn't realize how much she's been doing for Tiffany, or how much it's costing her, and how he'd give anything to be able to replay this night so he could say and do the right things. He stops just short of saying he loves her.

A HAIRDRESSER APPOINTMENT, a friend in from out of town, a TV show she wants to watch, even a sale at Macy's, any excuse will do. So long as it keeps her in the city.

She walks to the park, sits on a swing, tries to push herself. It's not as much fun alone.

Two bag ladies have invaded the playground.

Phil tells her his parents are starting to think she's past tense; they suspect he and Tiffany are back to living by themselves, replete with paper plates and TV dinners. He uses his most endearing smile to urge her into taking a ride to Cherry Hill with them. Tiffany doesn't even say please this time.

At the last minute it turns out to be the only time she can set up meetings with a new client.

Her father calls, concerned. It's been so long since he's heard from her.

"WELL, IT'S NOW OFFICIAL," Phil tells her. "They've moved the bed down to the dining room."

"What about one of those chair lifts along the banister?"

"My father insists this is temporary." He describes the way his mother screams, cries, pleads when his father's trying to redo the splint. "He must have wound and unwound that thing a dozen times before she gave in and said she felt comfortable." He talks about how simple exercises seem to have turned into Chinese water torture. His father stood there pleading *one more stair* while she howled like a wolf in heat. Forget that they were only taking three steps. She walked up four steps in rehab.

"In rehab there were rails on both sides," Ellyn reminds him.

"I've never known my mother to call it quits before."

She begins going for outpatient therapy three evenings a week, then two evenings a week. Phil suggests they look into the retirement community right near the mall. Cadbury? They'd live by themselves, but with an abundance of professionals around if . . .

"They don't let children live in those places!"

Damn right they don't. He goes straight home and writes out a check, deposit for next year's tuition at Clarendon.

The next time Tiffany sees Melissa, she's back to wearing her hair in that stupid ponytail. Her grandparents never again bring up the subject of her moving back in with them. Ellyn seems the only one who can't forget.

It's not as if she wanted this.

Mother wanted children, even if it killed her.

After TC the ovarian cancer sets in full force.

Five years old. She's upstairs supposedly getting ready for bed, but her brother and sister stuff pillows in her pajamas, march her downstairs and announce the baby's due next month. Her father dutifully laughs. Next month RuthAnn loses the baby. Pregnancy isn't something you fool around with.

Even so, she had her obligatory abortion. As did the majority of her friends.

Ellyn alternately pitied and looked down on women like Anita. She might have left home, might have tried to leave the glitzy church and monthly trips to the confessional back in Georgia or wherever the hell she was from, but abortion was still out of the question. She pictures Anita going to midnight mass with Phil's parents that first Christmas, holding her seven-month-old daughter in her arms. No longer living in sin, she takes communion.

CHAPTER THIRTEEN

"MELISSA HAS THIS NEW FORTUNE-TELLING kit she's soooo proud of. But, like, how many times can someone read your palm or look into this empty glass and tell you the name of the boy you'll marry? So I ask if she's seen *Evita* yet. And she has. Then I ask what she thinks about the way Madonna looked. And she stares at me. She thought Madonna always looks that way! Do you believe it? Doesn't she even watch MTV?"

Tiffany chatters away to her grandmother. She's here for spring break, and it's borrrrrrrring. All Grandma wants to do is sit on the back porch most of the day. At least there's loads to talk about now, almost a whole year of school and friends Grandma's never met. And Grandma talks back now; she doesn't just sit there crying.

She can't believe she and Melissa were ever friends. Or best friends, anyway. At least their spring breaks fall at different times, so she doesn't have to see Melissa much. Besides, Melissa's made all these other stupid friends now. All she talks about is Susie this and Susie that.

"Her name's Susan," Tiffany told her finally.

Riding her bike is fun (her father still won't let her bring the bike into the city). The people next door got this neat cocker spaniel. And the first few days are filled with planning their trip to the mall for her spring wardrobe. It'll be Grandma's biggest outing yet.

Grandpa drops them off in front of the Macy's entrance. They haven't even made it out of the men's store yet, and Grandma has to sit down. By the time they get to the jewelry counter even Tiffany realizes it's no use. They call Grandpa to come get them and Grandma sleeps for the rest of the afternoon. Tiffany calls her father.

Phil picks her up Friday night instead of Sunday.

Ellyn says she'd better stay at the office late.

"You've worked late every night this week," Phil comments.

Their eyes meet for a moment. Ellyn blinks, turns away. She runs her fingers through her hair, pulls it all back, and flips it over one shoulder.

Before they can get Tiffany off to bed she insists on giving them a play-by-play account of Cocky, the tricks she taught him, how far he'll run to chase a stick she's thrown, how far she can toss a stick, what he likes and doesn't like to eat. Most of which she's already told her father.

The next day Ellyn takes her to the big Gap store and outlet center on 35th St. Might as well make it as easy as possible. And on the off chance she doesn't see anything there she likes, Macy's and A & S are right across the street.

In the cab Tiffany complains nonstop about Melissa's probably even going to the ladies room with her mother and Melissa being proud on account of she's a Safety.

After spending half an hour ogling the jeans and shuffling through every top in every color, Tiffany takes an armload and heads for the dressing room.

"I never realized Gap had so many different styles," Ellyn comments, already envisioning an ad with all the different jeans hanging on a clothesline, the kids playing underneath it: caption, "a cut above."

Tiffany's way ahead of her.

She gets stopped at the door: only four pieces at a time. Ellyn grabs another four and goes in with her. Otherwise they'll be here all day.

Tiffany tries on every black t-shirt in the store, selects the six skimpiest. Six? Six. Let her father deal with this.

"If you want them that small, your old ones should fit," Ellyn teases.

Tiffany pretends she didn't hear.

Now for the jeans. Tiffany tries on pair after pair, discards two pairs, and then tries all the others on again. She looks in this mirror, then that one. Turns a pocket inside out, inserts a thumb at the waist to see how much room there is. Somehow, between last fall and now, she's learned that jeans look sexier worn low on the hips. Probably her friend Jessica's doing. Or Lara's.

Those jeans at Bergdorf's might not look so bad now.

Only one pair suits her.

Okay, fine. Fine. They'll jaywalk over to Macy's. And head for the restrooms while they're at it; her bladder's about to explode.

The bag ladies doing their laundry here every morning have half the sinks stopped up.

She's certainly not enjoying this, but can't help laughing when Tiffany emerges wearing five-pocket overalls.

She decides she wants them.

"You're kidding. And $125?"

"They're Calvins."

"Alvins would be more like it. You look like an elephant in blue-collar disguise."

"I think they make me look thin."

"If you want to look thin, I've found leggings are great."

"Give me a break! They're as bad as jeans with velvet stripes."

"What's wrong with those jeans we bought?"

"Everything! I knew they would be all wrong, and they were! I looked like I'd come from a boarding school on Mars or something."

"Why didn't you say that before we bought them?"

"Because I couldn't get a word in. You kept saying how great they were."

Ellyn takes a deep breath. She can remember nights she came home and found Tiffany wearing those jeans. Funny, though, now that she stops to think about it, she can't remember her wearing them at breakfast.

TC comes home and changes into old clothes after school. Not wanting to ruin the good stuff. It's a little trick Joan taught her.

"Okay," she tells Tiffany. "If you insist on looking like a waif, you might as well do so in black t-shirts and designer jeans." She opens and closes her pocketbook, redoes her lipstick, pushes a few hairs back in place.

Two hours and ten trips to the dressing room later, Tiffany emerges with the overalls and three pairs of jeans. Guess, Lizwear, and another Calvin Klein. *Know what comes between me and my Calvins? Nothing.*

And no one.

Ellyn suggests they look at shoes while they're down here. Not so much because she's in the mood for shoes, but she'll do anything to avoid another shopping trip.

The way Tiffany's lackadaisically scuffling along, she surmises the feeling is mutual.

They head upstairs to the casual shoes department. Ellyn goes off in one direction, Tiffany in the other. "Here they are," Tiffany calls. Ellyn puts down a loafer and goes over to look. Tiffany's holding up this ridiculous brown lace half boot with soles six inches thick.

"You can't wear those, you wouldn't even be able to lift them," Ellyn teases.

"They're Air-Ware. Which means light. Feel."

"I've never seen anything so ugly." She looks around, picks up a pair of ankle boots with soles not even half the thickness. "If you want a boot, how about something like these?"

"No. They have to be DMs."

"What?"

"DMs. Doctor Marten's. Like these, or these." She holds up a heavy-looking black shoe.

Ellyn picks one up, looks closer. She's never once worked on a shoe ad. And if this is what sells then she hopes to hell she never has to. But finally she agrees to let Tiffany try them on.

"They look like orthopedic shoes. God, Tiffany, I cried for two whole years because they insisted I wear shoes like that."

"I'M NOT YOOOUUUU!"

In a fit of barely controlled rage, Ellyn begins placing the shoes back in their boxes.

"I'm buying these!" Tiffany screams, reaching for the mate of the shoe she has on.

Gathering more strength than she would have thought herself capable of, Ellyn yanks Tiffany's foot up and begins undoing the laces, breaking a fingernail in the process. "You may, provided you first apologize to me, select one pair of appropriate shoes."

RuthAnn releases her. Ellyn freezes.

"You have no right to tell me what to do!" Tiffany screams, lacing up the DM again.

The salespeople discreetly look the other way. But a matronly lady sitting across from them pokes her head in. "You shouldn't talk to your mother that way, dear."

"She's not my mother! My mother's dead!"

"So's mine!" Ellyn shouts back.

This is insane. She gives in, or up, or whatever. While Tiffany changes back into her Nikes (God forbid she wear her best clothes when there's no one around to impress) Ellyn checks with the salesperson, is assured any unworn shoes can be returned, no questions asked. She charges one pair of shoes, one pair of boots, drags Tiffany down escalator after escalator, past the women holding tubes of lipstick delicately against their lips, and out the door so quickly you'd think the place was haunted.

As far as Tiffany's concerned, it is.

WITHOUT EVEN PEEKING IN THE BOXES, Phil packs up both bundles and places them next to his briefcase in the hall closet. He'll take them back Monday on the way home from work. Tiffany can make do with her old clothes.

Tiffany shrieks.

Without saying a word, Phil marches into her room, picks up a random t-shirt, and rips it down the center. He picks up another shirt. "Now, what did you want to say?" he asks, holding it at the neck.

Both Ellyn and Tiffany gape at him. Tiffany's backed herself against the far wall.

"Didn't you want to tell Ellyn something?"

Tiffany bats the tears back from her eyes. "I'm sorry," she mumbles.

"Louder!" Phil announces.

"I'm sorry."

"Sorry for what?"

"For yelling at Ellyn in the store. For acting up."

Phil balls up the shirt and throws it in his daughter's face, then steers Ellyn out of the room ahead of him. Tif doesn't emerge when it's time for dinner, and no one bothers to call her. It turns into a long, silent evening.

With an exaggerated yawn, Phil suggests they get to bed.

"In a few minutes." Ellyn hasn't looked up once from the pile of magazines she's been thumbing through ever since dinner.

Phil heads for the bedroom, saying he'll meet her there.

She picks up another magazine. Reads for twenty minutes or so. She supposes she has to turn in sometime.

"Tiffany at least needs an outfit or two for school," she says, standing at the dresser, picking out clothes for tomorrow.

"What have you been looking at out there, the fashion ads?" Jokingly.

"I should have done that before I took her shopping. I'd have had a better sense of what she needs."

"The only thing my daughter needs is some training in how to act civilized."

"And tearing up a shirt is going to teach her that? Right."

"It at least prevented another tantrum, didn't it?" She can almost see Phil's chest puffing up.

"Unlike in the store," Ellyn mumbles. She arranges some things on the dresser. "I should have just kept my mouth shut," she tells the mirror.

"No, *Tiffany* should have kept her big fat trap shut."

"Look," Ellyn says, sitting on the edge of the bed. AHer jeans are frayed at the knees, the turtlenecks are so tight you can see her nipples."

He jolts to a sitting position, slamming his shoulders against the headboard. "Is that my fault? Your fault?"

"No, it's not my fault. And don't yell at me." Grabbing her hairbrush, she marches off to the bathroom.

My daughter. Ellyn tries out those words in her father's voice, changing the inflection with each hard, angry stroke of the brush. As bad as last year's clothes.

Father seldom notices what they wear. Every August RuthAnn, cashing his paycheck, gives each child $50 for school clothes. Those years TC hasn't been through a growth spurt, it's manageable. But if the jacket's outgrown, that's $30 right there. Unless she wears one of Joan's old ones. With an eight-room house, they have no trouble keeping old clothes around.

Sometimes she takes jeans and sweaters from Joan as well. Joan's the one who has no castoffs, just the same $50, plus what she can make from babysitting.

"Look," she says, picking up the conversation where she left off, calmer now, sliding into bed. "You told me yourself how your mother used to do everything for her. Now all of the sudden she's the one having to wait on your mother. That's probably what's behind all this."

"She didn't even want to visit my mother in the hospital."

"We were the ones who said she couldn't visit at the start, remember?"

"Whose side are you on anyway?"

No response.

"She's a manipulative little brat, and I'll bust her ass if I have to, but I'll not have her expecting people to just scurry about for her benefit."

He turns toward the window, the covers forming a wall around him.

"She's entering adolescence. Give it time." Ellyn flops an arm across his chest.

"I've run out of time." Phil pulls away.

Ellyn turns over. Phil's appropriated all but a few inches of the covers. She can't even fall asleep in peace.

ELLYN BEATS PHIL HOME Wednesday night, finds Tiffany on the phone in the living room. Calling friends already? She left school less than three hours ago. That's another change – ever since Christmas break Tiffany's been on the phone night and day (including the one call per day they permit her those weekends they're in New Jersey). What the hell did people do before call waiting?

Bought the kids their own phone. Or screamed to get the hell off. Frankly, if she could get past personal associations, there are some pointers she might pick up from RuthAnn.

Stopping to talk with Abbey for a minute, Ellyn overhears a few words: clothes; nothing; she. And from the way she's whining, that's probably her grandmother she's talking to.

"She" doesn't trust herself to go shopping with the child again, but nobody asks her anyway. It's all been arranged: Melissa's mother will take both girls to the mall. As a matter of fact, they're waiting for Phil to drive her over. Phil's mother gives her $150. Cash.

Tiffany runs out and waits in the car for her father. If he's going to protest her buying things, she doesn't want to hear. At least she was smart enough to bring the backpack her father gave her last Christmas, and she cleaned it out so there's plenty of room inside. She only hopes she and Melissa go into the dressing rooms without her mother, and that Melissa hasn't turned into a snitch on top of everything else.

Yikes! The way she's dressed! Pink leggings with this stupid red floral pattern that make her look like she weighs 100 pounds. And then red high-top sneakers with hot pink socks folded over the top! How dumb can you get?

Melissa's mother guides them to Strawbridge and Clothier. Tiffany expected as much. Melissa's mother loves Strawbridge and Clothier. At least it's not J. C. Penney. But department stores always put those magnetic tags in their things; she doesn't stand a chance unless they get to the smaller stores. As long as a smaller store's crowded, all you have to do is walk out with a bunch of people, so if some alarm goes off there are all these others to suspect, and you can bolt.

Melissa buys a few stupid things, and they head for Gap Kids. Great! They have the same baby tees as they do in the city. She was worried they wouldn't have them out here. She picks up five of the six she bought the first time (they don't have the short-sleeved pocket t-shirt in her size), along with two turtlenecks. Melissa's mother doesn't understand why she has to try them all on, since she knows her size, but Tiffany makes up a story about how sometimes they're cut slightly different and hurries into the dressing room. Melissa follows. Not going to the trouble of undressing, Tiffany shoves three tees in her backpack, along with a black turtleneck. Melissa gapes.

Tiffany glares at her.

Melissa meekly minds her own business. She buys a pair of khakis. Tiffany buys one baby tee. They head for Macy's. Every damn piece has a theft tag in it here, but Tiffany finds a jeans jacket that's almost a twin to the one Jessica has, and blows $62 on it. Melissa buys two polyester blouses, one with that stupid sailor collar like only little kids wear. "You ought to get some turtlenecks," Tiffany suggests.

"They make me too hot."

Wouldn't you know it? Melissa gets two quarters from her mother and runs over to the candy train, just like a five-year-old! She puts one quarter in the machine stocking those fake M & Ms, the other in a chocolate-covered mint machine. They're out of jellybeans. Mrs. Canter offers her a quarter, too, but she politely refuses.

Benetton, T. J. Maxx. Limited Too, Designs, Children's Sample Shop, a few other places. By the end of the afternoon, Melissa's bought two pair of khaki trousers and a stupid-looking sweater and Tiffany's blown the rest of her loot, plus $7 she borrowed from Melissa's mother on two pairs of jeans. She's managed to stuff her backpack with two more t-shirts (Benetton), a vest (T. J.

Maxx, but it's Lizwear), and a mock turtleneck (Designs). She wishes she had nerve to take this great pair of jean overalls, but she doesn't trust herself with that much bulk. Her father will probably let her buy more in a few weeks anyway.

She and Melissa go into the ladies room. Melissa looks at two stalls before selecting one, and carefully covers the seat with toilet paper before sitting down. She goes into the next stall and piles everything into one of the shopping bags. They drop her off at her grandparents'.

SHE ISN'T BLIND, YOU KNOW. She can read a price tag. But everyone else seems to be ignoring the obvious, so Ellyn keeps her mouth shut. For the moment.

Monday she mulls things over, Tuesday she stews, Wednesday she goes for broke and calls her sister.

A quick rundown of the stealing, and Joan launches into her stock lecture on early childhood development, via Melanie Klein and the local Montessori school, with a few opinions from the health food co-op thrown in for good measure. Today's kids are forced to grow up too quickly, so they do impulsive things like stealing and lying in retaliation, blah blah blah. Living in the city only increases the tension, that's why she and Mike moved to Mamaroneck. "To date, it seems to have been a smart move, but I'm still knocking on wood with crossed fingers," she says.

"Happens in the best of families."

"Don't we know. I hope stealing's not hereditary."

"It's not. I never stole. And I don't think Geoff did."

"Great, one out of three. Which of my three do you think?"

"None. Your kids seem pretty secure."

Ellyn can hear her sister's breathing taking on weight.

"Believe it or not, Joan, you're the only kid I knew who went through a shoplifting phase. Or knew well, anyway."

"You've led a sheltered life."

"I always suspected you stole mainly to impress the other kids."

"And befriend them. Force them to include me. Actually the whole stealing club was my idea," Joan laughs. Two or three kids would go into a store together. One would distract the clerk, asking for suggestions about a birthday gift. After her friends had time to take what they wanted, she'd say she had to talk to her mother before buying anything.

"I can just picture you walking into that store with RuthAnn!" Ellyn jokes.

"Or Dad!"

"Or Dad."

Saturday morning. Joan's setting her hair. TC's reading. Neither one of them hears the phone ring. Dad comes into their room, his face red. One of the mothers caught her daughter with the loot.

Dad goes on and on about how mortified he is, how Joan's act reflects on the whole family and he has to do business in this town. He docks her allowance and grounds her for the next month. He makes her call the girl's mother and apologize, but he doesn't even tell RuthAnn about it. This is between him and his daughter. His *daughters*.

"I have to admit, Dad paid more attention to us that morning than he did through the rest of our childhood," Ellyn says.

"And we've been vying for his attention ever since, right?"

"Long before that. I remember you used to color pictures for him and tack them on the refrigerator, hoping he'd notice."

"No, I didn't. I never liked to draw."

"Sure you did, I remember . . . "

"I used to color with you sometimes. It was the only way I could think of to amuse you, and I used to have to watch you all the time."

Dad must have appreciated that, at least. Didn't he? Ellyn doesn't dare ask. Besides, she and Joan were neglected, whereas Tiffany . . .

Tiffany spends all day shopping, throws a tantrum, and ends up with nothing but a father one sass away from grounding her forever. Ellyn fills her sister in on the shopping trip. "I guess she's feeling pretty insecure, isn't she? Boy, that's a feeling I can relate to."

"That's pure fantasy!" Joan explodes. "The poor kid's so desperate she tells some stranger in a department store her mother's dead, and what do you do? You shout back that your mother's dead, too, then get her out as quickly as possible. All you were thinking about was how you didn't know what to do!"

"I give up."

"Don't give up, grow up! You're so damn competitive I don't believe it. And with a child! If you have to turn it into a contest, it's the memory of her mother you're competing with. But she'll never let you replace her mother, so you can't win. If children mean so much to you all of the sudden, go have your own child."

"I don't want my own child!"

"Of course not! You're afraid to nurse an infant, to have someone totally dependent on you. You think because Tiffany's past the toddler stage she won't be as needy."

"I said no such thing!"

"You didn't have to, Tiffany did."

"Correction: that's what you're reading into what I said Tiffany did."

"Any idiot could have read it correctly. Jesus, Ellyn, for a while there it looked like you'd changed. I hate to see you hardening again."

"What's that supposed to mean?"

"Look in the mirror! You're softer. Looser. Your shoulders aren't as rigid; you aren't trying to hide behind an inch of makeup. I noticed it the night you brought the boxes up. You've even had good conversations with my kids for the first time in your life!"

"They're getting older and easier to talk to."

"I knew you'd find some excuse the minute I pointed it out!"

Oh, screw it! "I'd better get back to work," she mumbles. "I can't afford to lose my job as well."

"Look, if nothing else, remember this," Joan says in closing: "Don't expect Phil to be all the things Dad wasn't. He's Tiffany's father, not yours."

"I'm looking for a lover, not a cough drop!" She slams the phone down.

CHAPTER FOURTEEN

WHY TODAY?

Because today's shot anyway. Might as well go home and ruin the rest of it.

She doesn't want her own child, she doesn't even want this child. Sorry to disappoint you, Sister Dear. O-U-T spells out, and she is not it. *My mother punched your mother . . .*

She stands beside the wrought iron umbrella stand, one of the few antiques in this apartment, awaiting the impending arrival.

Abbey says hello, Tiffany slinks off down the hall to her bedroom, Ellyn says goodbye.

"But I'm supposed to . . . "

"Not this afternoon! I'm here."

"Phil said . . . "

"You'll get paid, Abbey! Just leave. Please."

Abbey starts putting her coat back on. One of those calf-length coats gathered at the waist so that, even over jeans, she captures that evening-gown flow.

You'd think a drop of that style might have rubbed off on Tiffany.

Ellyn takes a deep breath. "Look, I'm sorry," she says, going to the door with Abbey. "I guess I was probably acting younger than Tiffany does, right? There's a lot on my mind right now."

"I get the same way around exam time." Abbey returns the chuckle. "Besides, I can use this free afternoon. I have to turn in four sketches by the end of the week, and I've barely started them."

Ellyn watches her bounce jauntily off down the hall. She thought, when Abbey suddenly cut her long dark hair into what used to be called a pixie, she'd lose all that bounce. But instead of hardening her features it makes her look elegant.

She's never felt so ancient.

She runs her fingers through her own hair, massages her temples, sits on the sofa to compose herself. The last thing she needs is to burst into Tiffany's room screaming, no matter what the temptation.

All you were thinking about was how you didn't know what to do! Joan had a point there. This time she's got to keep her focus on Tiffany.

A grownup would stay calm, regardless what happens.

She reminds herself not to immediately start in with accusations, give the child a chance to confess on her own. As she walks down the hall she concentrates on composing an opening sentence of more than five words.

"Why don't you show me your new clothes again?" she suggests, tapping once after she's already got the door open. Tiffany's settled in at the desk she's used maybe three times since she's lived with them, her homework spread out in front of her.

"I put them away already. They're, like, all mixed in with my other things," she says without looking up from the book.

Ellyn heads for the dresser. "I think we can pick them out."

Tiffany gets there first.

Ellyn backs down. If she expects Tiffany to respect her privacy, she supposes she ought to offer as much in return. "Okay," she says. "Why don't you tell me about the things you bought. You can start by telling me how much they cost."

"$157. I borrowed $7 from Mrs. Canter."

Ellyn grabs her wrist. Gently, but firmly. She asks again how much they cost.

"They were on sale!"

"Even sale items cost more than that."

"New Jersey's cheaper than New York."

"What do you take me for?"

Tiffany tries to stare her down. Fails. "So okay, I swiped some, you know. It's no big deal."

This time it's Ellyn's turn to stare.

Tiffany puts on a brave face, says okay, go ahead, tell on her.

Ellyn starts to ask what she thinks her father would say. *You have no right to tell me what to do*! For the rest of her life she'll hear Tiffany screaming those words, see the salespeople cautiously looking the other way, remember that meddling little old woman. If she's ever going to earn that right, it has to be now.

She sits on the bed. "Did you go on the stealing binge because your friends at school seem to have more than you?"

Tiffany edges toward her open schoolbook.

Ellyn asks if Melissa was with her, if Melissa stole too.

"Melissa won't even try anything on unless her mother approves of it!"

Ellyn puts an arm on her shoulder. She wants to suggest that maybe Melissa's close with her mother. That only six months ago she and Tips were close. Instead she points out that Tiffany's been through a lot of changes in the past few months. Her body's matured a lot sooner than Melissa's. "But stealing isn't going to impress her with how grown up you are, you know. The people who are impressed by stealing or cheating don't make very good friends in the long run."

Big deal, she can hear TC saying to that one. She doesn't steal, she doesn't cheat, there's not a single childhood friend Ellyn's still in touch with.

"I went to school with a girl whose parents gave her money and left her by herself. Cheryl, her name was. She had more clothes than anyone else in the class, and, boy, was she popular. She was the first one in the class to have her own phone, her own car. She'd treat everyone at the sub shop or the deli. I never liked her very much, but I couldn't put my finger on why. It took me years to understand that the only way her parents knew to show their love was to keep giving her more and more. And she, in turn, learned to buy her friends."

Laugh, smile, cry, do something! Tiffany's eyes don't even blink. It's her own damn fault if this "little talk" is turning into a lecture.

That day he catches Joan stealing is the only time he sits down and talks with them. And TC's only included because it's her room, too. He doesn't know what else to do with her.

One flimsy day, over twenty years ago.

"Were you stealing to get back at your father and me?"

Tiffany turns back to her schoolbooks.

Ellyn stands up, moves over to the desk. She can almost see Tiffany's face from here. "We – and by we I mean everyone, your father, your grandparents, and I – don't want to buy your love. We want to earn it." If she'd kept her cool in Macy's none of this would have happened. She's to blame as much as the child is.

"Remember the night your father spanked you? How I told you afterwards that he wanted you here, and loved you, but wasn't always sure what to do? Well, that goes for me, too."

Shit. Of all possible nights, why the hell did she have to bring up that one?

Tiffany's looking out of the corner of her eye. "I got a lot of work done during that week you were at your grandparents'," Ellyn continues. "And I was looking forward to the weekend to unwind. If I'd been thinking clearly, I probably would have suggested we wait a week before going shopping. As it was, everything got off on the wrong foot, and I guess I was over-reacting."

Silence.

"People do a lot of foolish things when they don't feel loved," she continues. "Not only stealing. Sometimes they start using drugs, or get sexually reckless. My first year in college was horrendous. It took me weeks to make girlfriends, let alone boyfriends. When a boy finally did ask me out, I slept with him the same night. I hadn't taken proper precautions, but I was afraid that if I didn't sleep with him no one else would ever ask me out."

Well, at least she has Tiffany's attention now. "As you might have guessed, I ended up pregnant. And had an abortion. But even then, I was so starved for love that I went straight from the clinic to a girlfriend's house. I felt no one gave a damn at my own home."

Tears are forming in the wrong eyes. Ellyn goes on to say that her real reason for having that abortion was not that she didn't want a child, but that she didn't feel capable of loving another person. "It's past history, anyway," she finishes.

She'd better get dinner started.

"Are you going to tell my father?" Tiffany asks when she's almost to the door.

Ellyn starts to promise she won't tell, then checks herself. "Do you want me to?"

"Please don't."

Ellyn's shoulders finally relax. Tiffany's looking directly at her for the first time all afternoon. "Okay. I won't." Then, feeling the need to play the responsible adult, she reminds Tiffany that she's only promised not to tell this once. If it ever happens again, all bets are off.

Halfway down the hall, Ellyn imagines she hears Tiffany mumble, "Thank you."

Not much to be thankful for. Had she expected Tiffany to break down in tears like a normal eleven-year-old, crying about how sorry she was?
For the stealing binge? For the day in Macy's? For all the things she has that TC never dreamed of?

There was a point to that abortion story; she wasn't being callous or trying to shock. She intended to finish by telling Tiffany that she's able to love people now, "You and your father are living proof of that." But somehow, by the end of the story, she felt more inclined to blurt out *Your mother could have had an abortion, too, you know; and if she had you wouldn't be here.*

She thought at the least the two of them would end up in a hug, their bodies rocking.

TC and her brother, ages five and nine, are jealous of their friends at school who have real mothers. They go through a stage of calling their stepmother "Mommy RuthAnn." It doesn't last long.

SHE CAN SEE IT NOW: she's taken Tiffany shopping. Tiffany runs out of the store carrying all sorts of clothes, still on their hangers, not even bothering to hide them, while she's running after her, calling out in this timid voice: "May I help you, please, may I help you? Please, please, please, please, please."

"May I help you?" she asks in the voice of the sixteen-year-old trying so hard to look older that she more than likely seems younger. But she's sixteen and has a copy of her birth certificate with her to prove it. She no longer needs working papers and parental consent.

It's the second "help wanted" sign she sees, in the window of a John's Bargain Store squatting between two gas stations in Forest Hills. The manager explains the position's already filled, but she's continuing to interview on the off chance another opens up.

"I'll be a potential customer. Approach me as if you're the salesperson. Show me what you'd do."

She sucks in her breath, takes three steps back then two steps forward, draws alongside the make-believe customer. "May I help you?"

"You'll never get any job that way!" the manager explodes. "It gives me a chance to say, 'No, you can't help me, I'm just looking,' or whatever. And you'd have no choice but to leave me alone. Never, ever, approach a customer with a question."

TC stands there, silent.

"Walk up quickly. Immediately begin commenting on whatever the customer's looking at. You could have told me how durable these plastic containers are. Make it so I'd be embarrassed if I didn't buy one."

TC's face turns red. She'll never be able to pounce on strangers, interrupt their thoughts, and start praising this junk. She'd almost rather chase after bratty children.

Feeling suddenly weak, Ellyn sits at the table. Puts her head between her knees. Takes a deep breath. Again. Again. Looks up to see spots, or dust particles. The Child's getting away from her.

SUSANNAH LIVES ON A FARM in Virginia with a family that has four children, two boys and two girls. The oldest daughter milks Susannah, stroking her neck while she works, and Susannah always gives a lot of good, sweet milk.

Then the family moves west in a covered wagon, and they can take along only one cow. Rosy, the calf that was always anxious to jump the fence and see the world, is left with a neighbor. There are hardships on the journey, but finally they get to a new home, and Susannah has another calf, Posy.

Susannah watches more and more settlers arrive, feeling sorry for the cows tied be-

hind the wagons. Then one day a cow's untied and put in the pasture with her. They stare at each other. It's Rosy! They're together again, on a farm almost as big as they had in Virginia. And Susannah is once again a happy cow.

Most girls TC's age are checking out the Beverly Cleary and Judy Blume books. Nobody wants much to do with a book written nearly two decades ago, with a tattered cover; it isn't even a mystery. That's the only reason she's permitted to borrow *Susannah The Pioneer Cow* again and again.

God, she hasn't thought of that book in years. It's what she was reading the day her father came in to talk to Joan. It's what she was always reading.

When Tiffany first moved in here, volumes from *The Babysitters Club* series lay all over the place. Either that series ended or Tiffany finds them too juvenile now. Most likely the latter.

Twelve, thirteen, fourteen, fifteen pass, without TC tacking up a note at the supermarket. "I know a lot of people who'd be more than happy to hire you," one of the women on the next block tells her. "And I'd be glad to give you a recommendation. Your sister was absolutely wonderful with my children."

Sure she was. So long as Joan was already saddled with one brat, the others would be a cinch. Might as well make some money while she's at it.

So TC's not interested in children, big deal! Some kids prefer math to English. She supplements her allowance by addressing envelopes for a penny apiece, or running errands on the bike she inherits from her brother. The only doll she'd had, aside from Barbie, was that walking monster, manufactured already at the toddler stage, too old to lie around in a stinky diaper. They'd wanted nothing to do with each other.

"YOU DON'T HAVE TO DO IT all yourself, you know," Phil says, coming home to find dinner almost ready.

Maybe not, but she sure as hell wishes she could.

"I finished up a long project at four o'clock; there seemed no point in hanging around the office tonight." Liar. She hasn't accomplished a thing in the past three days. Unless you call talking at a pre-teen deaf mute being productive. Or searching the freezer for chicken breasts. They were just beyond her reach when she gave up and pulled out a box of macaroni. Macaroni and cheese: it used to be Tiffany's favorite.

"Anita was that way, too." Phil kisses the back of her neck, and leans against the counter. Casual, relaxed, his long legs stretched to trip anyone passing.

Her neck feels stiff. She pours dressing on the salad, notices in disgust how heavy-handed her touch was, tries to drain off the extra, asks Phil to please call Tiffany in to set the table.

He opens the drawer to get the silver out.

"I said, call Tiffany in," she says, pushing the drawer closed tightly against his wrist. "She might have been too young to help her mother, but that doesn't mean she can't help me once in a while."

Phil looks up, confused.

THEY SIT. THEY EAT. Tiffany chatters about a French spelling bee at school. They gave the English word, then the kids had to know the French translation and spell the French word correctly. She tells them which words were given, which were missed, which kids misspelled them. She ends by mimicking the teacher's accent that's so heavy in class but, overhear her talking to another teacher in the hall or the cafeteria, and she has practically no accent.

Her father tests her knowledge by giving new words to translate and spell, and – to judge by his memory of high school French – she gets them right. Ellyn took Spanish in high school, German in college. The kids at Clarendon started French in first grade.

Tiffany's had a lot of catching up to do.

She doesn't let her eyes meet Ellyn's through the entire meal. Ellyn offers yogurt, the only thing they've got in the house for dessert, but everyone declines. Tiffany and Phil clear the table and do the dishes together. Ellyn can hear them in the kitchen, talking, laughing.

They finish in the nick of time. Tiffany makes a mad dash for her room, switches on the TV: *90210*'s on. Oh, cool! It's the episode where Brenda goes all the way with Dylan. She wouldn't have wanted to miss this for all the world.

TIFFANY PICKS UP HER RABBIT and crawls into bed, lets her father and Ellyn come in to say good night. "*Dites bonne nuit au lapin*," she says in perfect French.

"*Dormez bien, petit homme.*" Phil pecks the rabbit on one ear. Ellyn twirls a whisker around her finger.

Little man? He's nothing but a rabbit. And he's stuffed, besides. Not even as good as Carolyn's monkey.

Carolyn doesn't live in the building anymore. Probably couldn't fit in the elevator. She's the fattest woman ever, so fat only something like a monkey would want to be seen with her.

Tiffany drops the rabbit as if he's got cooties. Doesn't want to grow up to love a rabbit *or* a monkey. And for all she knows, it might even be a girl monkey.

No, it has to be a boy. She remembers, because it was about that time that she had to go to the bathroom bad one night, and her father told her to come on in. He'd just gotten out of the shower, was standing there all hairy. She laughed and told him he looked like a monkey!

Her father got upset. He didn't understand how much she loved monkeys in those days.

If that happened now, he'd probably spank her. He's not the same father he used to be. People change.

She wonders if she'll ever be so desperate for a boyfriend that she'll let the first boy who asks her out do whatever he wants, even if she's not taking pills or anything?

Christine and Di have steady boyfriends (though Di's on the verge of breaking up with Evan, so she might not count). Jessica and Lara talk about dating in fourth grade – nothing much, going to the park or the movies together, mostly just hanging out – but in fourth grade even the popular girls in Cherry Hill thought boys were stupid. Even when she started sixth grade, boys were the furthest thing from her mind. Well, not quite the furthest thing, but not worth bothering with.

Melissa probably still thinks boys are stupid.

She's different now, and she doesn't mean she's older or anything like that. Even Ellyn said she sees the difference. In Clarendon she stands the chance of really fitting in. But it means wearing the right clothes, and probably having a boyfriend. If she starts having boyfriends now, then by the time she's old enough to get pregnant she won't have to worry about boys not liking her and never having a boyfriend and stuff the way Ellyn did. She's practically in junior high school. That rabbit's probably what's holding her back.

She gets up, takes him over to the dresser, tells him to stay there. Sleeping with an old stuffed toy you thought you'd abandoned forever is a bad habit to get into. She wouldn't want any of her friends to know about this, so why continue the relationship?

The rabbit's button eyes stare at her from across the room. He should be glad she doesn't hang him up by his ears, that's what she wants to do. But that's kid stuff. And besides, it's not his fault.

"Go to sleep," she tells him. "Go to sleep forever." She rearranges the pillow under her head, closes her eyes.

April 29: Ellyn

There's an old lighting fixture they bought, at the street fair she thinks, and hung. It has a few bulbs and a rectangular cardboard shade with pictures of all sorts of creatures on it. Something's funny about this fixture. She finally realizes that the creatures, and a lot more, are alive and living in it. They only come out when the lamp's turned on. She tries to get rid of them, but they keep coming back in greater number. The lamp is also smoking. She turns it off and turns on the overhead light. No, that bulb's burnt out. No, it's not. There's a loose connection somewhere, it's flickering off and on.

She takes the lamp fixture, creatures sleeping since it's not on, back to the fair in the hope someone will help her. But it's snowing out now, everyone's gone. She sees some people she knows hurrying off to a restaurant, but they don't invite her to join them. Only the guard is left there. She tells him her story and he laughs. He says he can't help. She pleads. He looks inside and sort of sees the animals. She tells him the cat's hers, she didn't know she'd crawled in there. He says okay, he'll throw it away, and climbs on this green ladder to toss it out in the snow. She screams that won't work, he has to take it to the ocean and drown them. He laughs harder, tosses it out, and they watch in horror as the angry animals emerge and start crawling up the building to climb back in the window.

CHAPTER FIFTEEN

"YOU'VE GOT TO GET ME BRACES!" Tiffany shrieks. She shoves her toothbrush into the holder, leaves big globs of toothpaste along the edge of the sink, and gets the mat all jumbled up. But at least she's finally moved away from the mirror so others can use the bathroom. They should be grateful.

"You're too young for braces," Ellyn hears Phil telling her on the other side of the door. A boy he went to school with got braces when he was too young: the dentist extracted four teeth so there'd be room to push the others back. Then the kid kept breaking the wires. His parents finally had the braces removed. When he went to another orthodontist, three years later, they had to extract four more teeth.

"I'm not that stupid!" Tiffany counters. Ellyn can hear her grinding her teeth, probably demonstrating how they don't come together properly. She begins a list of other kids in her class who have braces.

Wait a few years, her father says.

"In a few years I'll be in high school. If I have to wear braces then, I'll die." She stomps off to her room to pick out her clothes for school and prepare her death mask. Ellyn emerges just in time to catch the exit scene.

Funny to think of it now, but that ever-so-slightly protruding bite was one of the first things she was attracted to in Tips. When she smiled her widest, as she did on the swings or that night in Chinatown, it looked as if her teeth were about to dig into her lower lip. It gave her a mischievous look she'd found irresistible.

"The younger she is, the easier it will be to wear braces," Ellyn tells Phil later that evening. "I didn't get them till eighth grade. It was agony to put on lipstick."

And Anita wanted Tips' ears pierced on her first birthday, but they decided to wait till she was old enough to decide for herself, and then there were two years of pleading and fights with his mother about it. How many times he wished he'd listened.

This time he buckles under pressure. Agrees to meet them at the office of the same orthodontist that, to hear her tell it, half her class uses. On Park Avenue, of course.

It's like arranging to meet at the Hard Rock Cafe. Teenagers chewing gum all around her, loud voices coming at her from all sides. Sweaters and jackets are balled up on the floor.

Tiffany sits down. Ellyn asks a boy who has his feet up on the next chair to please move them so she can sit beside her. Mortified, Tiffany thumbs through an issue of *Rolling Stone.*

"Did you get a lot of homework?"

"Enough."

It's as if she was here only yesterday: the nondescript grey Formica chairs that look like they're given new cushions twice a year, the reminders about keeping your teeth clean posted on the walls (if you look close, you can see traces of graffiti that have been carefully washed off), the receptionist barricading herself behind a glass partition (these days probably bulletproof). She glances at the picture of Cyndi Lauper covering Tiffany's face. "Was your grandmother excited about you getting braces?"

"I guess."

Comments of more than three words seem reserved, in public, only for people your own age. Unless they're older boys.

Boys in general get braces later than girls do. She remembers sitting around Dr. Pollak's waiting room with high school boys all around her. She'd let her eyes roam, picking out the one she'd like to go to the movies with, the one she could maybe study with, the one she'd like to go to the prom with. Of course some would be nerdy even after their bites were fixed.

Where the hell's Phil?

–TODAY'S ORTHODONTISTS LET YOU CHEW GUM.

–Your local orthodontist's: the meeting place for the "in" crowd.

It was the morning Tiffany was having her braces put on. Phil couldn't swing the time off, so Ellyn went with her, and sat in the – blissfully quiet – waiting room for nearly two hours. She finished reading the material she brought with her, then picked up an issue of *Seventeen.* Juxtaposition perhaps, but this orthodontic ad pretty much sideswiped her attention. Send in a headshot, they'll send back a composite of what you could look like after braces. Great idea. Except the braces themselves looked as thick and wide as the ones she'd worn. Christ, if Tiffany emerged with those she'd throw herself under a bus on the way to school. She double-checked the date on the magazine: last month. Whoever thought up that ad was probably still listening to "Rhinestone Cowboy" and "Lucy in the Sky with Diamonds."

At last Tiffany walked casually out. You'd need a magnifying glass to spot those thin tooth-colored wires.

Ellyn saves her file, calls up a new screen, sets it up white on black. She'll try anything to improve concentration. She wishes to hell she'd never mentioned to Ted that her stepdaughter was getting braces, and how much things have changed in the past twenty years. Wishes she'd never told him about that ad. She was sitting in his lavish account executive office, placing one arm on that solid oak desk of his, making small talk while waiting for some demographics to come up from Research. She certainly wasn't expecting him to take her comment all the way to The American Association of Orthodontists.

Small accounts are entry-level bullshit.

That ad did one thing right: before and after. She quarters off the screen. Box 1: a woman's face, showing the bite before braces; box 2: the same woman's face, after orthodontic treatment. But it's the bottom boxes that will be the key: box 3: braces as they were twenty years ago, the mouth full of metal; box 4: the almost invisible "designer" braces of today. She sketches earphones on the head in box four. Jots "No heavy metal!" beneath it.

Gritting her teeth. Fists clenched. She wants to yank that issue of *Rolling Stone* out of Tiffany's hands and rip it to shreds.

She spins around, studies the pale green Formica built-in shelves and file cabinets behind her. Tiffany is not in this room, on this floor, in this building, she assures herself.

–Keep heavy metal in the right place.

She wishes to hell she could.

–Adolescence isn't as painful as it used to be.

Not true; kids today simply have different ways of masking pain. From the distance it's almost unrecognizable.

–Seamless beauty.

–You'll have to kiss to tell.

What were those jokes that went around the school? They kissed and their braces locked; their lips touched and the sparks flew.

–It no longer hurts to smile.

Ha! Tell that one to Tiffany.

She goes to a new window, takes it from the top again, black on white. The head with earphones. They didn't even have walkmans when she was in high school. She remembers pleading for a clock radio after Joan packed up hers and moved in with her boyfriend. Christmas of her junior year they finally got it for her. It was over a year before MTV began: she had an unbelievable crush on Robert De Niro, John Lennon was still alive.

–It needn't all be heavy metal.

There! Maybe needs some cleaning up, but she likes it. Suggestive, the anger pushed aside to make room for the teeth to shift. She prints out three copies, walks over and gets a cup of coffee from the pot in the art room. Time for what used to be a cigarette break: inhale, exhale, think; inhale, exhale, think. Cup in hand, leaning against the wall, she looks around her.

Stanley, two kids, both probably in high school by now, but he seems to let his wife take care of them, never came in with stories of birthdays or little league; his ideas resemble blueprints: always technically perfect but, like the rest of his life, never seem to go that extra mile.

Bill, kids are still in the toddler stage. The only guy in the art room whose hair's in a ponytail. Probably hasn't had his own braces off more than half a dozen years. Maybe.

Carla, Lou, Jessica – all DINKS, all possibilities as well. Carla's in the middle of a huge Boston Market project, which probably rules her out.

Then along the far wall: Harriet, divorced, three kids, constantly complaining about her ex being late with support payments. She'd probably buckle under pressure if she had to pay that much attention to a child's teeth.

Ellyn's eye comes to rest on Andrea, probably the most feminine of all the artists here. But when all else fails, not afraid to dirty her hands with pastels and charcoal. Right now she's got the same picture up on two monitors, the light reflected in her curly blonde hair each time she turns her head. Where Andrea gets the money for that huge wardrobe is beyond her. Always perfectly coordinated, appropriately corporate, but with Abbey's flair. Andrea's one of her favorites, especially for cosmetic and fashion ads. She's a natural.

Ellyn hands over the copy. Give her a few days to fool around with it, then the two of them can bat ideas off each other.

She wishes she could hand over her life and let someone she trusts fool around with it. Andrea sure as hell wouldn't have gotten involved with a guy's daughter. "Kids are nothing but interference," she can picture Andrea quipping, making them sound like the snow people got from TV stations in the early 1950s. "But they aren't always," she might have argued last summer. Last summer, she'd probably have asked for Tiffany's input on this ad. They'd sit around the dinner table making up zany commercials. Tiffany's words might not be usable, but they'd at least point her in the right direction.

Tiffany would probably balk, accuse her of "using me."

An accusation, at the moment, not unfounded.

One day at a time, one tooth at a time. Hanging by a thread.

This is as bad as being in labor, she remembers Joan quipping. Christmas two years ago. Ricky was about to lose his first tooth, wandered over to have his parents take another look at it every two minutes. *Every time you get comfortable someone happens by to check on how you're doing*, Joan laughed, wiping her hands on a Kleenex.

Ellyn turned her head away.

Suddenly it's as if she's become her sister.

You think because Tiffany's past the toddler stage she won't be as needy . . . Afraid to nurse an infant . . . You can't win. Joan was sure as hell right about the last part.

TIFFANY STEALS A GLANCE at her father's face. Looks up from her perfectly twirled spaghetti and searches his eyes for signs. Has Ellyn told him about the clothes she stole? Over a month's gone by. It's probably just a matter of time, promise or no promise. Ellyn's different from what she was a few months ago.

"Oh, they're all the same," Lara tells her. "I've watched my father living with three different women, and I know the pattern, believe me. They treat you real nice for the first few months, then they start resenting your being there."

It's been more than a few months. It's been over six months. Almost a year, if you count from the time she first met Ellyn.

Lara had gone on and on about how lucky she feels. As soon as her father sees his girlfriend treating her and her brother and sister shitty, he breaks up with her.

She glances at her father again. He'd choose Ellyn over her, she's sure of it.

If she wants Ellyn out of here, she'll have to dream up ways to make her leave. Talk back to her all the time, steal money from her purse. Her father will find another girlfriend in, like, no time, probably someone not a quarter as nice as Ellyn, but she'll be nice for a while at least. They weren't all as bad as that one who took her to the park. Besides, she's older now, she can defend herself.

Anything would be better than going back to school in Cherry Hill. If she has to spend one more afternoon riding her bike or hanging out at the mall, she'll duck out of class and hitchhike to California.

Even at the start, the new girlfriend probably won't be as nice as Ellyn used to be. Di and Christine are always telling you how much they hate their stepfathers. And there's this one girl, Frances, who lives with her father and his boyfriend, never ever sees her mother even though she's still alive – they call her Frankie at home. She doesn't think she'd be able to stand it if Ellyn left and her father fell in love with some guy.

She doesn't want Ellyn to leave, she wants everything back the way it used to be, Ellyn and her father coming home from their offices and the three of them laughing together about the day. "Are you working on any dynamite commercials?" she even ventures to ask as they're doing the dinner dishes.

Hands immersed in hot, soapy water, Ellyn feels the heat shooting through her body. Thinks a moment. Stares at the child next to her: French braid, breasts growing out of their "AA" cups. The acne medication lies almost untouched on the bathroom shelf, as she suspected it would be. Morning, noon, and night, Tiffany applies a moisturizing cream, desperate to mask her freckles. This is not a child she could play on the swings with. Not a child who'd even think of racing them down the street.

She's already handed the orthodontist copy back to Ted. If she was going to ask for Tiffany's input, she should have done it two weeks ago. She's fed up with sucking inspiration out of a hollow relationship.

"Not at the moment," she answers.

CHRISTINE CATCHES UP WITH TIFFANY on the steps. "I am just so freaked! Do you believe this?"

"Believe what?"

"You mean you don't know? God, I thought everyone knew!"

"Christine, will you please tell me what it is everyone except me knows?"

"Lara's sister. She's pregnant!"

"Wow! And she's in, like, eighth grade?"

"Ninth. Jesus, didn't Lara call you?"

No, Lara didn't call her. Lara probably didn't think she was a close enough friend to bother calling. Tiffany feels like running off and getting pregnant herself or something.

"I tried to call you *all night*!" Lara explains later. "Who were you talking to?"

"I wasn't . . . " Ellyn! Of course. Ellyn brought some work home that just had to get finished last night, and she didn't want to stay in her stupid office later so she tied up the phone all night with her stupid computer connected to her office and call waiting turned off.

"You really should get your own phone, you know," Lara tells her.

She knows. And don't think she hasn't been pleading. Christ, you'd think she was asking for Versailles when they got her an extension phone in her bedroom.

What's even worse is that by now Lara's told the story so many times she doesn't feel like repeating it. She hears bits and pieces from Christine and Di and Jessica and everyone, but she'll never hear it all. Never!

Lara's father came home from a trip to Cincinnati and everything.

They're thinking of taking her sister over to France where you can just take this pill and get rid of the baby, no operation or anything.

"You know what my father would probably say? He'd say we can't afford it!" Tiffany announces.

"I'll bet if word leaked out to the neighbors he'd afford it pretty quickly," Di says. And Christine asks if that means she's not going to sleep with a boy till she's in college.

"Don't be ridiculous, of course not."

Except she can just picture herself, three or four years from now, calling everyone to tell them she and her boyfriend just went all the way and having Ellyn pick up the extension and listen to every word. She could have picked up the extension last night, even, if she'd gotten off the computer long enough for Lara to call. Or her father could have, except he had meetings all night and didn't get home till late.

"So who do you think it'll be?" Lara asks.

May 19: Ellyn

She's in a hospital. They're going to remove the bones between her teeth. It occurs to her this will hurt more than having a tooth pulled. But she'll be out, she won't feel it. She opens her mouth. She can already see the holes in her gum. She hears them talking, something about removing one testicle. She didn't think she had testicles, but guesses she must.

CHAPTER SIXTEEN

"IT'S NOT AS IF I CAN'T take care of myself, you know! Grandma used to leave me alone all the time."

"New York City is not Cherry Hill!"

"I've been staying alone since fourth grade!"

"And now I'm going into seventh grade!" Phil imitates his daughter's hysterical whine perfectly.

"I'm also twelve years old, in case you've forgotten."

"How could I forget? My ears are still ringing from that garbage you and your friends call music!"

The conversation comes to a sudden halt. Ellyn's the one who made his daughter's birthday special at the last minute by getting tickets to a Michael Jackson concert that had been sold out for months.

"Grandma left you alone for an hour while she ran to the supermarket. This is different," Phil continues.

"Who do you think I'm going to run into? A rapist? A kidnapper?"

"You wouldn't know a rapist if you fell over one."

"I have to learn someday!"

"The hell you do!"

"Maybe I should just go jogging in Central Park!"

"Maybe you'd like to play on the swings again!"

"You're frightened if Abbey's ten minutes late picking you up," Ellyn reminds her.

There was one time, once! All the way back in November. And Abbey wasn't ten minutes late; it was probably almost an hour. She paced back and forth between the two "No Parking School Days" signs, watched other kids get picked up, almost got run over by two boys from the hockey team on roller blades.

She's suddenly glad Abbey's leaving. Hopes she has so much schoolwork next year she flunks all her courses and doesn't even have time to comb her stupid hair. "Okay, so maybe I was afraid hanging around school alone," she mumbles. "But that was, like, before I knew the other kids." Head high, she proceeds to give all the details fit for them to hear: every time she's left the school area with friends during recess, every Saturday or Sunday she's gone out with a group of kids. She's different than she was last fall.

Yes, different. Her father sees the breasts starting to form. Ellyn sees a black Liz Claiborne vest with red and gold embroidery hanging in her closet.

"You let me stay home alone last time I had a sore throat, remember?"

"We let you stay alone for two hours, while Ellyn ran into the office and brought work home."

"I was still fine, wasn't I? I didn't, like, set the place on fire, did I?"

Tiffany's protests grow louder every night. Standard dinner conversation runs along the lines of "Erica's parents let her come home and hang out at the apartment alone." Talking with her mouth full.

"Christ, Tiffany. Yesterday it was Sandra's parents, before that it was Maxine's. Next thing I know, you'll be telling me Arabella Purpleheart's parents let her stay alone."

"I'm not making any of them up! It's true: Erica's mother lets her stay alone all the time."

"Well, then I don't have very much respect for Erica's mother."

No, Ellyn thinks; of course he doesn't. Hiring Abbey earns him a merit badge, shipping Tiffany off to live with her grandparents goes hand in hand with wanting what's best for her. A model father.

A model airplane. The glue gives you a quick high before it dries out. Geoff's planes collecting dust on his dresser till RuthAnn's had her fill of them.

"There's this note in the lobby," Tiffany blots her mouth with a napkin and announces over a half-eaten lamb chop. "This girl wants to baby-sit and she's, like, in eighth grade. That's only two years ahead of me."

Ellyn's already seen that note; every time the elevator's delayed, she finds herself rereading it: "My name's Jennifer, I'm in eighth grade at Steiner, responsible, reliable, etc. Babies love me! Hope to see you soon."

Not if I can help it, she tells herself, pulling her coat tight around her.

"Else's here twice a week, anyway. So I won't be alone," Tiffany continues.

Her father's so stupid he actually considers that. Else barely even speaks English; she's a Russian who had to get out of Russia quick. And she lives with these other Russians, and Russian's what they speak at home all the time. If there were ever an emergency, if a robber was trying to break in or they got mugged in the lobby because the doorman was talking to someone and not paying much attention, Else would be helpless. *She's* the one who'd have to call the cops.

"I don't want you taking the bus home alone," Phil says finally.

"Nobody's going to attack me on the bus! There are hundreds of people there! It's so crowded Abbey and I usually can't even get seats." Though one time there was a boy who tried to feel Abbey up; Abbey doesn't even know she saw, but she did. Anyway, she has eons yet before there'll be anything on her body to feel.

She explains how being with Abbey sometimes proves nothing more than a distraction. They spend all afternoon looking through fashion magazines, or Abbey plays with styling her hair, or they put on some new record. If she were alone in the apartment, or at least alone with Else, she'd probably get her homework done sooner. "And then I'd have more time to spend with you guys," she adds in a super-sweet voice, edging close to her father.

"You can never tell what you're getting into when you hire someone new, references or no references," Ellyn points out.

RuthAnn, yanking TC by the arm as she hurries from one store to the next. Geoff, supposed to walk her home from first grade, going off with friends and forgetting her.

"Give me a little credit, will you? I'd never leave Tiffany under the care of someone I didn't have complete trust in."

"Right. Exactly like what's her name, the one who took me to the park."

"Illana. And you weren't very nice to her, either, you know."

Tiffany stares out the window looking, she hopes, like someone who just might, one of these days, jump. "It's not like you won't be home till late at night."

"Okay, we'll make a deal," Phil says, more out of exhaustion than anything else. "You can come home yourself the two days a week Else's here, but you'll take a cab, not a bus."

"We can probably arrange for a car service," Ellyn suggests.

What a great idea! If the car service comes in a limo it could even up her grades. As if they have a chauffeur.

"It's conditional," her father continues before she can get a word out. "You have to find after school activities to keep you occupied the other three days."

"What? Brownies? Get real. I'm, like, too old for that junk."

"This isn't suburbia," Ellyn laughs. "I'm sure there are all sorts of interesting groups you could get involved in."

"Like RuthAnn made you do, right?" she asks with this super-wide grin. "She didn't want you hanging around the house and bothering her, so you had to stay as long as possible at school."

"As a matter of fact, that's not right. In eighth grade I was dying to join this journalism club, but RuthAnn wouldn't hear of it. I had to come right home and get dinner started."

Great. All of a sudden she's going to do everything different from her stupid stepmother.

Joan and her friends formed that stealing club.

Grudgingly, Tiffany enrolls herself in an aerobics program. It meets two days a week, days Else isn't here, and they play really neat music. Besides, she'd be following in her mother's footsteps. That should keep her father happy, shouldn't it?

They agree to leave her alone on Fridays. She'll more than likely end up at a friend's house, anyway.

At least she won't be bringing home little clay dogs and lopsided ashtrays. Ellyn had gone so far as to envision herself back in her own apartment, with Tiffany bringing some new masterpiece every time she comes to visit. She'd have to find a place to hide them all, and then be sure they were prominently displayed every time they got together.

PHIL MAKES DINNER RESERVATIONS for the three of them, only to have his daughter call and say she's at Lara's and was invited to stay for dinner. They can pick her up on the way home, can't they?

If it's not Lara, it's Jessica, Di, Janet, etc. The first few times Phil says okay, see you later, alligator (Ellyn pictures Tiffany scowling). Finally he says, no, it's definitely not okay. If she wants to spend time with Jessica then fine, Jessica can come to dinner with them.

Isabella's is one of those restaurants famous for letting people wait at the bar. Circulating's part of the action.

Phil asks the kids if they want Cokes. Tiffany says okay.

Jessica requests a Perrier with bitters. "Never ask for a Coke," she's telling Tiffany. "You can spot it a mile away. Perrier and bitters looks pretty real."

Drinks in hand, Tiffany and Jessica wend their way to the edge of the crowd, delicately nibbling at breadsticks from baskets on the bar. Ellyn watches them through the prism of a wine glass held to her lips. Jessica's hold-ing her glass out far enough to catch some guy's attention. And Tiffany, of course, follows her lead. She's even learned how to bat those extra-long lashes. Ellyn turns her glass slightly, changing the effect of light. One more drink and they'll look as if they belong there.

A boy and a girl run toward the entrance. Seven and eight? The girl's a quarter inch taller. Eight and nine? Half the crowd at the bar turns to gape at them. Tiffany and Jessica look the other way.

The girl's almost Jessica's height. Even the way she's dressed – tights, frilly skirt, one arm in her fuzzy jacket the rest of it dragging on the floor – she could have been Tiffany a year ago.

Was it only a year ago?

Phil suggested Louie's that night.

Sure, she adored the child. And sure, Chinatown had been a ball. But Louie's? They didn't even have a children's menu, it would cost $20 for Tiffany to eat a few shrimp and probably play with her pasta.

He was aware of that.

Ellyn washed her hair, tied it back, went easy on the makeup. Maybe people who stared at the child would look past her.

They were given a corner table, and Tiffany immediately got up, leaning on the windowsill, gazing out, commenting on passing dogs in a voice too loud for comfort. But it hadn't been as bad as she'd expected. People at nearby tables, if they noticed at all, seemed charmed.

Besides, Ellyn told herself, Tiffany was at the end of such childishness. Before too long she'd settle down, they'd be able to take her such places more easily. And she could hardly wait.

SHE SLIPS HER SHOES OFF, flexes her ankles, moves her stocking feet about under the desk. She flips through the folder in front of her, lets her index finger trace the lines of a face or a shoulder. Photos of old men, old women, wearing dog-tags.

One of the account executives was let go last week. Clients he'd been neglecting have been given to other execs, top priority. The old hurry-up-and-wait scenario.

Ted drew this one, turned around and dumped it in her lap. Medical alarm/alert devices, company's planning a national print and media campaign for the fall. Start from scratch, he said; get everyone she can spare working on it, and come up with something new and exciting.

What the hell can be exciting about living alone?

We can't all work on Revlon and Diet Coke.

What she needs right now is something she can sink her teeth into. A car dropped from a plane or going over a waterfall. Those suitcases run over by cars. That Minolta camera they blew up her first year of high school. Instead they hand her a false sense of security.

Oh, yeah? She pictures a house burning down, an old woman sitting calmly on the sofa as the flames come to within an inch of her, smiling and pressing this little button to summon help. A gentle reminder of the mothers and grandmothers we'd love to burn at the stake.

They'd never buy it. Anger's been "out" since Carter pardoned the draft-dodgers. Still, it was fun while it lasted.

She dials Research, sets up a meeting for tomorrow morning. Continues flipping through ten years' worth of brochures until a man in black ski mask catches her eye. He's prying open a window while a poised, well-dressed woman, late thirties, seems to be fingering a precious locket. The caption reads, "You might think if you're healthy, you're safe."

She flags that one. Dashes off a quick note reminding herself to bring this up at tomorrow's meeting. Could something of the sort could be targeted for metropolitan areas, buses, kiosks, cable stations. New York, Chicago, Boston, Detroit, Philadelphia, Los Angeles, San Francisco, Atlanta, Miami? It might even be used for latch-key kids.

Shit. There's Tiffany again.

In reality, Tiffany's on her way home from aerobics. She should get out of here soon, too.

Screw it! It's impossible to concentrate when you've got one eye on the clock. She calls the apartment, gets the answering machine, leaves a message that she's working late. Tells Phil to go ahead with dinner, she'll grab a bite on the way home, reminds Tiffany to double-lock the door. She slips her shoes on then off again. Turns her attention back to the copy.

Maybe she can even turn the stereotype back on itself. The elderly yet obviously healthy and well-groomed woman comes on. "My son and daughter-in-law are both lawyers, constantly on the go. But they worry about me. They wanted to be sure I could always get help if I needed it, so they gave me this little call box. They said all I have to do is press this button." She pauses. Studies the pendant. Looks up. Smiles. Her voice becomes animated. "I'm giving it to my grandson." A Macaulay Culkin look-alike comes on. Hugs Grandma. She puts the pendant around his neck. "He needs it more than I do."

That's right, get the whole family in there. "Our group had 21% fewer casualties."

How did that opening to the local newscast go? "It's ten o'clock. Do you know where your children are?" (Phil calls to say he'll save a plate for her. It's the least he can do). Open with the elderly woman sitting alone in an armchair, watching television. Announcer: "It's ten o'clock. Do you know where your children are?" The woman looks around her. Her children? Her glasses? Announcer: "Suppose you needed to get in touch with them." A shot of the product – that's what she was looking for. She picks it up. Doesn't press the call button, just relaxes with a big smile.

It's a quarter past nine, she's hungry, and she knows where her dinner is. She calls it quits. Puts the copy into her briefcase. Sleep on it.

She pulls the copy out, scribbles "get a good night's sleep" on her page of notes, sketches the alarm box on the night table. Packs up and darts out of there.

"I'm strung out at work," she says, taking a sip of wine as she places the tuna casserole in the microwave. "How about you and Tiffany go to Cherry Hill alone this weekend?

Instead of putting up the anticipated argument, Phil asks what she's working on.

A commercial to give children nightmares and char little old women to Pittsburgh rare, she wants to say. Instead she smiles. Private joke. Tells Phil one of the execs was fired, and she's picking up new accounts. Tight deadline.

Friday she stays at the office till 9:30, walks a few blocks along the deserted midtown streets, and grabs a cab. She stops into Indian Oven for dinner. Phil isn't crazy about Indian food, Tiffany says it makes her stomach hurt, and she hasn't had a good tandoori dish in months.

She walks into a dark, empty apartment. No back door to double-check. They're twelve stories up, with a gate on the one fire-escape window. Else was here yesterday, and must have spilled Mr. Clean or overused the floor polish – the ammonia smell, noticeable last night, is even worse when there's no other body here to absorb it. She cracks a window open to the familiar bus fumes, runs her finger along the bookshelf, checking for dust. Doesn't find it. She turns on the light in the kitchen; not even a roach crawls out.

No wonder Tiffany has her tape deck blasting between homework and dinner.

She goes ahead and checks the fire escape anyway.

Ridiculous as it is, she's tempted to change and head for the nearest bar. A sign her ideas are workable? Get a woman in this mood, and she'll dash out and impulsively buy one of those alert systems, the way women thirty years ago bought a new hat or dress? Her mother's generation.

She pauses, sits quietly for a moment, switches on the TV. Lucks out with *Mildred Pierce* on TNT. She puts on her nightgown and sprawls on the sofa with a glass of brandy.

Can't watch Crawford without thinking of *Mommie Dearest.*

She flips through a stack of old magazines, spots a Cover Girl ad, the heavy look of yesterday compared to the natural look of today. If she gets the orthodontics account this might be useful. She goes to cut it out, but her scissors aren't in the drawer. She gives up and rips the page out. It doesn't make any difference if it's neat or not, it's just for her own purposes.

Still, she'd appreciate it if her scissors could once in a while be where she left them. Is that too much to ask? She lived alone for close to a decade. She developed her own system for where things went – one pair of scissors in the top-left drawer of the kitchen counter, another in her sewing kit, batteries in the meat bin of the refrigerator, light bulbs in the linen closet. But Tiffany borrows the scissors to cut the tag off a t-shirt she stole, the batteries for her walkman. Ellyn reaches for the scissors and comes up with an AAA battery; month-old carrot sticks are in the refrigerator's meat tray. The remnants of her life are strewn in every conceivable place. It's almost as if she's been robbed again.

A man on the fire escape, after all. The back one, overlooking a courtyard that looks more like a landfill. He must have raised the window, bent the gate up with one hand.

It had been rather minuscule, as break-ins go. Took place in broad daylight. Real quick, in and out, like a rapist or a father whose daughter's asleep in the next room. No drawers had been emptied. All they took was the small television set, along with a camera, six or seven rolls of pennies from the kitchen drawer, and one pillowcase they'd probably thrown the coins and camera in. It was in those days before she had a computer at home. She'd been gone less than two hours, met a friend for lunch on a Saturday. Sharon. The same friend she'd gone to see the night she met Phil.

More than likely it was a junkie. Got what he wanted then went out the front door, down the stairs. She'd returned to find the door ajar – she kept two umbrellas in the corner there, and they often got caught in the hinge, preventing the door from closing. She walked in, admonishing herself for not having checked it in her hurry to run out. How could she have been so foolish? Not to lock the door. To walk in. As the police reminded her, that guy could still have been in there. Never, never, walk into an apartment when you find the door ajar. She'd been lucky this time, the cops said.

She didn't feel lucky, she felt violated. And since she'd been gone such a short time, she couldn't escape the sense that whoever it was had been watching her. For weeks afterward she found herself undressing in the dark, turning to look over her shoulder as she walked from room to room. She'd wake in the middle of the night and swear she heard furniture being moved.

At least in those days she worked through the discomfort. She wonders if she'll ever feel at home in Phil's apartment. And yet she feels guilty each time she stoops to pick up a book before someone trips over it or places her scissors back where they belong.

Come right down to it, she's the intruder here.

She imagines two cops showing up to arrest her: breaking and entering. The tall one pauses to look at Anita's picture over the TV, as Phil remembers him doing when they came to inform him his wife has been in an accident.

She gets up, takes a good hard look at that picture. And the one beside it, where she's holding her daughter, probably taken on the same day. What was it Phil said when she saw the picture at his parents' house – that her face was fuller than usual because she was pregnant? To look at her thin, drawn cheeks here, she'd have to be on cortisone before her face filled out that much. And the eyebrows here aren't as carefully penciled in. Obviously she didn't find it easy, working full time, caring for a child.

Ellyn turns back to the movie. No wonder she passed Anita's picture so many times those first few months with Phil, never giving it a second look. God, she doesn't even recognize herself.

July 6: Tiffany

She entered the contest mainly for her father's sake, since one of the prizes was a tiny plastic pig doll bank.

Now she's helping clean up the beach, but they say she can't go swimming because of something she said or did. She's confused, she's been so helpful. She points to some letters in the sand and asks if the judge knows what it says. He says no. She tells him it says "Ungrateful Little Wrench." That's why she did or said what she did. He says okay, she can "provisionally go swimming with the other wretches."

She doesn't think she can make it there in time, but her friend says let's try. They get to the beach, but she no longer wants to go swimming anyway. It's more of a watering hole. The others go in, she walks down and wets her feet in the mud. Her father, sitting on the beach with his legs drawn up and his arms around them, calls out to remind her she's wearing two watches. She says she's just wetting her feet. She's amazed, though, since some people are wearing blouses and not bathing suits. She supposes she could go in fully dressed. One of her watches is her grandmother's. She would take it off but she doesn't know where to put it. Her feet are muddy.

CHAPTER SEVENTEEN

THE HEAT DOESN'T LET UP. July's a real killer this year.

A year ago she'd been wishing she'd planned her vacation differently, that she could have spent the entire two weeks with Phil and his marvelous daughter. A year ago Tiffany had pleaded to stay one more week. "It's probably just as well," she and Phil assured each other, driving back alone.

It isn't just as well; it isn't well at all. For the next week she and Tiffany are stuck with each other.

"How about we hit the Museum of Television and Radio?" Ellyn suggests the first Monday they're alone.

"I've seen all that stuff already."

The Children's Museum?

Kid stuff.

Okay then, the Guggenheim?

She gets dizzy walking around there.

The Museum of Natural History?

She's not in the mood. Most of her friends are traveling in Europe with their parents, at summer homes in the Berkshires or the Hamptons, or at ritzy overnight camps. She's not only bored, she's deprived.

Joan's kids should be so deprived! Let Tiffany try going to public school in the city, or one of the cheap Catholic schools. Let her get mugged in the halls and be afraid to go to the ladies' room.

Oh, Christ. She wouldn't wish that on a stray cat.

Let her spend a day around RuthAnn, then.

They have to do something. Ellyn drags her to the Bronx Zoo, down to Soho for lunch and a tour of two or three galleries (she's bored after one, but Ellyn pulls her over to see the Escher on the off chance). The three of them go see Shakespeare in the Park. They meet Phil for lunch and then play around at the Seaport. Tiffany's barely cracked a smile.

Ellyn tries to tell herself she's worried, the closer it gets to August the more she's concerned about being back with her grandparents for a month. But she's at a loss for a way to broach the subject, and Tiffany hasn't mentioned it. She wonders if even Phil's parents will have the slightest idea what to do with this stranger Tiffany's turned into.

But then the second week is almost a throwback to last August. The three them are together on Martha's Vineyard. The house they're renting has a great view of the dunes, the weather's sunny but cool enough to leave the windows open and feel comfortable without air conditioning. Best of all, they're barely unpacked when Tiffany turns into a kid again. Morning and evening she roams the beach, searching for shells while Ellyn and Phil lie on the sand, close their eyes, and shut out everything except the sound of the waves. The salt air clears everyone's head.

Their last day Tiffany presents Ellyn with a white, scalloped fan shell, her favorite.

She goes back to work feeling glorious, but wary. At least Phil's charged with looking after little miss innocence over the next two weeks. Sure enough, by midweek life's become routine again. Tiffany has a long face at dinner, while Phil rambles on about the interesting street musician they saw or the great lunch they had. Ellyn goes for broke and asks for help with her latest commercial.

"You're the one who's getting paid to write it."

"I know, but I'm having more trouble than usual."

"You'll think of something." Tiffany pushes her lettuce aside to see if there are any more olives hiding underneath. She remembers those Red Lobster commercials that showed this great salad bar. She went there with Grandma and Grandpa once, and they didn't have a single olive.

Two nights later Phil makes a meat loaf.

Ellyn bursts out laughing. "That doesn't have an egg baked in the center, does it?" she asks when she can manage words again.

"Nope."

"Whew."

"Who'd do something so stupid?" Tiffany asks.

"A lot of people," Phil answers. "It's gourmet."

"It sounds yucky."

"It is yucky." Ellyn goes on to tell them about the time RuthAnn suddenly decided they should all play happy family and eat together, so she made a "gourmet" meat loaf. "Joan managed okay, but Geoff and I nearly gagged getting it down. Geoff made a dash for the bathroom without asking to be excused, and RuthAnn flew into a rage about how she'd slaved all day, the least we could do was be considerate."

"I totally agree," Phil tells them, straight-faced.

"So did Joan. Anyway, for the rest of the night Geoff was barging into our room, saying *I don't believe I ate the whole thing* and holding his stomach."

Tiffany doesn't get it.

Phil tells her it's from an old Alka-Seltzer commercial, one of his favorites when he was a kid.

Tiffany, sounding more like Joan every day, says nothing could make her drink that gunk. Phil asks Ellyn what she mostly ate.

"Peanut butter and jelly, grilled cheese, sometimes tuna fish. Anything we could make ourselves."

"For dinner?"

"Yep."

"That sounds pretty yucky, too."

"The lesser of two evils, let me tell you."

After which everyone chews with their mouths closed.

Ellyn wets her parched lips. Last summer this conversation would have gone on and on. They'd begin dreaming up weird food combinations, and jingles to go with them.

She heaves a sigh, carries plates out to the kitchen and puts water on for coffee. Last summer she also envisioned herself baking a cake and calling Tiffany into the kitchen to help her ice it. Afterwards she'd let Tiffany run her fingers along the inside of the frosting bowl, and lick them. TC had a friend in second and third grade whose mother let the kids do that, and it left her with a sweet taste in her mouth.

One more little adventure they never got around to. Everything happened so quickly.

AUGUST AT LAST! SHE THOUGHT it would never get here. They drop Tiffany off in Cherry Hill, have a month alone to gather their wits again, set their affairs in order.

The minute they round the corner, out of his parents' line of vision, Ellyn unbuckles her seat belt, Phil unbuckles his pants.

"You can't reach this far," Ellyn laughs.

"Neither can you. Don't worry. I only want him to come up for air. Get a little preview while he's at it."

"Coming attractions."

"This shift between the seats is the one thing I hate about this car. Every damn Volvo has it."

"It's part of their safety rep."

They're back in the city in time to shower, change, and head over to Tavern on the Green for dinner. It's the perfect night for it: high seventies, a bit on the humid side, no babysitter worries, enough people out of the city that they don't need reservations.

The food's not as good as remembered.

Still a nice night, still early. They walk home, high enough that they're both relaxed, not thinking very clearly. On Central Park West, they pass the homeless staking out their benches, one man elaborately arranging several boxes into a tunnel. But at least here no one accosts them; it's gotten so Ellyn will go out of her way to avoid walking along Broadway.

They enter the apartment, check the answering machine. Phil tumbles into the waiting bed.

Ellyn takes her time undressing, wondering whatever became of those nights he'd spend twenty minutes undoing her blouse or sliding off her pantyhose, rediscovering each part of her body as his hands passed over it.

She picks up her nightgown and hangs it back on the hook. It would only be in the way tonight.

She crawls in bed beside him. He takes her in his arms, instinctively reaches to put his hands through the nightgown's armholes. She can feel his cheeks puff out in the warmth of recognition when he sees it's not there.

His caresses grow hot and heavy. His arms are all over her.

She feels wonderful.

He sucks her breast, climbs on top of her. Enters. Comes.

He wanders off to the bathroom to wash up, returns to bed, gives her another quick but caring hug, turns over, fluffs his pillow, doubles it over to give his head more support.

She reaches over, tries to pull him toward her, let him know she'd like him to help her for a while.

He mumbles something about having to work tomorrow.

She lies back, stunned. Sure, she was the one who insisted upon minimal foreplay, worried about Tiffany being in the next room, especially over the past few months when Tiffany's seemed more and more withdrawn. But Tiffany's not here now, and she pretty much expected . . .

What did she expect? That it would be like last summer?

She can barely remember last summer.

She's too keyed up to sleep now, thinks maybe if she reads for a while. She picks up her book, grabs her robe, her pillow and the blanket folded at the foot of the bed. No need to put the light on and disrupt his deep, even breathing.

Twenty minutes' reading and her eyes feel heavy. She starts back to the bedroom. Stops. Maybe she'll curl up here on the sofa. Phil won't even know she's gone.

Better yet, she'll sleep in Tiffany's room.

She turns back the covers, exchanges Tiffany's pillow for her own, and crawls into the narrow bed. Silence. She overhears herself telling the child her grandmother isn't dead, trying out every word she knows to offer comfort.

She burrows deeper in, feels the imprint of Tiffany's warm body on the mattress. There's barely enough light to make out the design on the etched glass lampshade they bought last winter. The photo beside it might as well be etched on her retina: Phil and Anita flank their daughter, each with one arm each around her. Tiffany's seated on a carpeted stool, legs dangling, one knee scraped. She turns the stuffed dog she's holding upside down just as the photographer snaps the picture.

This was first on Tiffany's list of things to bring from Cherry Hill. Taken on her third birthday.

"You were there the day I turned three, too, you know," Ellyn whispers, reaching out to steady the fragile ceramic frame. "We didn't take a picture, but I remember."

She wouldn't have looked good in a picture, anyway. She lost weight, then more weight. There wasn't a bit of color in her face. Her hair was falling out. "My hair was the first thing your father was attracted to," she'd said over and over. Long, straight hair, like Anita's. Ellyn wonders if her mother ever wore that deep, rich shade of blue. It suits her perfectly.

SHE'S AWAKE AND IN THE BATHROOM by the time Phil gets up. He doesn't even seem to realize she didn't sleep beside him. Nothing like feeling loved, is there?

She throws herself into new campaigns, sits down with her copywriters and matches them word for word, stays at the office till nine or ten o'clock, takes longer lunches, strolls over to Jacques David to get her hair washed and trimmed. No, cut, washed and permed. Shoulder-length, with tight frizzy curls that bring out her auburn highlights every time she moves.

Phil stares. "What brought this on?"

"I don't know, impulsive, I guess."

"It's so different."

"It's a poodle cut. Actually, I used to wear my hair this way."

"When?"

"Junior high, part of high school."

By the end of the weekend he's enthralled by the feel of it. He buries his face in its softly scented mass, inserts a finger and unrolls a curl until it springs back. "Heel. Stay. Sit," he commands, laughing.

By mid-month Phil's extraordinary cooking talents are back in evidence and she's making the effort to get home a little earlier. "If Tiffany were here, she'd be picking out all the water chestnuts," she remarks, helping herself to seconds of a fabulous chicken and shrimp dish.

Phil refreshes his gin and tonic. He's been drinking more this past month than he has all year. "She's my daughter," he says, sitting down again. "I know her likes and dislikes."

"I was thinking about her, that's all. It's no big deal."

"What about me, damn it? Think about me for a change, why don't you? Your relationship's supposed to be with me!"

That sets everything in perspective, doesn't it? A long way from October, when Phil's mother went in the hospital for a simple operation, and he got her to come right over under the ruse that Tiffany needed her. He'll say anything to get what he wants.

He takes another long swallow of his drink.

She tells him gin and tonic used to be her favorite.

"It was Anita's before yours."

"I should have realized."

"As for me, I'm adaptable. I'll drink whatever's handiest."

"Great. Just great. Tiffany comes home and finds you passed out."

"I'll be fine by then."

Ellyn wants to ask what she'll be like by then.

Look where Anita is.

TIFFANY'S HOME. SCHOOL'S BACK IN SESSION. All the bigwigs are back from vacation, examining ads slated for the Christmas season, suggesting minor or radical changes. Ten phones are ringing at once.

Ellyn begs off the Cherry Hill junket, works straight through Friday night into Saturday, grabs five hours' sleep; other than that barely comes up for air. Finally she calls it quits late Saturday night.

She hops in the shower before heading out for dinner, turns on the radio while she's drying her hair. WNCN, Phil's favorite. She wipes her hands on a towel, moves the dial down to BGO. During a break between numbers, they go through the weekend's jazz calendar. Horace Silver's at the Blue Note. Ten-thirty show. She glances at her watch. If she doesn't waste a lot of time with make-up, and has a bit of luck hailing a cab, she can get down to the Village in time. She hasn't heard good jazz in ages – Phil's interests consist of classical, opera, and easy listening, and if she has to sit through his Frank-Sinatra-is-the-greatest-jazz-singer lecture one more time she'll swear off music forever. The Blue Note's exactly what she needs to unwind tonight.

She grabs two slices of cheese on her way out the door. Aside from blue corn chips, the food at the Blue Note sucks. Or at least it used to. And trying to eat at those long narrow tables, packed like the rush hour IRT, your elbow poking whoever's next to you each time you lift your fork . . . not exactly arranged to make a person feel graceful and feminine.

The cab goes down Ninth, runs into traffic from the theaters letting out. "Fuck you," a kid shouts, crossing in front of them, against the light. "Fuck you," the cabbie calls, "that light's for you, not your fucking father." New York, New York.

She doesn't get there till almost ten, so the only seats are at the bar – but that's okay, she's sat at bars before. And no cover.

By the middle of the set, when they finish "Song for My Father," she's feeling loose, leaning her head back, savoring everything. The guy beside her comments that Silver's at his best tonight. He heard him last month, and he was really playing tight.

"I only heard him once before. Must be four or five years ago."

Their conversation continues after the set. Names are exchanged. He offers to buy her another drink, she says she'd better eat something first, so they walk along Bleecker St. and find a place for supper. Turns out he's a real jazz aficionado, especially piano jazz.

"I searched all over the city for a copy of Brubeck's *Dave Digs Disney*," she tells him. "I finally found a clerk at Dayton's who was willing to make a tape for me."

"Why didn't you call me? I'd have made it for you." Brubeck's his second favorite, "next to Bill Evans."

After dinner he helps her into a cab. No propositions, no exchange of phone numbers, no life stories. Nothing but one hell of a pleasant evening.

She feels like a junior high school kid, sneaking a kiss in the movies, hugging good night as he walks her to her door. She'd almost forgotten how wonderful it could be to lie alone in the dark, remembering what a boy's lips and hands felt like. *You, you're the one, growing up now, Mary Ryan. You, you're the one, sometimes school is really tryin'. Getting notes about the boy you like, but he doesn't notice you, seems he's never gonna stop and there's nothin' you can do . . .*

She renews her membership to the Paris Health Club.

No longer giving a damn about the example she's setting, she doesn't bother making excuses most weekends now, simply says she needs time for herself. "Living alone and proud of it," scrawled on a napkin one night at the Museum Cafe, has become a personal slogan for that alarm/alert campaign.

Many's the Saturday night she comes home and gets back to work. In the pre-Tiffany, high-energy days, she was often at her creative best after midnight. She'd sit at her laptop with the TV in front of her, picture on, sound off. Some radio talk show would be broadcasting behind her. No one was looking over her shoulder, no one laughed at her unprofessional stance, images from the living, breathing city flowed through the room.

She also gains new respect for those long, restful Saturdays she used to take for granted. She sits around reading, rents an afternoon movie, catches up on correspondence, takes an hour-long bath, heads out for dinner then eases her way back into the bar scene. Hard to believe how much has changed. Mumbles is gone. The places on Amsterdam Avenue seem to have upped their prices, skimped on their dress code, and adjusted the music to make it seem like the din continues. Half the crowd seems to be looking for drugs, not sex, but she's not sure which half. She begins taking a book along.

Glancing down some bar or other, she often spots a woman standing at the edge of the crowd, a head shorter than the others, surveying the room with a stillness only absolute terror can produce. She's nibbling on a pretzel, a cheese stick. Looking closely, Ellyn can see a trace of braces binding newly polished teeth. Jessica. Tiffany. TC. Please please please please please.

"Get the hell out of here! Go home to Momma!" the inner voice hisses these days.

As if there is a Momma.

She mingles with the crowd in Memphis and a new place called Hi-Life where she wishes for earplugs, and it's so dim no one would notice if she walked in already in her nightgown. A woman crowding the bar beside her smells like RuthAnn.

TIFFANY RUNS BETWEEN THE BEDROOM and the bathroom all evening; she nods off for a bit, and then wakes up nauseous. Ellyn sits in the living room, holding a book in front of her face.

"You know how kids are," Phil comments, stroking her thigh. "One kid gets sick, and half the class comes down with the same symptoms."

She doesn't put the book down.

"Anita used to insist vomiting was something all women have to get used to. Every time Tiffany was sick, she joked it was training for morning sickness."

"I wouldn't know about that." All she can think of is that Pepto-Bismol commercial they had on TV when she was eight or nine, the one where they cut the stomach in half to show you how it looks inside. RuthAnn made the mistake of buying it once: seeing that gaudy pink bottle on their own bathroom shelf made everyone but Joan puke. It must have been a plot.

No Cherry Hill, she supposes. Phil's mother would more than likely catch Tiffany's virus. Assuming it is a virus.

She'd been counting on another free weekend. She'd planned on taking in the American Life show at the Whitney.

Four in the morning. Her anger hasn't abated long enough to let her fall asleep. She hears Tiffany go into the bathroom again, hears her gagging. She has nothing left to vomit up, but continues with those dry heaves. Okay, so this isn't some stomachache she's faked to get attention. Ellyn almost wishes it were.

Phil can't tell the difference between her and his dead wife, but she's willing, as he suggests, to give it time. His parents call her a money-grubbing hussy for short, and what does he do? Listen. He spends weeks using her body as a slot machine, while she patiently waits her turn and almost convinces herself that orgasm isn't important. She doesn't like his drinking habits, doesn't like his power ties, doesn't like his music. But a run-of-the-mill virus pushes her over the edge.

It's that simple.

October 7: Ellyn

Ted stops by the apartment, bringing with him a pile of copy she'd given him to put onto the disk for her. She assumed he'd send it down to Word Processing, but he's talking about having keyed it in himself. He came up to try to talk her out of this. He says he crammed all this on there but she's going to run out of disk space. Also, his union doesn't permit this. If these things are ever used the company can be accused of plagiarism.

She's having trouble understanding what he's talking about, then realizes he thought this was going to be a play. He even changed some of the names so they'd be more contemporary, better for a movie. It never dawned on him she might have written these.

They talk for a while and finally he understands. She asks him what to do, and he says she can always keep some on floppy disks, there'll be plenty of room.

Well, that's settled. Now she asks if this guy who's new in town called him. He says, yes, what a wonderful person. And he goes on and on about how much he likes Dave. He's also found him an apartment in Bayside – a big place, plenty of light. He's going to be driving him there today.

Phil announces he's going, too. Everyone starts asking questions. Finally it comes out that fifteen years ago Dave (who's not new in town, after all) had a child with Phil, a child that neither of them acknowledged. Now they're going to be living in Bayside, with this child, for another fifteen years. Then Phil will come back to her.

She doesn't want him to go, but also doesn't want to hold him against his will. She tells him, yes, he has to own up to this child. But she doesn't understand why it's going to take fifteen years.

Ted says look, I shouldn't have gotten involved in this. He refuses to drive them.

She's saying no, no, no, drive them. "But I will be in touch with you, won't I, Phil?"

He says he'll try.

She wants him to at least leave his phone number, but he won't.

Ted says he'll drive them if she wants, but he's not going to give them this apartment, maybe he'll give them some tiny place. And she agrees: don't help them that much.

She goes over to the coffee shop after they leave and runs into someone she dated years ago. He sits down and starts talking. He opens a plate he brought with him, shows her this beautiful salmon he bought, look at this gorgeous piece of lox. And his wife heated it! Have you ever heard anything so stupid?

She realizes he's just walked out on her.

CHAPTER EIGHTEEN

SHE TELLS DAVE SHE NEEDS her apartment. Tells Phil, over dishes, that she's moving back.

"Just like that, huh? Goodbye, it's been nice knowing you, don't forget to write?"

"Keep your voice down, your daughter's in the next room."

"She's got her stereo blasting. As usual."

"She can still hear shouting." Whispered.

"What is this, all of the sudden you're the only person who understands? Get off your high horse!"

"I don't have to put up with this!"

"Now you tell me!"

"I warned you from date one not to count on me."

"And Anita warned me the brakes were low. Who the hell listens?"

"I am not Anita!"

"Damn right you're not!" Phil storms out of the kitchen.

A wet plate follows him, hitting to the right of the doorway. As hard as she can hurl it, and it barely chips. Anita would have done better. She was more energetic, probably had more spunk. The sort of person who drove off each bridge as she came to it.

It wasn't a bridge, it was a fucking guardrail.

She suspected some problem with Anita's car, something he was supposed to fix, and didn't. Supposed to take precautions, and didn't. First pregnant, then dead.

"Mother wanted children, even if . . . " Dead wives, like fantasies, are easy to maintain.

Phil adored Anita.

There are no such thing as accidents.

SHE PULLS OUT A BRILLO PAD and scrapes the rest of the dishes, not giving a damn if that pretentious little gold rim rubs off. The metal splinters wedge themselves beneath her fingernails and she savors every lousy one. Phil's in the recliner next to the TV, his face buried in the latest issue of *Money*. She'd only imagined she heard the front door slam.

She and Geoff get into a fight over an Etch-A-Sketch their grandparents give them, and before you know it they're at each other's throat. Father runs in, screams at both of them, and then tells Geoff to give the toy to his sister. Red-faced, on the verge of tears, Geoff stomps out of the house. He runs in half an hour later, bubbling over with excitement. This photographer saw him on the street and took his picture. He's now a finalist in some "most beautiful smile" contest.

She'd only imagined herself stuck with the child.

Not for long, she's not. She goes off to the bedroom, soaks her hands, paints her nails bright red. With every nail she thinks of one more friend she might spend the night with.

Phil sheepishly walks in.

She exits. Gets a room at the Excelsior.

At eleven or so she goes over to one of the all-night drugstores for a bottle of nail polish remover. Red makes her feel cheap.

PHIL CALLS HER OFFICE bright and early the next morning. Apologizes for acting like a spoiled five-year-old. Thanks her for doing the dishes.

She says she'll stop by at lunchtime to pick up a few things she needs. The rest she'll get after she moves back to her apartment.

Please don't do this.

It's not as if she has no place else to go. She'll crash up at Joan's if she has to.

Phil asks for a little time to sort things through. Help make things easier on Tiffany. Please. Stay till the end of the month. Or, after a few days, if they see it's not working, he'll spring for the hotel bill.

She doesn't think that's such a great idea.

He apologizes again for the way he stormed out of the kitchen. For calling her like this. For how inattentive he's been of late. For all of August. For the gin and tonic he had last summer and the double Scotch he had last Christmas. For asking her to sublet her apartment. For every issue of *Money* he's ever read. For every time he's dragged her to Cherry Hill. For asking her to leave work when Tiffany's been sick. For not stopping to clean up that plate she threw. For his mother's illness. For asking her to sublet her apartment.

"You already said that one."

"Sorry." He apologizes for Christmas. Thanksgiving. Tomorrow. For the day it rained on them in Central Park. He continues his preposterous litany until he gets her laughing.

He's right, it's probably best for Tiffany if she stays out the month. "Does she know yet?"

"I told her you ran back to the office last night, and went in early this morning."

Just another joyous day in Mudville.

She decides to skip dinner. Calls and leaves a message she's working late. Has maybe one too many glasses of wine with whatever tasteless food she can manage to push down. Walks in after Tiffany's in bed, joins Phil in sitting zombie-like in front of the TV. After he goes to bed she stretches out on the couch and watches *The Tonight Show.* Closes her eyes.

"Ellyn? Ellyn!"

Her eyes pop open. Tiffany's looming above her. The TV makes the room now light, now dark.

"You were moaning or something."

"What time is it?"

"'Bout three."

"What are you doing up?"

"I was thirsty." She licks the orange juice off her lips.

Ellyn sits up. Flicks on a lamp. Gropes for the remote and turns the TV off. Silence. This isn't an apartment familiar with silence.

"My mother slept on this sofa sometimes. When she was, like, having trouble sleeping in bed."

Really? Or is that simply what Anita told her daughter? Ellyn wishes she had nerve to tell her something of the sort. But a five-year-old is different from a twelve-year-old. She pulls the blanket over her. "I was sleeping okay," she says. "I just wanted to be alone for a while."

"Oh."

The night air creates an aura of stillness.

Tiffany will suspect something, even if she doesn't say.

"Maybe I'm one of those people who craves solitude," she begins. "As a child, there was never space to be alone."

"You're leaving, aren't you?"

"Yes." Ellyn takes a deep breath, remembers the little girl with tears in her eyes. *Promise I'll see you again . . .* "Your father and I might be breaking up, but that doesn't mean you and I can no longer see each other," she offers. "We can plan some outings during Christmas break, maybe rent roller blades . . ."

Tiffany's already heading for her bedroom.

No way to bring Mother back.

She shouldn't be here in the first place. Not unless she's willing to acknowledge the child.

No getting back to sleep now. Her mouth feels like the inside of a garbage truck. She gets up and walks into the kitchen, carefully feeling her way without putting on a light, stepping around a gym shoe, a schoolbook, a second gym shoe, and a backpack. There's maybe a quarter ounce of juice left.

WHAT THE HELL'S WRONG with this city? The cab drivers seem to get more hostile every night. Muttering to themselves. Keeping that bulletproof barrier shut tight so she has to open the money slot just to make herself heard. Dropping her off where there's six inches of clearance. And all of a sudden Sloan's has hired cashiers with IQs of forty.

At least she and Phil are civil to each other. One or the other of them comes home and puts dinner on the table – though on the nights it's Phil's turn she often works late, grabs a bite and sometimes a drink before heading back to the apartment.

When eating together they exchange simple amenities in a level voice: pass the sugar, do you want more chicken, stay seated I'll put the coffee on. Some nights they even do dishes together. At about 11:30, right after the news, Phil goes off to bed. Ellyn sits in the living room for another hour or so, then goes into the bathroom and spreads moisturizing cream on her arms and legs before turning in. If Phil isn't asleep yet, he pretends to be.

If only she and Tiffany could find some innocuous middle ground. She hoped, now that she wasn't feeling suffocated by the relationship, they might draw close again. Or closer, anyway.

No such luck. For going on two weeks now Tiffany's acted as if she's alone with her father. Ask her to pick up a coat thrown on the sofa, and all she gets is a glare. What Ellyn wouldn't give to hear one more "You can't make me!" or "You're not my mother!"

Mother didn't mean to die.

Every so often she catches a glimpse of Phil during a commercial she's seen a hundred times: frown so intense his chin is quadrupled, eyes staring vacantly into space, lines on the forehead, hair sticking out. Hard to remember now that she ever found this man attractive. What you see is what you get.

Tiffany isn't a three-year-old.

Too young to understand. Daddy carries her on his shoulders, letting her touch the pipes over their heads in their basement playroom. Then they go through a few months where he barely hugs her. Suddenly he picks her up again, and TC's all excited, expecting some new game in this strange place. Except he pushes her forward, away from him.

"Kiss Mommy."

Mommy's in a box, like a Christmas present. And she doesn't kiss back. Her face feels cold. But still she looks so happy, so beautiful. *Peaceful*, Ellyn tells the child. *That's the word you wanted.* Not a word in the three-year-old's vocabulary. The child had no words to describe those lines in Mother's face when she lay in bed some days, either. *Pain*, Joan told her. But it's more than that. She sneaks another glance at Phil. *Anguish.*

TC bursts out crying. Her father puts her down and tells her to go sit with the other kids.

She's walking so slow she can't catch her breath. Instead of climbing up on the seat she crouches on the bare floor. Wishes she were still on the soft rug in mother's bedroom. Wishes there were dolls or marbles to play with.

People are not toys, Ellyn whispers, cracking five eggs and watching them sizzle in the frying pan. "This is what drugs do to the brain," she mumbles, stirring the broken yolks. She turns around, watching Tiffany lick the excess jelly off her knife.

"DON'T MENTION ANYTHING TO GRANDMA and Grandpa about Ellyn's leaving yet, okay?"

Why should she say anything? As long as she's quiet enough, she can be anything she wants to be – adopted, even – and no one tells her she's crazy or anything.

She doesn't think she'd have made it through first and second grade if she hadn't been able to imagine things being different than what they were. There was that day in first grade when they were writing birthday letters and she leaked ink all over her Brownie uniform. She had her arm in one sleeve of her jacket before she noticed.

Walking slowly, trying to hide the stain with her notebook, she pretended that before she got to the front of the room the door was going to open. A beautiful, tall woman was going to come in and say she's looking for Tiffany. She'd tell Mrs. Washington she's Tiffany's mother, and explain she'd been sick. She was hit by a car and had insomnia, didn't know where she was, but she's all better now, and she's come to take her daughter home with her. She wouldn't see Tiffany at first, because she'd be walking with her head down, but as soon as she spotted her she'd lift her up and kiss her.

As they walked out the door, she'd tell her how much she missed her. She'd promise that, starting the next day, she'd be going to a new school, a special school she picked out, the most expensive school in New York City. "And I want you to be the best dressed girl in first grade," she'd say before she even noticed the stain. Instead of going to the Brownie meeting, they'd drive over to the mall. Her mother would let her try on a hundred outfits, and buy as many as she wanted. She wouldn't make her stand still while she pinned the hem, either; she'd know her size by heart.

She reached the door, and her mother hadn't arrived yet. The last place she felt like going was to a stupid Brownie meeting. She wished she could go home instead, except her grandmother wouldn't know where to pick her up.

Grandma can't drive anymore. Her arm's paralyzed.

By second grade she'd given up on her mother. But every time she got scolded for not having her homework done or her grandfather spanked her or grounded her, she'd try to imagine herself living in New York with her father.

They'd maybe be in the park on a Saturday afternoon when he'd come to visit. She'd tell him how awful it was living with her grandparents. He'd get really upset about the way they were treating her. He'd take her back to the house. Park the car out front. "Now, I want you to go inside and get your favorite toys," he'd tell her. "Pretend you're taking them out to show me. Don't say anything to Grandma and Grandpa, we don't want them to suspect you're not coming back." Of course he'd buy her all sorts of new toys and clothes once they got to the city, but he didn't want her to be without her favorites: Isabel, Clue, Pictionary, that stupid rabbit . . .

WHAT'S A FIVE-LETTER WORD for feelings of remorse? A four-letter word meaning to loathe or detest? A five-letter word for hostility or indignation? She's gotten as bad as Phil's mother.

It used to be child's play. She and Geoff asked each other ad infinitum if they wanted a Hawaiian Punch. She hung around the dinner table with Phil and Tips, endlessly dreaming up commercials – the I Love New York theme playing while a woman steps in dog shit, a new cleanser that makes the toilet bowl explode, the toy for toddlers that boasts that its little plastic pieces are extremely easy to swallow, the candy commercial that shows a person getting fat right before your eyes – the weirder the better.

One stroke, and that's the end of it.

She has a nail half bitten off before she yanks her desk drawer open and searches for an emery board. Comes up instead with the pack of wintergreen Lifesavers she meant to take home three months ago. Supposedly, if you have braces and bite down on one of these in a dark room, you can see sparks. It only works with wintergreen.

"Stupid," Tiffany would probably say. "Immature. Kid stuff." She tosses them into the wastebasket. Probably stale now, anyway.

This whole goddamn office reeks of Tiffany. What was it she called this? A movie set. Sure it is: *King Kong.*

Can't even look out the window without the drafting table getting in the way, can't face the drafting table without picturing Tiffany sitting there drawing. One of the artists stopped by and handed her some graph paper: "If you draw on this, and it's good enough, it might get into a magazine," he told her. Tiffany was young enough then to believe him.

Bill, that's who the artist was. She amuses herself with the idea of having him fired. Never could tolerate that ponytail of his.

She looks up to find Andrea click-clacking over in those pert little heels she wears. "Want to go over the 'today's braces' head shots with me?" Andrea asks. "They're driving me out of my mind."

"Sure." She calls up "brace_hd" on her computer while Andrea wheels over another chair.

"Too old," she mumbles, keeping her finger close to the page down key. "Kids are getting braces younger and younger."

"There are a few younger shots in there." Andrea takes the keyboard, goes to the end of the file, and then pages back up.

Ellyn studies the new photos, keeps going back to one of a pony-tailed girl about twelve, smiling broadly. "Now I ask you, is that innocence or is that innocence?"

"That's innocence all right. But don't you think she's too young?"

"Not nearly as young as she looks, believe me."

"Most kids want to look older."

Ellyn gives an almost audible sigh and begins paging up again. "Sorry, sometimes proximity gets the better of me."

"Maybe proximity will help," Andrea suggests. She calls up the three headshots they've already chosen, cycles through the final shots in the fourth window.

Ellyn's looking at the physical resemblance, not the symmetry, wondering in the back of her mind if Tiffany will recognize herself. She can see it now: Early April. Tiffany's home from school with a virus she faked to avoid a math test. Lying on the sofa watching reruns of *The Young and the Restless.* The commercial comes on. Some career training institute or personal injury law firm. Then another commercial:

Marlene VerPlank sings "Embraceable You" as the faces of men, women and teenagers wearing designer braces flash across the screen. Thirty seconds, ten pictures. Near the end, a male voice interrupts: "It needn't be heavy metal. Call our toll-free number for a list of orthodontists in your neighborhood." The phone number, on the bottom of the screen throughout, turns the headshots into mug shots.

They've narrowed it down to two. Ellyn chooses. "Also, give me close-ups of the lower face."

"I was thinking the same thing. But I'd better get back to work if any of these are going to be ready before tomorrow's meeting," Andrea says. Ellyn's eyes follow her down the hall. By the time she's looking at her own monitor again she sees nothing but her own reflection.

Tiffany will at least know she started this, won't she? Assuming she gives a damn.

That TV spot's so obvious she'll probably find it condescending. Her original proposal called for the music, not the singer. Patterned after those Volvo commercials playing "Dry Bones" in the background.

Not on your life, every rep and his brother said. Not for daytime TV. They'd never understand subtlety.

She can't rationally explain it, even to herself.

She thought, once she broke with Phil, things would slip into place again. That sounds as childish as everything else these days. Maybe it's time to move on to an adult job. Editing or journalism. Cut out the jingles and nonsense rhymes.

If she doesn't pull this presentation together by tomorrow morning, she might have no choice but to look for a job.

She fishes the Lifesavers out of the wastebasket, pops one in her mouth. Chews it, pops another in her mouth, chews. Squeezing the pencil close to its point the way she did in second grade, she begins doodling circles on the page of copy in front of her. Lifesavers. A slinky. The Disney mouse ears insignia. "Embrace me, my sweet embraceable you," she sings, "embrace me, you irreplaceable you," scats a few bars she can't remember, "Ain't misbehavin', I'm saving my love for you. Winston tastes good like a [thump thump] cigarette should." Joan drops the needle onto the spaghetti-box record. All they hear is this grating sound.

"I told you it wouldn't work."

TC's heartbroken.

"Want to hear a fab song? Listen to this." Joan puts a Beatles record on. "I'll tell you something I think you'll understand . . . "

RuthAnn bursts in, screaming at them to shut that thing off. Don't they have any consideration? Their mother's sleeping.

Or was it dying?

All TC cares about is that stupid cardboard circle.

TC and Geoff paint a mural on the wall of Geoff's bedroom.

TC and this girl she can't stand come home from second grade and get into a scratching fight, drawing blood, and then more blood, Joan as referee.

Almost in high school already, TC and two friends, at a slumber party, dial random phone numbers at one or two in the morning, then hang up.

Ellyn chews another Lifesaver, reaches for the next.

Jesus! That's exactly what the twerp used to do, sit there chewing Lifesavers one after another until the whole pack was gone

She closes her eyes. Clenches her fist around that pack of Lifesavers so hard the pain shoots to her elbow. Feels the stiff, hard circles start to crumble. Takes a deep breath. Slowly lets it out. Blows a single kiss: goodbye, good riddance.

TC's gone for good.

Tiffany doesn't want any part of her.

Can't force the issue. All she can do is hope to stay in touch with Phil, try to be there if . . . No, *when*, Tiffany needs her. And meanwhile turn her attention to other things. Tomorrow's meeting, for instance.

EVEN WITH THE TWO OF THEM at it all day, they're still putting on finishing touches at nine o'clock. "Let's face it, Andrea: I'm brain dead," Ellyn says, watching the faces blur. "How about we grab a bite to eat, then come back and take one more look at these?"

"I might as well . . . It's not like I have anything better to do tonight."

"Sorry to hear that."

"I'm not," Andrea laughs. "The last guy was a real whiner. I'm saying goodbye and he's trailing me around the apartment, pleading with me to marry him."

"I know the type. Only the guy I'm with now has an angle – stay, please, the child needs you."

"Child, as in braces?"

"Child, as in let-me-at-least-be-the-mother-I-never-had. But yes, braces." On the way over to the nearest place they can get salads and a decent drink she recounts the tale of this adorable kid who'd *never be able to watch another commercial without thinking of you.*

Andrea comments that, thus far, she's managed to stay away from men with children, and especially those whose children live with them.

"I ended up caring more about Tiffany than I do about Phil."

"Accidents happen." Andrea breaks into this wide, impish smile. The food arrives.

Ellyn confesses she wants to bury herself in work and forget everything else. Only problem is that Tiffany's figured in so many of her ideas over the past year.

"Children are tough."

"Aren't we, though?" She talks about how remote Tiffany's become ever since the summer, how tense it's been since she's decided to get out of this.

"Sounds to me like she's growing up."

"I just wish she wasn't growing up so damn angry."

"Weren't you ever angry?"

"Angrier than I thought I was, I guess." Ellyn hears her own words, shakes her head, laughs. "Here I am, trying to control her life, when I can't even control the memories of my own childhood."

"Can't have one without the other?" Andrea jokes.

"More like: Can't lose one without the other."

"If there's any substance there she'll come back."

"Which one?"

"Whichever one's real."

Printed in the United States
221172BV00001B/1/P

9 780980 178616